The Secrets of Blaney's Mountain

Books by Thomas E. Lynn

Over the Transom
Tales in a Nutshell
Medley of Fiction - AbD

Books by Carrie Chesney

The Lander Series: Christopher
The Lander Series: Brody
The Lander Series: Jennifer
Medley of Fiction - AbD

The Secrets of Blaney's Mountain

Thomas E. Lynn &
Carrie Chesney

ISBN: 978-0-9822029-1-3
Westmorland Publishing

First Paperback Edition: September 2009

For Trudy and Lance who love, support and encourage us in all our endeavors. Also for Carrie's son-in-law, Jared Brooks who always wanted to be a character in a book.
But most of all, this book is for each other, for all the memories created while writing it.

Acknowledgments
We would like to thank the University of Tennessee in Martin for their cooperation and assistance. Our stay with you was enjoyable and educational. To all the students and staff who granted us interviews and tours, we are indebted and hope this work meets with your expectations.

Cover Art: Jeanette Pitt

Westmorland Publishing

8

Within that place so deep, so dark
Where unknown perils lie,
A world yet breathes of ancient
time
While spirits hover by.

Arcades of stone point the way
Beneath the clay and earth
Enticing them with memories
Of undetermined worth.

The Dig

"Come on, Sandy. It would be a shame to miss the trip after all the work you've done." Determined to persuade her friend, Valerie became momentarily distracted as she caught sight of herself in the mirror and paused to tug a few strays from the blue scrunchy twisted in her brunette hair. She didn't want it looking too immaculate.

"I just don't think I can stand a full week of having to deal with Michael Stanley Gant in such close proximity. He's like an albatross, always hovering over me. It'll be more like a prison sentence than an expedition." Alesandra grabbed her walkman, changed the CD, and jammed the headphones on her ears in irritation. Her polished fingernail jabbed at the button to turn it on. A loud squeal burst forth followed by silence as the digital window went blank. "Well, damn. Now my walkman's puckeroo." Ripping off the headphones, she tossed the machine on the desk in disgust. "It's the Gant curse. Even talking about him ruins things."

Valerie bit her cheeks to hide her amusement before continuing. "I thought you needed this trip. Isn't there field work you need to finish for your term project?"

"Please, don't remind me. Okay, so I don't have a choice. I have to go. I swear, Val, if you and Susan don't play interference to keep him away from me, I won't be responsible for my actions." She flopped her slender body on the bed in resignation, blowing upward in an attempt to scatter her auburn bangs from her eyes. "If I'm lucky, maybe the earth will open up and swallow him."

Valerie laughed outright. "That would solve things, wouldn't it? Listen, if you come, we'll try to maneuver him away. It won't be easy."

"You'd better." Alesandra lay staring at the ceiling, thinking. "You know, Val," she said in a subdued voice, "I know you guys think it's funny, but he genuinely makes me uncomfortable. Almost a claustrophobic feeling, as though I won't be able to breathe if he doesn't get out of my space. I feel like screaming bloody murder every time I see him coming."

"I'm sorry, Sandy. We'll do our best."

A knock on the dorm door was quickly followed by Susan's blonde head popping in. "Hi, girls. What are you up to?"

"Sandy's coming on the dig," Valerie announced, pleased with her success.

Susan's eyes lit up, and she grinned. "That's fabulous. We're going to have a great time."

Alesandra looked at her dubiously. "There's a condition," she warned. Susan's eyes pivoted back and forth between the girls, waiting to be filled in.

"Oh right, right. We have to keep the dweezle away from her as much as possible."

Susan instantly realized the futility of the task. "Yeah, sure. How in Hades are we supposed to do that?"

"Can't you talk to him--ask him questions--get him interested in something else, push him off the mountain?" Alesandra pleaded.

Susan saw the desperation in her friend's eyes and sat on the bed next to her. "We'll figure something out. I'm glad you're coming."

"Thank you both. I'll be eternally grateful."

Even from a distance the sprawling mountain loomed large and foreboding. They approached along a two-lane highway with perilous twists and curves causing them to occasionally lose sight of it, but it always reappeared seeming closer with each new sighting.

The travelers consisted of a small portion of Professor Blaney's archaeology students, albeit the more enthusiastic portion. The spring outing provided an opportunity to devote a week to exploring, inspecting and chipping away at the old, majestic mountain for remnants of mankind's history.

Alesandra Davis sat in the middle seat between Valerie and Susan, the only girls in the group. In the front seat next to the professor sat Max wearing his trademark loud Hawaiian shirt. Jared, Michael, Brandon, and Lewis rounded out the troupe. Excited about returning to their excavation site, conversation had not ceased since leaving the university at Martin, Tennessee, more than three hours earlier.

As they neared the mountain, restlessness emanated from their enforced confinement. Everyone rolled their eyes as Lewis called from the back seat for the tenth time, "Dude, are we there yet?"

The van pulled into the parking lot of the hotel that would be their temporary home for the next few days. Professor Blaney proclaimed, "Altogether now…" and the entire group hollered, "Lewis, we're here."

Laughing, they erupted to run free and stretch their limbs.

Blaney gave them a few minutes to work the kinks out while he registered and picked up the room keys. Returning, he summoned them together. "All right, everybody. Gather round. Girls, here's your key. Jared and Max can bunk with me while you other boys take the third room." He distributed the keys and suggested, "Let's get the luggage to our rooms, then grab something to eat before heading up the mountain."

The girls were happy with the arrangement. The same could not be said for the male faction. Waiting until the professor was out of earshot, Jared and Max voiced objections.

"I don't see why we have to stay in the same room with him," Jared sulked.

"Same here," Max muttered. "I'd rather be with the other guys than listen to the old man snoring all night."

Lewis tried to calm them down. "Let's quit crabbing. It's a financial thing. We can only afford three rooms, right? Since two of us have to share a room with the professor, and since you're upper classmen and all that, you win. With seniority comes privilege, you know."

Jared still wasn't happy. "We understand the reasoning, but being the generous guys we are, we're willing to trade. We're amenable to giving you a chance to get on the Prof's good side and earn some brownie points."

"I don't think so, dude. Look at it this way; you two drew the shorter straws."

Leaning closer and speaking in a low tone so only Max and Jared could hear him, Brandon added, "Besides we have Gant, so we're no better off than you."

A typical science dweeb, Michael Stanley Gant was tall, thin and wore plastic rim glasses that continually slid down his nose until he remembered to adjust them with his index finger.

The girls giggled, glad they weren't involved in the dispute. "I don't think Professor Blaney is old, anyway," Susan said. "He certainly isn't as ancient as Dr. Turner." The others found humor in the comparison. Jacob Turner, head of the Chemistry Department and familiarly recognizable by his long white hair and bushy eyebrows, could have been a twin to either Mark Twain or Albert Einstein. Susan turned to the girls and added, "I think he's a hottie, Professor Blaney I mean."

Carl Edwin Blaney, 36 years of age, had authored several books on the subjects of paleoecology, geological aging and modern archaeological field methods. In his younger days, he researched in the Guatemalan highlands. The bachelor seemed content to spend his remaining years as a university resident, his energetic appeal consistently luring highly promising students to select archaeology as a major.

After moving their gear to their rooms, they congregated in the hotel restaurant. Eager to begin their quest, they ordered nothing more complex than sandwiches.

Sitting across from Lewis and Brandon in a booth, Alesandra watched with amazement at the speed with which the boys consumed their food. "Lewis, you're supposed to eat it, not inhale it," she commented.

"Why? It's not exactly candlelight and wine." He reached across the table and snatched the pickle from her plate.

"Maybe not, but I think you're at least supposed to open your mouth."

"The sooner we get out of here, the sooner we get to…what's the name of that mountain again?"

"Who cares what the locals call it?" Jared answered. "Doesn't much matter. It's been Blaney's mountain for almost ten years now, and we are propitious enough to have been selected for exclusive membership in the Blaney Bunch."

Max started to sing, "'til the one day when the fellow met this mountain, and they knew that it was much more than a hunch..."

The girls giggled and pitched in to finish the famed theme song with him, "…that's the way we all became the Blaney Bunch."

With lunch out of the way, the group collected their climbing gear and traveled to their objective, The Mountain.

Gathering his crew at the foot of the climb, the professor led the way, Jared and Max closely on his heels. The three girls followed next with the other boys bringing up the rear.

Indians once lived on the mountain, comfortably at home with bears and smaller animals, their traces making it ideally suited for field trips. His voice drifted to those trailing behind, pointing out signs as they gradually ascended the slope.

Alesandra gave up listening to the professor's discourse after a while. She concentrated on putting her feet on solid ground, careful to avoid slipping on loose stones. It was occasionally necessary to dig in with her point ax for an anchor to pull herself up a particularly steep incline.

After an hour they halted on a relatively level outcropping of rock to rest. Dropping their backpacks, they stretched and searched for smooth places to sit. The sun was hot, and hands began rummaging for water bottles.

"Go easy on the drinking water," Professor Blaney cautioned, "we still have a long day ahead."

Alesandra felt someone slide into place next to her, immediately realizing her worst fear. For some reason, this three-named oddity fancied himself as her protector, always volunteering to do things for her and driving her batty in the process.

"You can have some of my water if you need a drink," the dweeb offered.

Quickly scanning the area for her friends, she wondered how he managed to get so close to her. No rescue party magically appeared ready to leap to her aid. It figured. The first time she needed them, they disappeared. She hoped it didn't prove a portent of their reliability.

"No, thanks," she tried to wave him off. "I have plenty."

Visibly disappointed, he lingered. "Okay. But don't forget my offer."

She couldn't even bring herself to look at him when she spoke. Casting her eyes in the opposite direction, she indicated he was unworthy of her attention. "I won't. Thanks again."

He walked back to his gear. The group stood, ready to resume the climb when the other girls returned.

"Where were you, Val?" Alesandra hissed as they fell into step together.

"I had to pee. Why? Did you miss me?"

Alesandra seethed. "While you were gone, *he* moved in on me. I can't believe you deserted me at the first opportunity."

"I'm sorry, Sandy. It wasn't intentional. Nature called."

"What did he say to you?" Susan asked.

"That's not the point. You weren't here when I needed you."

"Well, Sandy, what did you want me to do? Take him with me?"

Alesandra knew her expectations were unreasonable, and she heaved a sigh.

"So," Susan persisted, "what did he say?"

"He said I could share his drinking water with him." Somehow, it didn't sound so bad when she said it aloud.

Susan came to an abrupt halt, grabbed Alesandra's arm, and with mock solemnity exclaimed, "Oh, my gosh! How awful for you. I had no idea he could be so cruel. No wonder you're so uptight."

Alesandra realized how juvenile she sounded. She began giggling at her own childishness, and her friends joined in.

The group resumed their climb until they reached the first excavation site. "It's still early, people," the professor said. "That gives us four or five good hours to work."

Groups had previously visited here, as evidenced by the number of unfilled holes and gouged out layers of sedimentary rock strata. The students fanned out, each with pre-assigned locations to continue the work of prior visits.

Alesandra took her time, wandering around the site to recapture the feeling before beginning anew. Finally settling down to the job at hand, she found her previous work area near a large boulder undisturbed since her last visit. She extracted a probe and digging tools from her gear.

Already preoccupied with the project, she set to work. This particular area proved rewarding the last time, providing several invertebrate fossils and animal bones. Following proper field study procedures, she kept notes regarding the location, type of soil or rock encountered and probe depths. She also took photographs as significant findings warranted. Thus engrossed, she failed to sense the arrival of Michael at her side a few hours later until he softly spoke to her.

"Alesandra, I've found something I think will interest you."

She looked up, irritated by the disruption. Seeing who it was, she prepared to lash out but stopped short. Something in his look, something in his voice, coaxed her to cooperate. He bent down and reached for her hand. "Shhh, don't talk. Just come with me."

Refusing to take his hand, she followed him to a slight indentation in the side of the mountain. He pointed to a smooth portion of the wall in front of them. With his fingers he scraped away some of the sedimentary covering until tiny glittering mineral flecks adhered themselves to his hand. He held them out for her inspection.

Alesandra leaned closer, peering at his fingers. "What are they?" she whispered, puzzled at the discovery.

"I'm not certain, but they could be small particles of gold. Look at their sheen. I don't know what else they could be. I wanted you to see them before I called the professor over." The yellow flakes drifted to the ground as he waved his hand in the air. Mesmerized by the shimmering specks, she touched the rock wall, delighted to see more of the granules attracted to her hand. A gentle wave of her fingers, and the golden dust hung in the air as though suspended before floating like feathers slowly to the ground.

Her eyes large with excitement, she stared at him, momentarily forgetting her dislike for the young man. "Michael, I don't know much about minerals, but I don't think gold is normally found in this part of the country, and I've never heard of it drifting like this."

He pushed his glasses back with one finger and seemed to wilt before her. The nerd persona firmly back in place, he replied, "I know. It probably isn't important, after all. Do you think the professor should be told?"

"Oh, of course I do," she quickly answered. "He is the expert here. I don't know what it is, but I think it's fascinating." Michael might indeed be a milquetoast because of his apparent ineptness at mingling with other people, but she saw something in his eyes that was new to her. Perhaps she detected a glimmer of independence and a desire as strong as her own to learn as much about earth sciences as possible. After all, he had to be one of the professor's most promising students, or he wouldn't be along on this trip.

Alesandra stayed while he went for the professor. The entire group converged to stand in wonder, watching as Michael scraped the golden particles off the rock wall to momentarily float, then drift as air currents caught them before settling slowly to the ground.

The professor peered at the wall. “No doubt about it,” he said, “this is interesting. Personally, I've never seen anything like it.”

“I was thinking we could take some scrapings back to the university. We can run them through the mass spectrometer to determine the mineral composition.”

“Absolutely. Meanwhile, I think Michael and Alesandra are to be congratulated for their discovery.”

She tried to interrupt. “No, Prof. This was Michael's find.”

“No need to be modest, Sandy.” He dismissed her protestation with a gesture. “These minute particles appear to have certain properties found in the element of gold, and it is definitely unusual. Nevertheless, we must remember that gold is normally present in ore veins, and these particular flakes might well be in a mineral filament ending unceremoniously right where we found them.”

Talk of Michael's find had everyone animated, making attention to the jobs at hand futile. As their working day drew to a close, their enthusiasm made the trip down the mountain much quicker than their ascent, and they arrived ready for their evening meal in good spirits.

At dinner, for the first time in his life, Michael was the center of attention, and he basked in it. Since an entire millennium would likely pass before it happened again, he savored the rush. All eyes were on him, wanting him to recount the find over and over again. They marveled at the properties of the substance; how it glittered, how it floated.

After dinner, when they separated to their own rooms, the girls were instantly on Alesandra.

“So, Sandy, tell us all about your new partner,” Valerie teased.

“Yes, Sandy. One minute you need to be protected, and the next, you're colleagues with a new discovery to shake the geological world.”

“Stop it. It was Gant's discovery, not mine, and I hardly think it'll be anything earth shattering. It's probably just something off the periodic table we haven't personally seen before. And stop calling him my partner,” she said with a glare. “He was the one who found them and insisted on showing them to me. That's all it was, so please don't try to make anything else of it.” She picked up her hairbrush and started to pull it through her glossy auburn strands.

“Right, right. You had nothing to do with it,” Valerie agreed sarcastically.

“Sure, we understand.”

“Look, I have my own work to do on that mountain.” She wondered why she was forever destined to defend herself where Gant was concerned.

"Doesn't it sound to you like she's protesting a bit too much, Val?"

The hairbrush flew through the air, missing Susan by mere inches, and the tormentors collapsed onto the bed in gales of laughter.

When the lights went out, Alesandra lay in her bed thinking about the day and about Michael Stanley Gant. They were the same age, but he didn't seem to fit in with the other guys. Maybe it was because they thought he was a geek with those horrid glasses and quiet ways. She felt a smidgen of sympathy for him in that respect. He was probably a lonely guy. However, she didn't feel the need to respond to his incessant overtures. She sincerely wished he would leave her alone. She tried to make her feelings on that as clear as possible without being downright rude.

Images of the gold flakes filled her mind. An anomalous feeling that the shimmering flakes seemed somehow alive intrigued her. Falling asleep, she dreamed of flying silently among the clouds. A sharp pain in her side interrupted her peaceful flight.

"Come on, girl. Get dressed. We've got an early day."

She opened one eye and looked at her roommate. "It's too soon to be morning."

"You're absolutely right. The sun isn't even up yet, but it will be soon. Rise and shine. You snooze, you lose."

Alesandra dragged herself from the bed and took a cool shower in preparation for the hot day ahead. Toweling her hair dry, she opened the bathroom door to find the beds made and the room empty. She quickly pulled her clothes on, tying her hair back as she hurried to join the others for breakfast.

With barely enough time for a doughnut and half a cup of coffee, she found herself on the slope once more plodding upward into the gray opacity of a morning mist. Professor Blaney's voice wafted back to those in the rear of the column, but no one paid attention. They already knew what to watch for, and they hadn't yet reached the dig clearing. Good-natured bantering was in full sway as they neared the site, everyone anxiously ready to get on with the day's work.

Blaney, eager to get another look at the gold granules, attached himself to Michael. With tools in hand, they worked to accumulate a generous quantity of the mineral for lab testing.

Alesandra settled into her own project site, silently hoping Michael and the professor would become so mutually absorbed in the new found flakes that she could work undisturbed and progress with her own research.

Several hours elapsed when Max suddenly broke the silence with a second discovery. "Hey, Professor! Come check this out!" Resuming his working posture, Max brushed carefully at a flat stone lying partially buried. Blaney knelt beside him, eager to see what was being unearthed. Close inspection disclosed the appearance of rudimentary ridges and jagged notches.

"Max, this looks like a rock carving or some sort of picture writing."

Line carvings had been exposed during previous field trips here. It seemed plausible this stone could be more of the same with variations. In fact, Max and Jared both specialized in linguistic communication of Native American civilizations, and the new discovery fit right in.

Blaney stepped back out of the way, and Jared moved in to assist Max.

Time passed all too quickly. Alesandra loved the hours spent on the mountain digging as well as the evening sessions in which everyone met to compare notes and discuss the happenings of each day. Camaraderie grew stronger among them, for even with their divergent scientific interests, they shared the same enthusiasm and exhilaration. Michael's doting attention seemed less irritating, and she relaxed and enjoyed the evenings. In spite of her earlier apprehensions, the field trip filled her with satisfying pleasure, making her glad she came on the venture.

Max sat next to Alesandra, keeping his body in close contact with hers. He leaned closer to whisper in her ear when the professor called for their attention.

"Okay, folks, everybody's having a good time, and I want to keep it that way. Tomorrow we're going to break away from the routine and have a change of scenery. We're going to move higher up the mountain for some good old down-to-earth spelunking."

"All right! Now we're cooking!" Brandon and Lewis, both amateur cavers, had heard tales of past members of the Blaney Bunch exploring inside the mountain, and they itched for their turn. Tomorrow would be the day for which they waited all year.

High fives resounded, and the professor laughed, enjoying seeing his students so jazzed.

CHANGE OF SCENERY

Blaney gathered his bunch together on a grassy slope at the bottom of the mountain. "Okay, everyone. Listen up. I know you're excited about getting to the top, but first there's some rules we need to cover."

Valerie dropped her backpack on the ground and sat cross-legged next to Susan, who was flanked on the other side by Alesandra. Moments later, Michael Stanley Gant arrived and parked himself on Alesandra's other side.

Leaning in front of Susan, she glared at Valerie. "This is your fault."

Valerie saw her mistake, and winced. "Uh oh. Sorry, Sandy."

Piqued, Alesandra folded her arms. With effort, she tried to concentrate on the professor's words.

"Now I know we only plan on being inside for a few hours, but we're going to take some precautions. Lewis, why don't you handle this?"

Always glad to have an audience, Lewis took charge. "The professor brought helmets for everybody. Pass 'em out, Bran." Brandon grabbed the pile and started handing them to the others while Lewis continued. "Keep it on your head at all times, in case of falling bits of rock and stuff in there." The students put the brimless hats on their heads. Each came equipped with a battery powered lamp strapped on the front and a black plastic case in the back holding three C-cell batteries, all held firmly in place with elastic. "Light is your most important resource when you're inside. Even more important than water, so use it wisely. Conserve when you can. You should also have a flashlight with you in case you need it for additional wattage."

"Hey, if we put Max in front to lead us, we won't need lights. His shirt probably glows in the dark," Jared suggested. Laughing, everyone turned to stare at Max in his hot pink shirt covered with large white hibiscus flowers.

Max held his arms out wide, giving a clear view of his shirt, as though it couldn't already be seen. "It's a classic."

Lewis, usually the class clown, got the group back on track. He took his caving seriously. “I know it’s hot outside, but everybody should put on a warm sweatshirt or jacket. The air inside is a lot cooler with no sunlight to generate heat. Oh, and don’t forget to put on your leather work gloves. They were on the kit list. It gets pretty muddy in there. Now, we’ve got one more thing here to hand out. Bran, the bottles please.”

Brandon grabbed a cardboard box filled with white plastic wide mouth bottles with yellow screw-on lids and dispersed them to the group.

“What are these for, Lewis? We already got water bottles.”

“Dude. These are for water coming out the other end. We might not be long enough to need ‘em, but just in case, we don’t want any of you guys taking a whiz in a corner in there. The lid is yellow to remind you what it’s for. Don’t want you getting it confused with your drinking water. If you have to go, use the bottle and pack it back out again.” People often took what Lewis said with a huge grain of salt, but he wasn’t kidding around now.

“How come, Lewis?”

Brandon cut in, “Salt and sugar in human urine can throw the entire ecosystem out of whack. A cave has no way of renewing and cleansing itself. No rain to wash things away, no sun or wind to help decompose. What you leave stays there. And if you find you have to do something else in there, we’ve got some doggie bags with us too. Just ask.” Brandon reached into his pack and pulled out a handful of Ziplock storage bags. “Seal it up, double bag it, seal it again, then wrap it in foil and pack it out.”

“Ewww, that is so gross,” Susan turned her nose up.

“Not as gross as leaving it there for everyone else for the next hundred years. Think of it as taking the dog out for his evening walk, minus the dog.”

“But, Brandon, we aren’t going to be in there that long,” Valerie pointed out.

“Crap happens, dudette.” Lewis answered, putting an end to that discussion.

A new eagerness burgeoned as the group climbed higher through the mist of dawn and set up an overnight camp near the mountain summit. Individual tents marked their bivouac, and they bustled to ready themselves to enter the cave.

After putting on warmer clothing, they gathered at the mouth of the cave. Blaney reluctantly permitted Brandon and Lewis to lead the way because of their experience. “Never mind that you’ve both done this before,” he pointedly warned them. “None of the previous groups suffered any accidents, and it is important for all of us to observe common sense safety rules. Always remember who is ahead of you and who is behind you. Look out for each other, and I mean this, do not leave the group for any private exploring."

Brandon and Lewis glanced at each other furtively and frowned, both determined not to leave at the end of the week until they explored every nook and cranny of the cave's interior.

"One final word before we go in." Blaney looked at each face to make sure he had their attention. "The only thing you take is pictures. The only thing you leave is footprints. Don't get any clever ideas to bring back a piece of rock as a souvenir. This is non-negotiable - doing so will seriously affect your grade. Is that understood?"

The group nodded in agreement, and Blaney gave the cue. Reaching up to flick his headlamp on, Brandon set his feet on the path that had been trampled by years of Blaney's students before him, leading the way with confidence. In single file, they ducked beneath the waist high threshold of the entryway, entering the dark world. Alesandra found herself lagging behind the other girls, followed by Michael, with Jared and Max bringing up the rear. Michael, never overly talkative, seemed quieter than usual. Alesandra presumed his mind was still engrossed in the puzzle of the strange mineral flakes.

Twenty minutes into the cave, the ground changed to a thick carpet of loose rubble which shifted precariously beneath their feet. Susan's foot slipped, causing her to stumble.

"Take my hand, Sue." Valerie reached back and clasped her firmly, helping her over shallow depressions not fully shown by the headlamps. The air grew steadily cooler as they moved deeper into the mountain, and steam resulted from every breath.

Alesandra loved the adventure of penetrating a world that never saw sunlight, a place where early man probably sought shelter from wintry snows. "I hope we get a chance to take a closer look at the walls and flooring of this passage," she commented in a low tone. "How can I find any human artifacts if we keep on the move?" She stumbled in the semi-darkness and immediately felt Michael catching her before she could fall.

"Thanks," she said over her shoulder.

With damp darkness surrounding their meager illuminated area on all sides as though ready to swallow them, they eased past rock formations that often resembled human forms. Walking crouched under low ceilings, their lights produced eerie shadows on the walls. Limestone creations resulted from water dripping, then crystallizing, to form stalagmites on the cave floor. Subterranean treasures reflected orange and white sparkles of organic acids acting on underground calcium deposits.

Each explorer cautiously avoided touching the many shapes surrounding them. Even the sound of a human voice could interfere with centuries-old growth causing stalactites dangling overhead to topple. They clambered down a few rocks and entered a narrow tunnel. A rockslide left a shambled pathway of loose stones and larger boulders to slither around before regaining the main corridor. They loved the challenge, but progress finally halted for a breather.

"We'll go on a little farther," the professor advised. "This tunnel comes to an end in about another twenty minutes. You'll have some time there, then we'll turn back."

"Isn't there another area we can check out?" Brandon asked, disappointed the corridor was nearing its end so quickly. "I mean, there has to be a connecting passageway somewhere. Why else would the Indians have come in here unless the tunnel went somewhere else?"

"You may be right, Brandon, but an adjoining tunnel has never been located," Blaney told him. In fact, no one had ever suggested such a possibility, but he had no intention of allowing this small and virtually inexperienced assemblage of students to branch out in search of another inner corridor. He had a safe, horizontal route, and he wasn't varying from it. "At the end of this tunnel is a small cavern. We can examine the surroundings there and satisfy our scientific curiosities."

The prospect did nothing to pacify either Brandon or Lewis. With a single conspiratorial look, they sealed a pact to ferret out a new tunnel. After a few minutes of rest, the group pushed onward to the inner extremity of the cave.

While the two amateur cavers huddled and conversed in whispers, the others began to explore the small grotto. Michael's eyes studied the walls' composition, searching for veins that might contain his golden particles. Finding none apparent, he felt anxious to return to the exterior so he could continue his work there.

Alesandra pulled her flashlight from her backpack and flicked it on to examine markings on a section of wall.

"Are you interested in aboriginal languages?"

Startled, she jumped, letting out a squeal. She glanced up to see Max leaning closely over her shoulder to observe the object of her scrutiny.

"Geez, Max. You scared me. Don't sneak up like that."

He settled his hands on her shoulders reassuringly and let them linger there. "Sorry, Sandy. So, you interested?"

"Yes. I'm interested in all aspects of the culture, but this is your main focus, isn't it?" She gazed at his handsome face as he moved closer beside her, welcoming the proximity of his athletic body. Max had transferred to UTM during the winter term. She wasn't sure if he played football, but she certainly hoped so. She would love to cheer him on.

"Yup. It's what I'm going to do my master's thesis on. I noticed similar markings at the cave entrance. These in particular appear to be line drawings, certainly of a Cherokee origin."

Her eyes lit up as she asked, "Can you read this?"

"I can probably interpret some of it. These drawings represent a complex system much like our own Roman alphabet. Around 1790, the Cherokee developed an alphabetic system, so these were obviously created more recently." He warmed to his subject, and she was captivated.

Blaney checked his watch and saw they had spent an hour in the chamber. "Everyone remember your positions. The order we came in is the same way we'll go back – Brandon and Lewis in the lead."

The temperature seemed frostier as they stretched tired limbs and prepared to move out.

Alesandra reached over her shoulder, trying to return her water bottle to her pack. Fingers deftly took it from her and tucked it inside, then slid the zipper closed. Looking back at her helper, she gave a half smile. "Thanks, Michael."

"No problem."

The group retraced their steps, discussing the things they had seen inside. They quickly reached the difficult part where progress was impeded by the former rockslide. One by one, they gradually worked their way through the maze of boulders and squeezed through the crevice back into the cleared corridor.

Alesandra was squirming past the jumbled mass of jagged rocks when a rumble emanated from the bowels of the mountain. Deep below them, a shifting of plates occurred. Each movement resulted in sequential adjustments of rock layers along a faulted line, forcing the walls of the tunnel to weaken. The floor trembled, violently tossing the group into rock and each other.

Alesandra felt arms protectively surround her as Michael tried to use his own body to shield her from flying fragments. Without further warning the ground gave way, and the rumble became a roar as the floor beneath them gaped open and swallowed them.

As swiftly as it started, it was over. When the mountain ceased shaking and the dust began to settle, Blaney rose to his feet. The air, thick with silt particles, made breathing difficult. Along with the sounds of shifting rock and small loose stones looking to find purchase, he was vividly aware of moans, whimpering and a cacophony of coughing to clear throats and lungs.

Giving his head a moment to clear, he asked, "Except for bumps and bruises, is everybody okay?" A chorus of voices responded. "Okay, let's have a head count. Lewis?"

"Here."

"Brandon?"

"Right here, sir."

"Susan?"

"I'm here."

"Valerie?"

"I think my leg's broken," she whimpered.

"Okay, we'll get you out as soon as we can." He continued with his roll call. "Alesandra?"

Silence.

"Sandy? Are you okay?" Susan called.

More silence.

"Sandy, answer me. Are you all right?" Alarm rose in her voice. "I don't see her. She was right behind me."

Blaney made his way back into the tunnel followed closely by Lewis and Brandon. "Okay, Susan. Don't panic yet. Let's finish the head count. Max?"

"I'm here and so's Jared."

"What about Michael?"

"No, sir. He was right in front of me, but he's not here now."

"They must be under the rocks. We have to find them," Jared declared as he flashed his light on the pile of boulders that now separated he and Max from the rest of the group. Recognizing their dilemma, Max started to lift and heave the rocks he could manage.

Valerie's pain, compounded by fear for her friend, caused her sobs to increase in intensity. Susan clasped her hand and assured her, "Take it easy, Val. We'll find them."

The professor, Lewis, and Brandon arrived at the point where their classmates disappeared and immediately threw themselves into moving rocks, searching for any sign of Alesandra and Michael.

As Valerie's cries took on a note of hysteria, the professor turned to Brandon. "Get her out of here, now."

Brandon took Susan's arm, and the two of them helped Valerie out of the cave, leaving the others to focus on the task at hand without distraction. Rocks and boulders dislodged during the cave-in lay scattered, blocking the tunnel corridor that now extended deeper into the mountain.

The four men worked together to maneuver the fallen rock, but their willing hands were inadequate to budge the boulders. When it was clear Michael and Alesandra couldn't be found, Blaney resigned himself to the need for professional help. He tried to remain calm for the benefit of the students, but the burden weighing on his shoulders was almost unbearable.

Brandon was at the mouth of the cave, ready to head back inside to help when the group emerged into the bright sunlight. Blaney called his remaining bunch together with a heavy heart. He saw Valerie in her tent out of the hot sun, lying on top of her sleeping bag.

"How's she doing?"

"No broken bones. I think she just wrenched her knee, Professor. I gave her a couple of Tylenol. She needs to rest in the shade for awhile so she doesn't go into shock. She should be all right, though."

"Thanks for taking care of her."

The group peeled off the jackets and extra pants now that they were back in the hot sunshine.

Blaney ran his fingers through his disheveled hair as he addressed the Bunch. "Listen, from this moment on, you stay in groups of two. Each of you has a partner. Do not go off on your own for any reason."

Turning to Max and Jared, he gave explicit instructions. "I need you two to hike back to town. Call 911 and the National Cave Rescue unit while you're there. Then wait until they arrive, and lead them back up here to us. Think you can manage all right?"

"Absolutely. No problem."

Without another word, they hooked their backpacks over their shoulders and headed down the mountain.

"What about us, Professor? What can we do?" Brandon asked.

"You and Lewis are getting your wish, to an extent. You can start to search for another tunnel. Maybe we can find an alternate way to reach them. I know you're anxious to explore, but please, don't stray too far from camp, and do not go back into that cave. There's still danger, and the last thing we want is to have to look for you, too." He knew they comprehended the seriousness of the situation and trusted them to stay out of trouble.

His eyes sought Susan and found her with Valerie, comforting her and wiping her tears away. With everyone occupied, at least for the moment, and frustrated he could do no more, Carl Blaney rubbed an arm across his sweaty forehead and wandered to a nearby sycamore tree, leaning against it in an attempt to stay vertical while indulging in his first moments of privacy.

He accepted the possibility that future excursions of his study groups were in jeopardy. However, uppermost in his mind was a genuine fear for the safety of Alesandra and Michael. He knew full well the perils within the unmapped confines of caves, and if they were injured, the risk factor escalated. He didn't need anyone to tell him that the chances of rescuing them dwindled with each passing moment. Unable to restrain it any longer, he leaned over and retched.

As swiftly as it started, it was over. When the mountain ceased its shaking and the silt began to settle, Alesandra found herself in total darkness. Dry air teemed with dust particles swirled about her, and she coughed to clear her throat. Groping for her helmet to turn on the lamp, she discovered the headgear was gone.

"Susan! Val!" she called, frantic to locate her friends. Reaching tentatively into the unknown blackness, she felt someone underneath her. The deep resonant sound of her unknown companion's initial moan indicated it was neither of her girlfriends. With effort, she managed to roll off of him, her body screaming in agony. She reached in the dark to grasp his arm and shook it none too gently. "Who are you? Are you okay?"

"Who's there? What happened?" the low-pitched voice responded.

"It's Sandy."

He turned his head in the direction of her voice. "Alesandra. Are you all right? Are you hurt?"

She bit her lip in abject dismay as she identified the voice of *Michael Stanley Gant*! Of all people. "I think I'm broken. Everything hurts," she moaned. "There's rocks and stuff all over, and it's hard to move. I think there was a cave-in. The floor just sort of collapsed."

Michael lifted a hand to touch his throbbing face, wondering if his nose broke when her head smacked into it on impact. It sure felt like it. To his surprise, the bones seemed to be properly aligned. Suddenly aware of the surrounding silence, he asked, "Where's everybody else?" He tried to rise but fell back as pain shot up his left arm and across his ribs.

"I haven't heard anyone else."

He felt her clutch his right arm and heard the trepidation in her voice. Suppressing his own anxiety, he attempted to soothe her. "You sure you're all right?"

"I'm frightened."

"I know. It's okay to be scared, but we can't just lay here. We have to find the others." He valiantly managed to sit up and tried to shrug off his backpack, but his left arm refused to cooperate. The agony ripping through it made him gasp. He was not too foolish to admit he needed help. "Sandy, can you sit up?"

Tears streamed down her cheeks as she pulled herself to a sitting position. "It's my ankle. I can't move it. How am I going to do cheerleading with a broken ankle? What if it doesn't heal in time? I'm going to lose my place on the squad. My career is over."

Immersed in his own pain, he grappled to maintain a voice of reason. "Sandy, if we can't find our way out of here, you'll be missing a hell of a lot more than cheerleading."

"Oh." She hadn't thought of that. "You mean we're going to die in here?"

"Only if we don't get ourselves up and moving." He reached over to touch his left arm, dangling at his side at an awkward angle. "I need you to help me get this backpack off. I can't move my arm."

Aside from feeling battered about, she realized her only real injury was her foot. Leaning toward him, she slid the strap off his right shoulder without difficulty. "Can you slide it off your other shoulder now?"

Gingerly, he removed it while shifting the mangled limb as little as possible and fumbled to open it single-handedly. He finally gave up and told her, "Rummage around in there. See if you can find the flashlight, my first aid kit, and a notebook."

She located the flashlight and switched it on, illuminating dust particles still drifting in the air. "What do you want me to do now?"

"We need to put my arm in a sling. It's fractured pretty badly."

She shone the light onto his arm and gasped when she saw it. "Oh, my gosh. That's terrible. You must be in so much pain."

"We're going to use the notebook as a splint. Okay, now very carefully, you'll have to straighten my arm so we can get it in there."

Three times she reached out to take hold of it, and each time recoiled, afraid of hurting him more. Finally, drawing a deep breath, she did as he bade her.

With a short scream of pain, Michael toppled backwards, unconscious.

"Oh, geez. What have I done now? Wake up. Don't do this to me. You've got to get us out of here." Panic fluttered in her stomach, and tears sprang to her eyes.

Hands slapped at his face until his eyes slowly opened. A bout of nausea hit, and he turned his face to the side to vomit.

Managing to refrain from the exclamations of disgust that threatened to spew from her, she turned away in silent revulsion, certain that practically barfing on the girl whose attention he sought might not win him many points, and at the same time feeling guilty that she caused him so much distress.

He wiped at his mouth with his good hand, and turned back to her. "Okay, I think I'm ready now." He took the duo-tang folder from her and wrapped it around his swollen arm, holding it in place while she tied it with twine. "Thanks, now open the first aid kit. I have a couple of triangular bandages in there."

"Right." Returning her attention to the kit, she found the white bandages rolled neatly inside. "You'll have to tell me how to do this."

Following his directions she laid the sling across his chest and over his shoulder. After tying the knot firmly in place, he told her, "Okay, now I need you to take the second bandage, and tie it around me like a sash. I've managed to pop a few ribs out of place, and it will also hold my arm more securely."

With her ministrations completed, he turned his attention to her. "You said your foot hurts? How bad is it?"

She realized that while tending him, the throbbing in her foot seemed to subside somewhat and wasn't nearly as painful as it had been a few minutes before. "Still sore, but probably not broken, thank goodness. I can hardly turn cartwheels with a broken foot."

Michael shook his head in the darkness. Here he was, worried about getting out alive, and she was worried about gymnastics.

"Think you can stand on it?"

"Not sure."

"Well, try. We can't get out of here unless you can."

"Then I guess I'll just have to, whether it hurts or not."

"Take another look in my pack, and see if you can find a length of twine."

"What are we gonna do with it?"

"So we don't get separated. Tie one end around your waist and the other around me." For the first time, they looked at each other. "Your face is dirty, and where's your helmet?"

"I don't know. I guess I lost it in the fall."

"How could you lose it? Didn't you have the chin strap done up?"

"Well, I did when I first put it on, but it got sweaty and uncomfortable, so I undid it when we were looking at the cavern. I didn't want my skin to break out."

"Heaven forbid, we wouldn't want that to happen. Preventing a blemish is far more important than safety," he jeered.

The flashlight caught him in its beam, and she noticed that he too was missing something important. "Where are your glasses?"

Reaching up, he felt a welt on the bridge of his nose where his glasses were supposed to be. "That's a good question. I guess they're with your helmet." He removed his own helmet and handed it to her. "Here, put this on. I imagine there's still going to be a lot of falling rock. Don't want anything to hurt that pretty head of yours."

Somehow, in the dark, Michael wasn't as loathsome. Given the choice she would rather be stuck with him than on her own. She drew strength from his composure and gave him a half hearted smile, not certain whether he could see it or not. "Are you blind without them?"

"Well, I won't be able to kick back and read you a novel, but I can make out just about as much as you can in the dark," he grinned, trying to dispel her fears. Letting his hand rest on her arm, he told her, "Don't worry, we'll be fine."

She pulled the twine around her waist and tied a knot, then attached the other end around him. Picking up the flashlight, he gave them each a thorough going over, examining the scrapes and bruises suffered during their fall.

Alesandra watched his face in the light from her headlamp. He wasn't nearly so geeky without the glasses. In fact, dare she think it? He might even be what some considered – nice looking. She gave her head a quick shake to dispel the notion.

"Now, let's try to figure out where we are." He aimed the flashlight slowly around the room, looking for signs of others buried under the fallen debris, but saw none.

"We have to be beneath the tunnel we were in before. We definitely fell downwards," Alesandra said. She watched as he played the light up the walls. The thin ray shone murkily against a high ceiling, then displayed random patterns of rock scattered throughout a spacious underground chamber. Powdery particles continued to sail on faint wisps of air in the lingering aftermath of the shock.

"Looks like the chasm closed as quickly as it opened. Either that, or a lot of rock fell into it during the cave-in. Which ever, we can't exit by the same route we entered. We have to find our own way out of here."

"Maybe we should shout for them, in case they can hear us."

"In light of what's just happened, I don't think that's a good idea, Sandy." It was the first time she heard him use her nickname. "Things might still be unstable, and shouting could cause another collapse."

"Oh. I never thought of that. I wonder what's happened to them. I wonder if they're all right." Her fear for her friends caused her voice to tremble.

Michael continued with his outward optimism. "It doesn't look like anyone else was trapped in the cave-in." He tried to convince her, but she was having none of it.

"We don't know that. They could be buried in another part of this cave. The question is, what do we do now?"

"This flashlight isn't going to last forever. We have to conserve our batteries. If the headlamp is on, the flashlight is off."

"All right. That's sensible," she agreed as he turned his flashlight off. He stood and reached down, taking her hand to help her to her feet.

Trying not to put her weight on her sore ankle, she suggested, "Listen, maybe I should lead since you don't have your glasses."

"Lead on, my lady."

Chapter 3

Chamber Of Gods

Valerie and Susan were distraught with concern for their friend. When they exhausted the first bout of tears, Susan pulled out her sleeping bag and stretched out next to Valerie.

"Do you suppose they're alive?"

"Oh, Val. They have to be," she said with uncertainty in her voice, then dredging up more confidence added, "We have to believe they are. Otherwise, we'll never make it through the next few hours. They're fine."

"Okay, they're fine." They lay silent for a few minutes, both willing it to be true. "Poor Sandy."

"I know. It's a dreadful thing to happen. And we convinced her to come."

"I don't mean that. I mean, of all people for her to be stuck with in there, it had to be him. She's probably wishing she *was* dead."

"Who could blame her? Who would ever want to be stranded with Michael Stanley Gant? As if the cave-in isn't bad enough, add him to the equation, and this has to be the worst experience of her life," Susan commiserated.

Valerie reached out and grabbed Susan's arm in sudden astonishment. "Oh, my gosh! Do you remember what Sandy said back at the dorm that afternoon? She said, and I quote, 'If I'm lucky, maybe the earth will open up and swallow him!'"

Susan's eyes grew large at the implication. "Wow! They always say be careful what you pray for, you might get it. I guess she shouldn't have been standing so close when she got answered."

"Sue, you know if she comes out of this alive there's going to be hell to pay. We'll never hear the end of how awful it was to be trapped with him."

"I know, but I'd rather have her complaining, than not have her."

Michael followed closely behind, holding Alesandra's steadying hand as they scrambled over boulders. As uncomfortable as the touching was to her, the need to find a way out was paramount. Knowing they were reliant on one another to accomplish that, she rose above her aversion, pushing her personal qualms aside. The pain in her ankle gradually subsided, and she no longer needed to hobble.

They inspected crevices for possible openings, and she frequently pointed out dangerous ground to keep him from tripping. As they came to each new junction, he paused to lay a small row of stones and piled a few together at the end like a small cairn to mark their path.

"Seems to be warmer here than it was up in the tunnel with the others. Do you notice it, or is it just me?" she asked. She stopped and handed Michael the helmet to hold onto as she pulled her sweatshirt over her head. He wasn't too blind to see how nicely shaped her breasts were as her arms lifted in the air. She took the sleeves of the shirt and tied them around her waist.

"Michael?"

"What?"

"I said, isn't it warmer down here?"

Embarrassed at being caught in the distraction, he refocused on her face and handed the helmet back. "Oh. Yeah, now that you mention it, it is. It's a sign the mountain is breathing."

"What do you mean? Mountains don't breathe."

"Sure they do. Caves breathe silently."

"You're not serious."

"Sure I am. You see, cool air seeps out along the rocky floor, and warm air flows in along the ceiling. That's why we feel alternating currents of warm and cool air, just as if the mountain was breathing."

Tripping over a rock outcrop concealed in the shadows, she fell to her knees. He was right there at her side, helping her back to her feet. "You all right?"

"Fine. Just another bruise to add to the multitude already there."

Michael looked at the green face of his Indiglo watch glowing brightly in contrast to the utter blackness surrounding them. "Let's take a break. We've been going for almost two hours straight, and my arm is killing me." He dropped onto a rock and leaned back, gritting his teeth. Wanting to be a hero in her eyes, he refrained from letting on just how much pain he was in, but it was getting to him. They sat next to each other and drank from their water bottles. When the bottles were back in the packs, he switched off the helmet lamp.

Darkness enveloped them as they sat together listening to the internal sounds of the mountain. Eerie echoes reverberated off the rock walls, and from somewhere came a faint but intriguing echo of rippling water. Natural curiosities permitted their imaginations free reign where they considered all possible sources for the sounds, from nocturnal creatures such as bats to reptilian denizens of the underground.

"Of course, you know it can't be any living creature. Too far from the food chain. No type of life, reptile, insect or otherwise to be found more than maybe a few hundred feet in. In all probability we're hearing noises made by loose shale or pebbles still settling after the quake."

She took comfort in his words and relaxed against the wall thankful for the opportunity to rest. She felt her strength returning and was strangely content to be in this time and place. "Do you think anyone was ever here, in this very spot before us?"

He squeezed her hand as if to insure his presence. "I wondered the same thing, until I saw these." He flicked the beam back on and illuminated a nearby wall, exposing several geometric figures preserved in soft gray clay.

"Michael!" she gasped. "Those are drawings!"

The mountain offered a variety of landscapes, from dense forests to small streams meandering through vistas of wildflowers, both sharply contrasted by craggy karsts. The mountain itself was not excessively high in elevation, but its trails were steep and rugged, making the summit nearly unattainable to ordinary hikers. That, and its Cherokee history, were the main reasons Blaney selected it for their field studies.

Preoccupied with his thoughts, the sudden explosion of sound as a helicopter appeared over the crest of the mountain startled Carl Blaney. He walked to the edge of the clearing about ninety feet from the camp. Brandon and Lewis were soon at his side, and Susan appeared from her tent to watch.

A man and woman jumped clear of the chopper and carried a stretcher between them, loaded down with supplies. Blaney ran forward to greet them and signaled for his able-bodied students to assist.

Mixed emotions of relief and self-reproach overwhelmed him as he joined the newcomers while the chopper blades slowed to a stop. Dropping the coils of rope from his shoulders to the ground, he extended a hand in greeting.

"Thanks for coming. I'm Carl Blaney, and these are my students."

The rescuer gripped his hand firmly. "Sorry we had to meet under these circumstances. I'm Roger Gunnison, and I'll be heading up this operation. This is Dr. Giselle Hawkins, and she's here to transport your injured gal to the hospital. Why don't you give me a rundown of what we're looking at here?"

Blaney had just finished explaining the situation when Susan arrived at his side. "Professor, should I go with Valerie in the helicopter?"

He ran a hand over his head in exasperation, not knowing what anyone should be doing any more. "I guess so, Susan."

"Hold up a minute," Gunnison cut in. "Can you cook?"

Susan crinkled her nose, not understanding the purpose of the question. "Yes."

"Then we need you here. We have a lot of people on their way up this mountain needing hot coffee and food all through the night. I've brought supplies with me." He reached out and laid a hand on her arm. "This isn't some piddly little job. We have to keep the energy of our rescue team at full steam until we have those kids out of there. Can you handle it?"

"Yes, sir."

"Good. Send those two fellas of yours out to start gathering firewood. You're gonna have to keep that fire going all night."

Susan nodded. "I'll get right on it. I'm just going to say goodbye to Valerie first."

Gunnison nodded, and she left them. Turning to Blaney, he said, "Why don't you show me where the cave-in happened."

Blaney secured his helmet and led the way.

"This area has numerous interconnecting caves and underground hollows. Some of them might connect to the one that gave way, so there is always the chance your two students will find their way out without any help from us. Tell me," Gunnison asked, "Uh…just how experienced are they?"

"Well, I'm pretty sure this was their first time, but I think they're both cool under pressure. That's not what worries me."

They stood in the cave's corridor, perusing the area of the accident. "I know. Their safety is uppermost in all our thoughts. Here's what we're gonna do. My guys will work in here removing as much of the rock as possible. Then, they'll try to drill through the remaining barrier so someone can climb through, see if the kids are there, and whether they can be pulled out."

"We didn't want to do that…"

"I know, and you were wise not to. It's dangerous, even with the right equipment and manpower. The positive thing here is that we have well trained people who know what they're doing. If anyone can get them out, they can." Gunnison exuded confidence, allowing the professor to grasp at a small strand of hope.

"Thank you. I'm grateful for your help. I just want those kids back alive."

"Meanwhile," the other man continued, "when the rest of the teams arrive, a field search will begin for adjoining caves and openings. Some of your people can join in that if they want. The more manpower, the faster we cover the mountain."

Gunnison was a take-charge guy, a real dynamo who issued

commands swiftly and competently. He knew what to do and how to get it done. The team had barely reached the campsite before he'd delegated tasks to everyone, and the rescue was under way. Blaney hung back, impressed and thankful. Within minutes, he too was put to work.

J. D. Evans, a large burly man and an experienced hiker and woodsman, headed up the Field Rescue Team. He carried a walkie-talkie on his belt and had a map of the mountain spread on a fold-a-way table that had been dropped off with another load of equipment on a subsequent journey by the helicopter. Jared and Max returned to the site with the rescue team, and Evans included them as part of his crew.

Wilbur "Bubba" Grubbs was the second in command from the Field Rescue Team. Older and grayer, he fit the mold of a typical mountain man. Brandon and Lewis were assigned to his team. He chattered incessantly to the boys about other rescues in which he participated. They, in turn, peppered him with questions about unexplored caves in the area.

They leaned over the map which had already been divided into grids, and assignments were made so the mountain would be thoroughly covered in a systematic manner. With a second map in his hand, along with his Garmin GPS, Bubba guided his team to the first grid of their assigned area.

He told the boys of Indian myths in which ancient Cherokee spirits allegedly visited the mountain. "Even to this day," he went on, "folks hereabouts claim to hear the echo of tribal drums in the night and ghostly lights that come and go. Brighter than the sun, they say. 'Course you might not hold with ghosts and the like, but I believe in those old Indian stories. I'm part Cherokee myself, you know."

Brandon nudged his friend with a wink in Bubba's direction, as he urged the old man to divulge more tales.

"You might think this is foolish talk," Bubba said, "but don't close your eyes and ears to strange things you happen to run across in these woods."

Alesandra and Michael found themselves in a small chamber dominated by various pillared growths resembling grotesque structures. In addition to the usual icicle-type formations hanging from the cave ceiling or extending upward from the cavern floor, they observed some of the dripstone formations to be translucent and fragile. The colors ranged from alabaster white to hues of dusky red and brown.

Warm air flowing into the cavern along the low ceiling had formed a fine mist that reacted with the limestone to produce a soft veneer of clay. Ancient artists left a legacy preserved in the malleable sediment. Geometric figures and recognizable outlines of animals decorated the rock walls.

"So, we're not the first humans in this cave after all." Her disappointment was obvious.

"That's true, but just imagine how long ago these carvings and pictographs were placed here, and by whom!"

The awe in his voice captured her, and she realized how superficial she sounded.

"I know, you're right. Let's take a closer look." She studied the glyphs, noting the primitive lines and elegance of simplicity. With reluctance, she finally turned away. "I'd love to spend more time studying these, but I guess we need to carry on, or we'll never get out of here."

Her casual words suddenly impacted them both with a ring of truth. As if by signal, they resumed their search for another exit from the room. Straying as far as he dared while still being able to explore within the beam of her headlamp, he spotted an exit.

"Sandy, over here."

She turned, and saw him beckoning her. He pulled on the twine that still connected them, and she allowed herself to be gently tugged to his side. They moved forward along a narrow passageway into the murky darkness, frequently stooping to avoid overhanging stone draperies, then twisting to squeeze past ornate, multi-tiered towers blocking their way.

Michael coddled his arm as much as he could while they trekked. The pain that shot through it whenever it bumped against rock brought a few yelps from him, but he tried to brave it silently. He didn't want her to think he was a wimp.

Rounding a column they came to a junction, and he stopped abruptly.

"What's the matter? Is it your arm?" She knew it must be agonizing for him, but he complained so little. In spite of the fact that she didn't like him, compassion still surfaced. And the reality was they had to work together to survive.

"No, look at this." He pointed to the ground.

She saw a row of stones exactly as he laid them. "How did they get there?"

"I laid them the last time we came through here. We've just gone in a circle."

Her shoulders sagged in frustration as panic quickly returned. She felt her throat tightening as tears blurred her vision. "Great. Just great. Now what? We're never getting out of here, are we?"

Hearing the tremors in her voice, he stepped closer and stroked her upper arm with his good hand. "Hey, it's okay. Don't get upset. We aren't in trouble yet. This is the reason I've been marking the trail. It's showing me we took the tunnel to the right last time. This time we'll take the one to the left and hope it gets us out." He stooped to set another row of stones.

She led the way through the darkness. “Do you feel it?” Her voice was soft.

“What? Feel what?”

“The breeze.”

Her body blocked the first hint of moving air but as she moved aside to let him in, he felt a noticeable change. “It's an air current originating from the cave,” she said. “We must be heading deeper into it.”

He waited while she pulled her sweatshirt back on and they continued moving forward, stumbling every so often as loose rock fragments were encountered or slipping on the mud covered stone. During their blacked out resting periods their eyes adapted to their new environment. Increased visibility revealed various outcroppings jutting from the walls of the tunnel, and their journey proceeded with more assurance. A soft glow lit the passage ahead until it opened into a tall chamber with smooth clay flooring. The high ceiling produced an eerie illumination, exposing their surroundings to view.

“It's just like twilight,” she said, caught in a moment of marvelous splendor.

Michael untied their tether and wandered away. “Sandy, come and see this.” He pointed toward a ribbon of water stretching before them, dark and glistening, and narrow enough they could easily lob a rock to the opposite shore. “This might be the source of the water sounds we heard before.”

Sharing his excitement, she hurried to his side and knelt to dip her hands into the water. She lifted the cool liquid to her lips and tasted it. “It's cold and fresh,” she said. “There's no mineral taste.” She shrugged out of her backpack and extracted her water bottle. “May as well fill it while we're here. The water's not stagnant. It's a flowing stream.” She lifted the bottle and took a long quenching drink, then dipped it back in to fill again. With the full flask tucked into the knapsack, she rose to her feet.

“This is magnificent, isn't it?” he asked.

“If you think it's great now, you should see it with your glasses on. It's really quite breathtaking,” she murmured. They gazed at the overall immensity of the cavern, caught up in the wonder of their discovery.

Hearing a small splashing sound, she turned and asked, “Are you thinking what I'm thinking?”

He nodded with a smile. “I'm thinking there might be fish in this river, and we haven't had anything to eat since breakfast.”

“Great. Now, how can we catch one, and if we do, how do we cook it? We can't build a fire.”

“If we have to, we'll eat it raw.”

“Oh, gross!”

He laughed. “You've had sushi, haven't you? Sushi is uncooked fish.”

"All the sushi I've eaten came ready-made with rice and soy sauce, and we don't have anything like that. Besides, it made me sick later." She wasn't eager to eat whatever they were able to catch without cooking it, but she was hungry.

"Trust me. I don't think it'll be a problem. First things first, though. We have to catch one before we worry about cooking it. Help me get my pack off, please."

She stepped closer and unsnapped the plastic buckles that held the straps in place, allowing the pack to slide down off his shoulders without having to work around his broken limb.

With his good hand, he rummaged through it and dug out an extra shirt and shoelaces. "Now, I'm going to need your help with this."

"Okay, what are we doing?"

"We're going to make a net. Come on."

She knelt next to him and followed his instructions, tying the sleeves of the shirt together. One shoelace looped around the collar and tied to the knotted sleeves at the other end. The other lace caught up a piece of the shirt tail, and fastened to the sleeves also, in effect making a parachute-designed net. Taking the ball of twine he handed her, she knotted the loose end to the shirt and unraveled a long length to use as a casting line.

He tugged her pack closer and asked if she had anything useful for their endeavors. Reaching inside, she pulled out her digging tools, her notebook, a textbook titled *Foundations of American Prehistory*, a half-eaten candy bar, and several essential items of makeup. She laid out her treasures, feeling suddenly sheepish as she compared them to his well-prepared kit.

She carried the net to the water's edge. "This is ingenious. I hope it works."

"Have faith, Sandy. Of course it will work." Selecting a relatively narrow part of the river, Michael used his good arm to show her how to cast his make-shift net into the water, allowing it to float in the current. "Then again, crossing your fingers can't hurt."

He stepped back and watched as she quickly kicked off her shoes and socks, rolled up her pant legs and waded into the steam.

The black water was impossible to penetrate with their eyes, but trout were known to inhabit underground cave streams. Minutes seemed like hours without success, and they were disheartened. The only positive thing she could see was that the cold water felt good on her sore ankle. She stared at the coruscated canopy overhead, wondering what would become of them.

Running his thumb in a caressing motion over the Mattock grubbing tool in his hand, he commiserated. "Sorry, Sandy. I really hoped this would work. Maybe it wasn't such a good..."

The net tugged, and the twine nearly jerked from her grasp. "Whoa!"

"What? You've got one?" He saw the tension pulling her string taut.

"Yes!" She squealed in delight.

"Well then, pull him in. Harder!" He watched her tugging as the fish fiercely struggled for its freedom.

She grabbed the shirt tightly, throwing it onto the bank where it continued to flop around. He knelt next to it, and waited for her to join him. The Mattock had a prying pick on one end and an adz blade on the other. Alesandra held the fish down with one hand and squeamishly looked away while he chopped off its head.

"You'll have to strip the flesh into filets and remove the scales. I can't do it with one hand."

"Eww. I don't know if I can."

"Of course you can. You're a brave girl."

She poked at it with one eye closed, and he laughed. "Don't worry, he won't bite. I took care of that. Here, this might help." Opening a small leather pouch hooked to his belt, he extracted a Swiss army knife and passed it to her.

She located a flat rock and in the half dark prepared the fish for cooking, just in case they were somehow able to build a fire.

"Good job. Now let's see if you can catch another one."

Feeling more confident now, she grabbed the net and waded in, casting it into the river again. It wasn't long before a whoop of joy signaled the catch of another fish, and she presented him with her prize.

"Another trout," he told her. "We'll have to be careful about small bones. You've done a great job, Sandy."

She smiled but conceded, "I couldn't have done it without you. I wouldn't have a clue what to do. It's your smarts that are saving us. I'm very impressed."

He grinned at the praise, remembering the first day he laid eyes on her. She was leaving Hardy Graham Stadium after a football game last fall. The sun cast golden highlights on her beautiful red hair, and her cheerleader's skirt flipped around her hips as she walked. Damn, she was pretty. He was a goner, right then and there. Of course, a guy like him could never do more than dream, but if he is going to dream, he might as well dream big. His fascination increased when he found she was in three of his classes. Science seemed to be her interest as well, and that gave them something in common. From that day on, he tried to win her approval. Now, he finally had it.

"I'm sorry we don't have any flour to roll our dinner in," he apologized. "But, I think I have something we can cook them on. At least they won't be completely raw." Ferreting through his backpack, he pulled out a Ziploc bag. It contained what looked like cups from a cardboard egg carton.

"What are those?"

"Fire starters. Stuff the egg cartons with dryer lint, then pour on paraffin wax. Break 'em up into individual pieces, and you can start a dozen fires. They burn a lot longer than paper, long enough to let wood get a good blaze going. And since we have no wood, we'll hope they burn long enough to cook us some fish."

"That's so clever. Where did you learn all this?"

"I was an eagle scout. I guess that's why I have this stuff with me. Blaney said we'd be camping out overnight, so I came prepared. That, and the fact that my parents sent me on Outward Bound wilderness survival camps four summers in a row."

"Really? That must have been terrific. I always wanted to do something like that."

He pulled a fork from the backpack and held the fillets over the small flames in an effort to cook them. "I guess it all depends on your reasons for going."

"What do you mean?"

"The only reason my parents sent me was to get rid of me," he confessed bitterly. "Simply couldn't tolerate the idea of having me around for a full two months. Two weeks were more than enough for them."

Alesandra felt something deep inside her move. Sympathy, not pity. "I'm sorry, Michael. I can't even begin to imagine how awful that must feel. I guess I've been very lucky. I have a family that gives me a lot of love and security." She studied him, and the thought again crossed her mind that he wasn't so geeky without the glasses. Maybe there were reasons for his inability to socialize well. Maybe there was a person in there that wouldn't be so bad to get to know. She started to feel guilty for all the times she brushed him off without giving him the chance she would have had he been attractive or popular. She never considered herself shallow before, but she was suddenly seeing things about herself she was not particularly proud of.

"Well, Michael, if I had to get lost or stranded with someone, I'm glad it was you." She watched as an embarrassed smile spread across his face.

They ate and talked, not unlike their idea of a meal in which cavemen sat around a roaring fire after a hunt.

"Feel better with something in your stomach?"

"Much better, thank you. That was probably the best fish I've ever tasted. Gourmet dining at its finest," she declared as she leaned back on her arms and stretched her legs out in front of her.

"Glad to hear it. As great as this spot is, we should probably get our things packed up and get moving. We still have to find our way out of here."

She nodded in agreement. "You're right, of course. But I can't help wishing we had time to look around more."

"Nothing says we can't come back another time." He watched as the idea took root in her mind and blossomed into a grin. "Come on."

Although the light emanating from the cathedral roof was less than during normal daytime hours, they saw a number of side chambers leading out of the cavern. Michael let her choose which one to explore, and assembled his line of rocks with a small pile on the end stone, continuing to mark the path as he had been doing.

Alesandra switched on her headlamp, but once they left the main cavern, her light was noticeably dimmer. "I think my batteries are running low."

"Okay, we'll change to the flashlight now." He unclipped it from the swivel hanging on his belt and switched it on, significantly increasing the brightness.

They threaded their way across rock-cluttered flooring and around bizarre shapes. Alesandra found it impossible to dismiss the treasures they might be overlooking in their desire to escape the darkened inner clutches of this cave.

Absorbed in her thoughts, she suddenly became aware of a fluorescence ahead starkly contrasting the darkness to which they had grown accustomed. Her step quickened and she passed through a narrow portal into a spacious room where the surrounding walls appeared illuminated. Stranger yet was the fact that the irradiation remained after they extinguished their light.

"Michael, what do you think is causing this?"

He was less in awe of the phenomenon but took his time in forming a response. "I suspect we're seeing a form of reflective energy caused by our own light rays. I don't know what mineral properties are being excited here, but we're undoubtedly witnessing something that's lain dormant for a very long time."

Everywhere they aimed their beam, it produced an increased level of light intensity, and soon the entire chamber abounded in artificial brightness.

"It's as if we flipped on a switch of some kind," she said.

The subdued lighting within the chamber made it easier to pick their way around the sediment and loose rock fragments littering the floor. When the chamber began to darken, they directed a beam of light at the walls, illuminating a new section of the cave. An eddy of cool air caught their attention.

"There must be an opening somewhere ahead." Michael motioned in front of him, and they set off in that direction.

They made their way by instinct, pausing to rest for a few moments at a rise in the flooring. Alesandra glanced around aided by the reflected cave light and suddenly leaped to her feet in amazement.

"Michael, look!"

She pointed toward a gallery of stone pillars, eerily reminiscent of ancient altars and godlike idols. She counted seven such formations, each similar in size and situated in a semi-circle. Her imagination could easily have portrayed them as praying figures. Shadows gave the image of a host of deities congregated to conduct a ceremony of divine purpose. They forgot for a moment that the stone structures were not real, in spite of their appearance.

She wanted a closer look. Michael watched as she ran her hands over one of the columns before exclaiming excitedly, "There are indentations here," she whispered. "I think they're man-made. I feel distinct carvings that I don't think are of natural origin."

"You mean like pictograph designs?"

"Well, yes, but more like symbols or perhaps even writing of a sort."

As Michael moved next to her, his eye caught sight of the time on his watch. "Sandy, I think we should get some sleep before going any further. It's almost midnight. You must be exhausted. I know I am. This looks like a good place, and we can give our batteries a rest."

"I am kind of tired. I'll be back in a minute." She hoisted her pack and headed for a dark corridor that led out of the cavern.

"Wait a minute. Where are you going?"

Her cheeks flushed, and she reached into her pack withdrawing the white plastic bottle. "After all that water we drank at the river back there, I need the bottle."

He gave a brief nod of embarrassed understanding. "Good thinking. I'll meet you back here in a few minutes." He pulled out his own yellow-capped bottle and headed for an alcove in the opposite direction.

Decidedly more comfortable, Alesandra reveled in the chance to lie down and close her eyes. Using their backpacks as pillows, they each chose a place to bed down, making themselves as comfortable as possible on the stone floor. She watched as Michael settled on the other side of the room. As she felt the cave chill set in, the enormity of the dark unknown made her uncomfortable, and she found herself wishing he was closer.

"I don't bite, you know."

"Uh, well, I didn't want you to uh, get the wrong idea. You know."

His stammering shyness made her giggle. "No, I don't know," she teased.

"Sure you do. Here we are, all alone, in the dark. I'm a guy and…you're a girl."

"It's nice of you to notice I'm a girl."

"Of course I noticed. Even with all your scrapes and bruises, torn clothes, and dirty face, you've still got those…uh, it's hard to miss."

The giggle returned, echoing in the chamber. "Dirty face? You're not so clean yourself, even if I can't see you in the dark."

"I'm sure we're both a mess," he said, grinning at their easy banter. "Let's try to sleep."

In spite of her realization that they were certainly alone in this place, there remained a stray feeling that someone watched them. She knew she was being ridiculous, but spoke anyway. "Michael, would you mind sleeping here next to me? I'd feel better," she admitted timidly.

Without a word, he came to settle beside her. "Better?"

"Yes, thanks. Wait a minute, finish that sentence."

"What sentence would that be?"

"I've still got all those…and then you stopped. What have I got?"

"Did I say that?"

"Yes, you did. Finish it."

"Sorry, don't remember."

"Finish it."

"Okay, let me try to remember."

"Think harder."

"What you have is all those cute curves in all the right places," he admitted, then waited to be slugged.

Alesandra smiled as she rolled over, putting her back to him. "Thank you," she said, pleased with the answer. She waited until she heard his breathing change signaling he was asleep, before she shifted closer for warmth and a sense of protection. It amazed her to realize that only this morning she couldn't tolerate even breathing the same air as Michael, and now here she was depending on him and seeking his comfort, not that she would admit it to anyone else. Absolute darkness made it easy to fall asleep in spite of the fact they were possibly in the presence of primeval gods. It was a sobering thought and the last thing she remembered until she slowly woke the following morning.

Liberated

"It's startin' to get too dark to see much anymore. Let's bunk down here for the night and start again at sunup." Bubba Grubbs shucked off his bedroll and pulled out his walkie talkie. "There oughta be plenty o' dry wood around to build us a fire. Why don't you fellas gather some while I check in with headquarters."

Brandon and Lewis dropped their gear and set off to the nearby wooded area to collect fuel for the fire. Grubbs reported in, then built a decent campfire for them to cook some of the food he had packed, all the while regaling them with more stories. The boys listened avidly until it was time to sleep.

The older man flipped his bedroll open and laid down. After a quick visit to the edge of the woods to water the trees, Brandon and Lewis tugged their sleeping bags out and unrolled them. Lewis got in and fidgeted, trying to get comfortable. Grubbs' stories played repeatedly in Brandon's mind, and the idea of sleeping among the mountain's ghosts without a shelter caused stirrings of anxiety. He spread his sleeping bag close to Lewis' and lay down.

"Dude, why don't you just crawl in with me?" Lewis mocked. "We got a whole mountain here. You don't need to lay on top of me."

"Sorry, man. Didn't realize I was that close." He shifted his bedding a few inches away, but only a few. When he was snugly ensconced inside, he asked, "What'd you think of those stories he was telling us?"

"You mean the stuff about the Indians? I thought that was pretty interesting. He's not bad for an old coot."

"I mean about the unexplained lights at night and the ghosts and stuff."

"I doubt it's true, Bran. He's just yanking our chain."

"You think so?"

His question was met with silence while Lewis thought about it. "Yeah, he's just funnin' us."

A forest animal cried out, a little too close for comfort. In an instant, both boys were standing, still wrapped in their sleeping bags. Without a word, they hopped their way around to the other side of the fire and settled next to Grubbs.

"We're gonna sleep over here. Too many rocks in the ground on the other side," Brandon told the old man in explanation.

"Uh-huh," Grubbs replied, smiling as he rolled over and went to sleep.

Susan finished filling the thermos bottles with coffee for the umpteenth time for a rescue worker who gathered them in a pack and carried them to the cave entrance. She arched her back to stretch her sore muscles and noticed the brilliance of the spring night sky. Millions of stars twinkled, and she wished on every one of them for Alesandra and Michael to be found safe. A tear slipped down her cheek, unbidden. It helped that Gunnison gave her a job to keep her moving, but the horror of the situation never left her thoughts. Soon, the first tear was followed by a second and a third.

A sound near the trees to her left caught her attention. She didn't realize anyone else was around. The rescue workers remained congregated at the cave for what seemed like endless hours now. Peering into the darkness, she thought it looked like Professor Blaney's yellow windbreaker just inside the edge of the forest perimeter.

He had been on her mind throughout the day and evening, too. How awful it must be for him to bear the weight of the tragedy on his shoulders. Folding her arms against the chilling night air, she strolled toward him. Her foot snapped a twig, the sharp sound crackling above the ever rustling of the aspen leaves overhead.

Carl turned his head and saw her. As she came closer, the moonlight showed her wet cheeks, and his guilt intensified. "Susan."

"Professor. Are you all right?"

A huge sigh left his chest, and he quietly admitted, "I don't think so."

"Me neither." Following her instincts, she opened her arms and slipped them around his waist, laying her head on his shoulder and snuggling into his neck. "I'm so sorry. I know this must be more awful for you than for any of us."

Carl knew he should stop now. Common sense shouted to pull away and keep her at a distance, but he felt so vulnerable and her arms comforted him. He let his own wrap around her, offering her succor in return. "It's the worst moment of my life. What if something has happened to those kids? What if we find them too late? What if…?"

She heard the choke in his voice and lifted her head to look into his eyes. "It's not your fault. I know you feel like it is, but it's not." Her hand lifted to his cheek, her thumb gently stroking.

"Of course it's my fault. I'm the one ..."

"No. What happened to us in there was a fluke of nature. There's no way anyone could have foreseen that. You would never have let us go in unless you firmly believed we'd be safe."

He hung his head. "I was wrong. God, I was wrong."

"Shh, shh," she gentled him. With a hand on either side of his face, she lifted it until she was gazing into his blue eyes.

He was touched by the depth of compassion he saw. And when her lips brushed against his, they were warm and inviting. Thoughts of what he should do, what he needed to do, fled his mind, and his arms embraced her more tightly as her tongue sought entrance to his mouth. He parted his lips and let her in, his hands moving up her back and burying themselves in her soft, blonde hair as he tasted her.

Susan brushed her fingertips through the dark hair on his collar. She wanted to soothe him, to find some way to take his pain away. And somewhere in it all, she got lost in the kiss, wanting it to never end. "I've wanted you for so long," she whispered to his lips.

Her back felt warm pressed against another body, an arm snugly wrapped around her with a large hand settled comfortably on her breast. It felt hot. Her eyes flashed open with sudden clarity, and she wiggled her way out of the embrace, trying not to disturb him. As she lifted his hand from her, the heat of his skin surprised her.

Her movement released the pressure her back had provided against his injured arm, and the suddenness woke him. "Is it morning already?" He rubbed his eyes and took a moment to discern where he was. "It's so cold in here." Even his voice shivered.

Alesandra turned on her light and saw a sheen of sweat beaded on his brow. "Michael, are you feeling okay?" She placed her hand on his cheek. "You're burning up."

"Can't be. Don't have time for this. We've got to get out."

She pulled his water bottle from his pack and let him drink the still cool mountain water before pouring some onto a tee-shirt and bathing his face.

He brushed her hands away. "Stop it. I'm fine. Just cold. We've got to get up and moving. That will warm me up."

With a frown creasing her forehead, she watched as he insisted trying to sit up. "I think you're getting sick."

"Sandy, just help me out of here. That's all I'm asking. The sooner we get out, the better."

She helped him sit, and he waited a moment for the dizziness to subside. His determination to get her out of there, to be her hero, made him refuse to surrender to the fever. As his head cleared, he reached out and picked up one of the reflective rocks. Slowly turning it over in his hand, an idea began to take shape. "I wonder..."

"You wonder what?"

"I wonder if this is in any way related to the mineral I found at the dig. It has that same golden glow."

"Too bad we can't take some with us," she murmured, disappointed. She repacked the bottle and shirt into his pack. "You heard the professor. You could end up losing your credits if you take it."

"Only if he were to find out about it. He won't know if we don't tell him."

"I don't know, Michael."

"C'mon. Aren't you as curious as I am?"

She shifted her weight from one foot to the other, and back again, wondering if it was the fever talking. "We'd have to make a pact."

"All right. Let's be fair to both of us. I want to learn all I can about these rocks. You want to come back and check out those glyphs. I say our journey within this mountain is never to be discussed with anyone else. No one hears what we've seen or done."

"Sounds good to me. Everything we've seen and the route we took will be kept secret at all costs."

"Sort of like, 'What happens in Vegas, stays in Vegas.'

"Exactly. And you will come back again with me?"

He was elated. She actually wanted him to accompany her on a return trip. That meant more alone time with her. It was more than he dared hope for. "Of course I will. Remember, that means no Val, no Susan. I know how girls are. This is strictly between you and me."

"Understood and agreed." She wondered if he would even remember this conversation when the fever subsided.

He tucked the precious rock in his knapsack and let her lead the way down a long and narrow passage branching off from the chamber which opened into a second, smaller chamber with an array of artistic draperies hanging overhead. When she stopped without warning, he bumped into her and jarred his arm, sending shafts of pain shooting through him. "Argh!"

"Oh, my gosh! I'm so sorry." She winced in guilt. Michael Stanley Gant was still not her favorite person by any means, but oddly enough, she was no longer as repulsed as she used to be, and her inborn compassion made her regret causing undue physical pain. She recognized all he had done to help them find their way out, and it demanded that she at least show him some kindness.

Grimacing, he leaned against the wall for support and waited a few minutes in silence, hoping the throbbing would soon start to ebb.

"Are you okay?"

"I'll be fine. We've got a bit of a problem ahead of us now." He knelt down, inspecting the wall in front of them. "The only way out is back the way we came, or through this hole. It's barely large enough to squeeze through, but I think we can make it. Take a deep breath, and let's give it a try."

A moment of rationalization struck. If she went first and got wedged in, what then? Would she die here? On the other hand, if he went first and got through without any problems, it meant she would get through easily. However, if he got wedged in, the opening would be sealed off, and she would be stuck inside forever.

Michael assessed the dilemma confronting them. He had to manage to worm his way through the hole and its connecting tight tunnel without using his arms to hitch himself along. He awkwardly doffed his gear, took the helmet from her head and put it on his own. Lying on his back, he worked his shoulders through the opening and used his feet to propel himself like an inchworm.

Left on her own in the dark, she removed her backpack. It would be her job to push both packs through the tunnel once he made it out the other end. The glow emanating from his lamp inside disappeared soon after she lost sight of his feet.

Deep rumblings once more emanated from the earth, and the floor started to quake. He would be trapped inside that tunnel forever, and she would die here alone. Hysteria took hold, and she screamed.

Michael was jostled in his cocoon by the trembling earth. Alesandra's shrieks of fear echoed, and he heard rocks tumbling behind them in the chamber. Knowing her reaction was aggravating the situation, he needed to get back to her, to help her. If only she would stop screeching long enough to hear him.

"Sandy, shut up. Stop screaming. Grab my feet, and pull me out of here." Working his way back in reverse proved much more difficult, especially with his surroundings so unstable. He continued to call to her, hoping she would hear him and obey.

Formations overhead broke loose and crashed to the floor. Rock pelted her from every direction. With her hands over her head seeking to protect herself, she noticed the light reappear from within the tunnel and his feet popped back into view. Bending, she grabbed hold of them and with all her might, tugged him back into the chamber with her, still fretting and wailing.

Rolling onto his good arm, he levered himself to a sitting position. She helped him to his feet, and he immediately pressed her against the wall, using his own body to shield her.

"Stop it, Sandy. Stop screaming. You're only making it worse." He wrapped his good arm around her neck and pulled her to his shoulder, whispering words of comfort in her ear as she settled. "It's okay. We're both fine. Shh. It's okay now." He held her as she wept. They stayed that way until the shockwaves ceased, and the rock shower ended.

When silence settled she finally whispered, "I was so scared. I thought we were both going to die this time."

"I know. I'm sorry. We're fine. Shhh. No worries. You can't scream like that. It just makes the ceiling collapse."

"I'm sorry. I didn't think. I'm sorry."

"It's okay. We're both fine, and we're going to get out of here." His voice exuded a confidence he didn't feel, but she required him to be strong for her. His fever made him dizzy, and although he would not admit it, he leaned against the wall as much from his own need as hers. When he felt capable, he pulled away and attempted a smile.

"Okay, let's try this again. If the passage is still clear, we can crawl through it. You'll have to push the equipment in ahead of you." With a finger under her chin, he lifted her face, wanting to be sure she was all right.

She nodded and wiped her tears. He stepped back and allowed her to move away from the wall. She bent to clear the debris that now littered the floor in front of the mousehole.

Minutes later, Michael was on his back and squirming his way inside again. She thrust the backpacks in after him, wanting out before another quake started. They might not be so lucky the next time. Scrambling on her hands and knees, she suffered another bruise on her shoulder before she, too, emerged on the other end.

They found themselves facing a steep incline covered with layers of aragonite crystals. They looked like icy feathers, reminding Alesandra of the frost patterns on the windows at her grandmother's house in Pennsylvania in the winter. In reality they were anything but soft. She reached out and gasped in shock as the crystals sliced into her hand like razors.

"It's no good, Sandy. It's too steep, and our light is fading. We can't climb and carry the flashlight. We need to take two of the batteries out of the helmet lamp and replace them with the ones in the flashlight. Hopefully, that will give us enough light to see what we're doing."

He removed the helmet, and she undid the battery casing, then opened the flashlight and spilled the batteries out into her hand. Leaving in one of the weakened batteries, she replaced the other two with stronger ones and turned the switch on, making it shine significantly brighter. With the torch light and the expended batteries stashed into his pack, she strapped the helmet onto her head, pulled on her leather work gloves, and once more attempted to climb the slope.

"We've got another problem. How are we going to get you up this cliff with your broken arm? You can hardly climb it."

Refusing to relinquish his quest now, his scientific mind considered the steep angle of the incline and weighed the options. "Ok, you have to climb up first. Take your time, and choose your pathway carefully. When you get to the top, toss the rope down and help me up."

Progress was slow, but steady. When she finally hiked herself over the ledge at the top, she rested for a moment before pulling off the bloody gloves and looking at the damage on her tender palms.

"Sandy, you okay?"

"Yeah. My hands are a mess, but I'll live." Compared to his broken arm, she really had nothing to complain about. "Hang on, I'll toss the rope down."

After tying one end securely around her waist, she tossed the loose end down to him and sat herself on the ground, bracing her legs against a rock for anchor.

With only one hand, Michael was unable to tie a bowline and had to be satisfied with a simple overhand knot. He twisted the rope length around his wrist before grabbing hold to keep it from slipping out of his hand. "I'm ready. Let's give it a go." He planted his feet on the slope and leaned forward as he scaled it, trying to make the job as easy as he could on her in his weakened condition.

Her shoulders strained under the weight, but she continued to tug with all her strength until finally his head rose above the ridge, and they were face to face. He crawled the last few feet and collapsed next to her to catch his breath.

Finding a single hallway beckoning to them several feet from the rim of the slope, their progress was quickly impeded by a new feature of the underworld. Clusters of round popcorn calcite growths covered the passageway floor, making their journey hazardous.

"Slippery road ahead, gal. It's going to be like walking on beads." He didn't add that he already felt tipsy.

With her hand firmly clasped in his, they picked their way through the passage until the air that brushed against their faces no longer carried the damp smell they were accustomed to. Cool and refreshing, it signaled an opening into the outer world.

Coming out of the cave in rotation for a break, Gunnison saw the sun rising on a new day. He wiped at the perspiration as it runneled through the grime on his face. The night had been long and arduous. Stretching to loosen tight muscles, he wandered into the woods to relieve himself before washing and grabbing something to eat.

They had still not made contact with the trapped students, visual, verbal or otherwise. He refused to let it show, but Gunnison was worried. Nineteen hours elapsed since the cave-in, and who knew what they would find when they finally located the students.

Susan saw him coming and ladled a bowl of chili for him. "Sit down, Mr. Gunnison. You must be exhausted."

"Thanks, Susan." He took the proffered food and sat at a makeshift table. A bag of bread rolls sat open in front of him. He grabbed one, dipping it into the meaty sauce.

"How's it going?" she asked timidly.

"Slow, I'm afraid. We have to be careful, or we'll exacerbate the situation. Can't afford another rock slide in there."

"No sign of them yet?"

"Not yet. I'm sorry. I know that's not what you want to hear. Hopefully, in the next few hours we'll reach them." He dug the spoon into the food, devouring it in short order and holding the empty bowl out for a refill. "How are you managing out here?"

"Fine. That lady over there," she pointed to an older woman with a long gray braid, "Martha Sue, showed up late last night. She's been helping me stay on top of things and let me get a bit of sleep while she held the fort down. She's a godsend."

"Yes, she is. She runs a restaurant back in town. Terrific lady. Always the first to step up when help is needed. Thank goodness we don't need this kind of help often."

Susan sat on a bench opposite him and looked him in the eye. "Mr. Gunnison, tell me straight. What are the chances we're going to find them alive?"

He looked at her squarely and assessed her strength. Convinced she wouldn't wither into a heap of tears, he told her the truth.

"Injuries in caves are rare, but even minor ones can be fatal if the caver is so far underground or in such a constricted position that he's not able to get out of the cave in time. You were in there. You know how cold it is. The constant low temperature frequently causes a victim to quickly lapse into unconsciousness."

"And Sandy and Michael have been trapped since yesterday morning."

"Yes." He left her to her own conclusions, watching as she bravely wiped a tear away before it could fall. "But until we know differently, we pray and hope for the best."

"Yes, sir. Let me get you some coffee." She went back to the fire, keeping her back to him as she fed more wood to the hot glowing coals and poured him a cup of steaming liquid. When she returned, she handed it to him and quietly said, "Thank you for being honest with me and not treating me like a kid. You're right. I'll just keep hoping and praying."

Gunnison nodded as he stirred sugar into the coffee, working hard to stifle his own misgivings for a happy ending.

Once again on his back, Michael worked his way through the final tunnel toward the sunlight that enticed him from the other end. With freedom just a few feet away, his excitement ground to a halt when he found the exit obstructed. Sticking his head through the opening in an effort to get a better look at the barrier, he drew in his first deep breath of fresh air. To his dismay, a granite slab stood like a guardian less than two feet from the hole effectively blocking the way. Seeing the proportions of it, he knew attempts to dislodge it would be futile.

"Pull me back," he shouted. He felt her grab hold of his ankles and tug him back inside. He sat up to face his partner in grime.

"Sandy, we did it. We've made it. This leads outside."

Her eyes lit with excitement, and she missed the reservation in his voice. "Well, what are you waiting for? Let's get out of here."

"Just one problem. It looks like we've got a rock wall blocking the entrance. It's going to be a really tight getting out, but I think we can do it." He worried about the difficulty of trying to squeeze out with his injured arm, but he didn't share that with her.

"You go ahead first, and I'll push our packs out, just like last time."

Nodding in agreement, he lay back down and tucked his head out of sight. "Here goes nothing." Making his way through the tunnel for a second time, he struggled to push through the aperture at the other end.

Alesandra watched as his feet left the tunnel. She waited for the light that would fill the space he vacated, but it did not come. "Are you out?"

He grunted in frustration. "Remember when Pooh Bear went visiting Rabbit, and he ate too much honey?"

"You mean when he tried to get back out of Rabbit's hole? A large bear in a very tight spot?"

"That would be it. I'm stuck."

Midday found the rescue group enlarging the passageway by dislodging and removing some of the larger rocks and continuing to shovel loose shale away. They searched for a weakened area in which to insert a probe and possibly communicate with the trapped students. Gunnison planned to lower men down into the cavity to bring them out, but occasional soft rumblings underground threatened additional tectonic movements.

Dread seized her heart and squeezed it tightly. “Oh, no you don’t’. Don’t you dare even go there with me, Michael Stanley Gant. You are NOT stuck. You can’t be stuck. I won’t let you be stuck.” Finally, being so close to liberation she refused to be stopped now. Huffing, she scurried through the tunnel to look for herself and assess the situation. With her head outside of the tunnel, she flipped onto her back so she could look up at him without breaking her neck. Taking a few deep gulps of fresh air, she found it easier not to lose control. Panic would not get them out of their predicament. Her mouth screwed up as she sought a workable solution to getting Michael unwedged.

“Okay you tubby little cubby all stuffed with fluff, am I supposed to be Christopher Robin and read to you until you get unstuffed enough to squeeze through, or am I supposed to be Gopher and use explosives to blow you out?”

“Definitely not Gopher, if you don’t mind. I don’t think my poor body could take any more battering.”

“The problem is, you’re too tall. I think if you were to sort of squat down about six inches, you’d have more room for your shoulders and could get through easier.”

He tried to follow her instructions, but what he truly wanted was to simply collapse and sleep. The exertion of the past few hours wore him down, and he struggled not to give in to it. Squirming first one way and then another like a circus contortionist, all the while trying to favor his arm, he finally eased free of the restriction and took a deep breath.

“Hurray! The Pooh is free,” she laughed, feeling giddy at her own proximity to liberty. She scooted back inside, grabbed the backpacks and pushed them out ahead of her. Michael did his best to help pull them clear of the opening.

“Okay, Piglet, your turn. Come on.”

“Piglet!” she exclaimed, as she wiggled out into the long sought sunlight. “I don’t look like a pig.”

“Indeed you don’t. But piglets are small and cute and pink, and besides, who else accompanies Pooh on all his adventures? It’s always Piglet.”

“All right, I’ll be Piglet,” she conceded, shading her eyes with her hand. The brightness of the noonday sun hurt after the abysmal blackness in which they had been living, and she dug in her pack for her sunglasses.

Using his feet, he gathered rocks again, larger ones this time. She watched as he distanced them apart to form a large circle, placing the last one in the center.

"What are you doing?"

"The final sign. 'I have gone home.' It marks the end of the trail. Baden Powell has it marking his grave in Kenya. And for us, it's going to mark the entrance so we can find it when we come back. I've placed them far enough apart that the circle isn't obvious unless you're looking for it."

"You're clever for a bear of very little brain."

Michael grinned at the praise as he stood back and surveyed the location. "The entrance isn't readily apparent at all. It just looks like a rock-faced wall. If you didn't know there was a gap behind it, you'd never guess it."

Sliding open a zippered pocket on his backpack he pulled out his GPS and a small notepad. "Okay, Sandy, I can't see without my glasses, so I need you to read the gizzie for me and record the bearings. If we don't do a little orienteering now, we'll never find our way back here, and this is one place we don't want to lose."

In the light of day, she clearly saw the flush of his cheeks and the sheen of sweat on his upper lip and forehead, indicators of the fever he was still fighting. "I'll take care of it," she promised.

After noting the bearings he asked her to, she sat back on the grass and sucked in a deep breath. "This air smells so good, doesn't it? And it feels so dry." She took off her windbreaker and lifted her sweatshirt over her head. "Wait, I hear water." Rising to her feet, she wandered around a bend. "Hey, Michael, come here."

He followed the sound of her voice to find her bent at a small stream soaking her hands.

"I'm covered in blood from those aragonite crystals cutting my hands to shreds."

"I guess band-aids are pointless. You'd need about a hundred."

Without being asked, Alesandra opened his backpack and found the damp tee-shirt she had used to bathe his face earlier that morning. Dipping it in the cold mountain stream, she lifted it to once again minister to him. "Why don't you lay down in the sunshine and rest a bit?"

Settling on the grassy slope close by, she laid back and lifted her face to the sun with her arms extended over her head. "Sunshine feels great, doesn't it?"

"No arguments here." His eyes focused on her chest, watching it rise and fall as she breathed in the fresh mountain air, and not for the first time, fever be damned, he wanted her. She lay stretched out, just like she did in his fantasies, and he wanted to crawl over to her, and onto her, and make her his. Instead, he kept his distance while she basked in the world that greeted them; the sound of chirping birds, the gentle rustling of breezes through tall pines growing in reckless profusion everywhere around them.

"They must be frantic with worry about us," she said.

"Yes, I imagine they are. I'll bet Brandon and Lewis are tearing through those rocks to get deeper into that cave. They must have been disappointed it wasn't them who fell through instead of us."

"I'm more concerned about Val and Susan. I hope they aren't hurt." After a few minutes of silent pondering, she turned to look at him. She debated whether to speak, but decided it was right. "Michael, before we go back, I want to say thanks. Thanks for everything you did in there, for looking after me. I'd probably still be sitting in that first chamber, crying and hungry, if you weren't there with me. I appreciate it, and I won't forget it."

Instead of being cocky and tossing it aside as though it were naught, he simply replied, "You're welcome." He lay back on the grass, thoughtful for a moment before adding, "I'm kind of glad I was the one who fell through with you. I mean, in spite of our harrowing adventure, I got to be trapped with the prettiest co-ed on campus. Every guy's dream, right?"

She laughed and sat more upright, leaning back on her arms. "You know, even in the light of day, you aren't such a bad looking guy without those glasses. You ever think of contacts?"

Michael's eyes grew large at her words. Did she really say that, or was it the fever talking? It was the closest thing to a compliment he ever received from a girl. "You can bet I'll be thinking of it now."

He closed his eyes. Fever or not, he knew that while she was grateful now, going back to the real world would overshadow that. Alesandra was who she was, and reunited with her friends and social atmosphere she would quickly revert back to the girl she had been two days ago; looking right through him as if he did not exist. He would not think any less of her for it. It was the way things were. He had lived it too many times to believe otherwise. Her words were like a butterfly—beautiful and treasured while he had them, but he knew they would flutter away. Furthermore, although he trusted her not to tell about the pilfered rock in his backpack, he didn't really expect her to keep her word to return to the mountain with him.

"Well, Pooh?" she said with reluctance. "What now? Do we go hunt a heffalump, or do we sit here and wait to be found?"

"I'm not sure how far I can go, but we don't want to be found here at the portal. Let's start working our way down the mountain toward town. We're bound to run into someone."

The sun was high overhead as they crossed broken trails and sporadic clearings. When he stopped frequently to rest, she checked the

GPS and made notes.

Time dragged and hunger gnawed at them. She recognized his fortitude in trying to carry on was to impress her, but he was growing weaker with each step. Knowing it was up to her to put an end to it, she announced she was too tired to go on any further and wanted to rest in the shade of a small glen, out of the glare of the afternoon sun until they were found.

"If this is where we're going to stop, I need you to do something."

"Sure, what is it?"

"See that rocky clearing in front of us? I want you to build three separate fires in a triangle pattern."

"Okay, and I'm doing this why?"

"It's a universal search and rescue code. If there are any overhead search parties, they'll see it and know we're here."

"All right. Got any of those nifty little fire starters left?"

"Probably so."

She sifted through his pack and found the bag of starters, then gathered enough wood to get the fires burning. He called instructions to her as she built the first fire, and she managed the next two on her own. When she had all three blazes going with plenty of smoke rising, she rejoined him in the glen, close enough to keep an eye on them.

"Pooh, I'm starting to feel rumbly in my tumbly," she complained. Retrieving the partially-eaten candy bar from her backpack, she broke it in half and shared. "I'm still hungry."

"Don't worry, Piglet. I think we just found lunch." He pointed to the edge of the clearing and smiled.

Following the direction of his finger, she bounded to her feet with delight. Plump red raspberries covered the vines in profusion. Using the helmet as a basket, she worked quickly to fill it. "I love raspberries. They're my favorite," she told him.

Confident he had done all he could to take care of her, he lay back to rest. When she returned to his side to share her harvest, she found him fast asleep.

The field search team scrambled over ridges and gullies, calling out periodically and blowing their whistles in case the two lost kids could hear them. The mountainside consisted of rolling hills and granite blocks grown over with crusted earth and foliage.

Lewis discovered a hollow rock face indentation that possibly led deeper into the mountain. Overjoyed, he made a tentative entry only to find it was a shallow porous opening no more than ten feet deep. "This place is crawling with caves."

Bubba Grubbs nodded. "Most are false caves, like that one. Still, there are others once used by Johnny Rebs to hide from marauding Yankee patrols. The woods are full of old minnie balls and rusty bayonets."

The boys kept one eye open for their missing classmates and the other peeled for Civil War relics. Grubbs' stories fascinated them and created even more interest in returning to explore the many secrets of Blaney's Mountain.

She saw his eyes opening, and reached into her backpack to pull out the water bottles she filled at the last stream. "Here. Drink. You need to stay hydrated."

He took the water bottle gratefully and guzzled down the cool liquid. More than three hours had passed since leaving the cave.

"You don't suppose we'll have to spend another night out here before anyone finds us, do you?" she worried.

"I don't think so. It's still early." He watched the tension drain from her shoulders as she relaxed. "Wait a minute. Did you hear that? Listen."

The sound of voices broke through the sounds of nature they'd grown accustomed to. Listening closer, the words became more distinct.

"Michael! Sandy!"

Alesandra leaped to her feet and shouted excitedly to attract their attention.

Gunnison and Blaney sat at the table, and Susan served them each a bowl of chicken stew along with a plate of hot buttered biscuits. She saw the look of defeat shadowing the professor's countenance, and it dragged her own spirits down.

Static burst out of the walkie-talkie on Gunnison's belt. "Grubbs to Gunnison -- come in."

He snatched the radio and held it to his mouth. "This is Gunnison. Go ahead."

"Uh...your two lost birdies are back in the nest. They're a little worse for wear, but both are safe."

Gunnison stood and shouted, "They're safe. They've been found." The words were drowned by the cheers that followed.

The message was quickly relayed into the dark confines of the cave, and workers poured out, tired and relieved. A successful rescue was forever the highlight moment of their efforts as an emergency team.

Blaney rose to his feet, and Susan flew into his arms. Embracing, with tears of joy on both faces, they were oblivious to protocol. He felt the mantle of guilt lift from his shoulders, and nearly sank to his knees in relief.

Max's voice sounded hoarse. He had alternately blown his whistle and shouted for Michael and Alesandra in hopes they would be close enough to hear. He and Jared had been out on the mountain since returning with members of the rescue team early the previous afternoon.

Thoughts of Alesandra monopolized him. Finding a woman was not his reason for enrolling at UT Martin, but then he had not expected to find someone like her. He believed she returned his interest. He was unprepared for the possibility of losing her in the cave. To think he might never see her again tore at him.

Group leader, Jeb Corley, pulled his walkie talkie from his belt. Max jogged over to hear the transmission.

"*Your two lost birdies are back in the nest. They're a little worse for wear, but both are safe.*"

"Jared, they've found them," Max shouted, smiling and waving for his friend to join them. "Thank God, she's safe," he murmured.

On The Shelf

"Thanks, Max. I had a great time." A gentle breeze blew across the campus of UTM, and Alesandra tucked her blowing hair behind her ear to keep it out of her face.

"Me too. So, how 'bout Thursday night? You up for a movie?"

"Sure. I'd like that."

"Great. I'll pick you up here at 6:30. We can go out for coffee after."

"Terrific. Oh, look. Val's back." She perked at the sight of her friend and immediately started to head in that direction.

Not willing to let her go so easily, Max grabbed her hand and pulled her back. "Thanks, Sandy. See you later." With his arms around her, he turned what she intended as a chaste kiss into something deeper before finally releasing her. She gave him a parting smile over her shoulder as she jogged away to meet her friends.

Against his better judgment, his feelings for her continued to grow stronger each passing day. He wanted Alesandra Davis and was determined to have her. In his mind, she was already his. He came too close to losing her in the cave-in, and it only served to increase his intention to secure her heart.

The open courtyard at Cooper Hall served as an informal meeting place and study area for those who preferred the outdoors to stuffy climate-controlled dormitory rooms. Graduated terraces and a rock-lined pool augmented the aura of college life, and it was here the girls often shared confidences away from prying eyes and sensitive ears.

"Valerie, I'm glad you're home." Alesandra hugged her roommate, then sat on the stone bench next to her with Susan on the grass at their feet. "When did you get back?"

"Brandon picked me up from the hospital this morning. We just got here about half an hour ago. Here, let me hug you again." She draped her arms around her friend and squeezed. "I'm so happy they found you and that you're not hurt," she gushed.

"I'm fine. Glad to be out of there, though. You can't believe how wonderful it is to feel the sunshine and breathe fresh air again. What about you? Susan wasn't sure whether your knee was broken or twisted or what."

"No, no. Tore a lot of ligaments, but it got me a ride in a helicopter, and that was cool," she grinned. "And having Brandon come back for me wasn't bad either."

"Brandon, huh? He's pretty cute."

"Go for it, Val. Brandon's a good catch," Susan encouraged.

"I think I will." The threesome giggled. "What about you and Max, Sandy? Is that a happening thing? I noticed him coming on to you when we were at the mountain, and that kiss just now looked pretty promising."

"Might be. He was actually starting to make his play before the trip. Now he's being more forward about it. He's taking me out Thursday night."

"This is cool. We're both dating members of the Blaney Bunch. Now we just need Susan to hook up with someone. Let's see, that leaves Lewis, Jared, or how about Michael Stanley Gant, Susan? Yeah, yeah. Now there's a match made in heaven."

"Please," Susan rolled her eyes. "I can do just fine on my own, thanks. I have my eye on someone. I'm just not ready to talk about it yet."

"Oh, come on," Alesandra pleaded. "Fess up. Who is it? Do we know him?"

"Yes, and I'm not saying another word. I'll tell you when I know if it's going to turn into something."

"Pinky swear?"

"Yeah." She stuck out her pinky and linked it with the other girl's to seal the deal. "I've been waiting to hear more about what happened with Sandy at the cave-in." She nudged her friend with her foot. "You've hardly said a word, even on that long drive home. I figured you couldn't very well say how horrendous it was with Michael right there in the van. But, he's not here now, so you can tell us all about it."

"It must have been terrible for you being trapped in that rockslide." Valerie sympathized and tried to console her.

"We weren't actually trapped in the rockslide. It was not knowing if anyone else was trapped or hurt that was most upsetting. We hunted for the rest, but didn't find anyone. And then his glasses were lost in the tumble, not that it mattered. We couldn't see much in the dark anyway."

"Well, we were scared spitless. We were so afraid you were dead and that we'd never find your bodies, but nobody would say it out loud."

"Yes, and poor Professor Blaney. He was just devastated over the whole thing," Susan added. "I've never seen a man so distraught in my life. I don't know how he would have handled it if you hadn't been found."

"Well, after we couldn't find anyone else, Michael simply took charge and said we had to find a way out. We had a tough time of it for a while. I had a twisted ankle that I was afraid I wouldn't be able to walk on, and of course his arm was badly broken."

Susan posed the question the girls were most interested in. "So tell us, how did the nerd react to the whole experience, and to being alone with you? He must have thought he'd died and gone to heaven."

"I'm sure he did. In fact, I think he said something to that effect. I couldn't believe I was stuck there with him. I almost wished the mountain had finished me off."

She watched as a pretty blue butterfly alighted briefly on the bench next to her before fluttering away on a gentle breeze, and her mind shot back to a few days earlier when she sat on a hillside telling him she was grateful for what he had done. Her cheeks flushed with shame as she listened to herself now. She was being scathingly unfair to someone who had been good to her—someone who in fact saved her life in spite of his own personal suffering.

"To be fair, he was a nice guy and really rather heroic. In fact, without him, I probably wouldn't have survived. He saved us both."

Susan and Valerie cast surreptitious glances at each other in surprise. "So, tell us about it. What did he do?"

"He used his head and let common sense prevail. He spent a few summers with Outward Bound, so he had all kinds of skills and a well stocked backpack that came in handy. He took care of me, even with his broken arm. He showed me how to devise a net and catch fish for our meal, so I think he did pretty well. He took care of all my needs, and complained very little of his own."

"All of them, Sandy?" Valerie asked with a coy smile.

Alesandra rolled her eyes at the question. "He was a perfect gentleman. And I wouldn't expect him to be anything but. He's a decent guy." As the words left her tongue, she remembered his comment about her curves being cute and in all the right places; that, and a memory of a hand upon her breast brought a whimsical smile to her lips.

"Darn, huh?" Valerie teased.

Sandy threw her a dirty look in mock reproach, and they all laughed at the absurdity of it.

The members of the Blaney Bunch waited anxiously for the decision of the university administrators regarding their group's activities and Professor Blaney's culpability.

Two weeks after the group's return from the ill fated adventure, Carl Blaney's doorbell rang. Tugging a T-shirt over his head, he went to answer it.

Susan stood, nervously waiting, a smile ready on her lips. Carl opened the door and stepped aside to let her in.

"Susan. You shouldn't have come here," he said in surprise.

"Are you mad?"

"No, of course not."

"Are you glad?"

In answer, he put his hands on her waist and pulled her closer. Her arms looped around his neck as he set his mouth on hers. They had both played it cool since their return from the mountain, and it seemed an endless two weeks. With hunger, he consumed her, wanting more. "You feel so good in my arms."

"Mmm." She was thrilled by his response. Things were definitely looking good for her heart's desire. "I've missed you, Carl."

"I've missed you, too. It's been so hard to see you at the campus and not be able to say or do anything. I've wanted to, believe me."

She pulled back and looked in his eyes. "Really?"

"Yes." He covered her mouth again, and let his hands wander into her hair. When he had to make a choice between stopping to breathe or dropping her on the floor and taking her right then and there, he tipped his forehead against hers and fought for control. "Sorry. I should at least ask you in first." She giggled as he led her to the living room. "Can I get you anything? Would you like something to drink?"

"Sure, a soda if you have one, or just some cold water would be fine." She looked around the room, admiring his taste in furniture. "You listen to good music. Who is it?"

He went to the kitchen and returned with two cans of pop,

handing her one as he sat next to her on the sofa. "Dave Koz. I like a little sexy jazz when I'm kicking around the house on weekends."

"I heard the administrator's decision this morning. I just had to come. I'm so happy they aren't holding you responsible. It would have been so wrong for them not to absolve you."

"I'm pretty damned relieved, myself. At least I still have a job. I'm afraid it's not totally good news, however. They've curtailed any further excursions to the mountain."

Susan's brows knit together in consternation. "They can't do that to us. We have so much time and study invested there."

"Well, they can and they have, I'm sorry to say. They said they're going to look for an alternate 'safer' site for us."

Susan turned sideways, laying a hand on his shoulder. "But, Carl, you've been going there for years. It's *your* mountain for Pete's sake. Everyone knows that." She wanted to console the hurt that was evident in his features. Her finger smoothed its way across the worry lines on his brow. "I'm so sorry. It's not right. They'll come to see that. Just give it time. They're simply reacting to a scary situation and all the media hype. I'm sure the Chancellor's concerns about the school's reputation had something to do with it." She took his drink from his hand and set it, along with her own, on the coffee table. Moving into the corner of the couch, she pulled him to her, settling his head on her chest. His arms slipped around her waist as he felt her fingers working their way through his hair, comforting him. "Things will all work out in time. It's going to be fine."

He let his eyes close as he listened to her soothing sounds. "Susan, you know you shouldn't be here. We're breaking every rule in the book."

"Don't you want me here?"

"Yes."

"Then I don't care what the university says is right or wrong. I'll be discreet and do whatever I have to in order to protect your position, but I want to be with you. I've had a thing for you for a long time, you know."

He lifted his head and gazed into her eyes. "Have you, now?"

She nodded, and a sexy smile slowly spread across her face. "Yes, I have."

"Well, Miss Ellison, people think I don't notice things unless they're a few millennia old, but I can assure you, I've noticed the way you fill out those jeans, and the way they move on you, and I've thoroughly enjoyed it."

She giggled as she lowered her mouth to his, and he slid further up her body until she was lying beneath him.

The summer semester began, occupying their minds with chemistry, finite mathematics and dynamic Earth sciences.

Disappointment swept through the close-knit group at the temporary shelving of The Blaney Bunch. The members commiserated together, feeling disciplined for something beyond their control.

The boys gathered in the lounge at McCord Hall, where a few of them dormed, to discuss the issue. Jared was the most outspoken. "They know we need first-hand research for our projects, and there aren't many similar sites in this area to study. They're holding the professor accountable, and we're all stuck paying the price with him."

"I don't want any other site," Brandon complained. "Blaney's Mountain is ideal as far as I'm concerned. Our projects are based on data from that particular site. Besides, we uncovered some great artifacts. That place is rich with undiscovered treasures."

"Not only that, Dude," Lewis chimed in, "you want to get back into that old cave."

"Yeah," he enthused, "I do. There's something about it that fascinates me, and I want a chance to check it out."

Jared stared at Michael. "If there's anything unusual about that cave, this is the guy who would know. How about it, Michael?"

"How about what?"

"Is there anything special about the caves in that mountain? You certainly saw more of them than anyone else here. Fill us in."

"Oh. Well, it was pretty dark in there. Couldn't see much and didn't have my glasses anyway. Lost them in the cave-in."

"Did you find any more of those crystals?" Brandon prodded.

He tried to be nonchalant. "Nope, but uh...I guess we saw a lot of rocks."

The boys laughed, but Brandon pressed for more. "You know, you never did tell us where or how you got out. I looked around the area where we found you, and I didn't see any cave entrances there."

"We didn't come out there. We'd been wandering for awhile when you found us. I'm pretty sure we told you that at the time."

"So, can you find your way back? I'd really like to get in there and take a look for myself."

He looked at Brandon through his new contact lenses with an incredulous expression. "Bran, we were so glad to see the light of day, we didn't care where we were. We could have been in Canada for all we knew. All we cared about was getting out, not getting back in. The last thing Sandy and I wanted to see was the inside of that place again. What did you expect me to do? Pull out a GPS and start taking bearings? Make a little map of how to find it again? Get real."

The seniors laughed at the ludicrous image Michael painted. "Get over it, Brandon," Jared advised. "He hasn't got a clue where he was. He was too busy ogling Sandy to notice anything else."

"There you go," Michael agreed amiably. "I was pretty sick, too, if you remember."

Max stayed noticeably quiet during the discussion, his back stiffening at the mention of Alesandra. He suspected Gant of holding back but decided not to question him further. For now. His eyes squinted as he studied the sophomore, judging him to be far more astute than the dull, unsophisticated college geek everyone else presumed him to be. He didn't need Michael Gant to tell him about the mountain. Dating Sandy opened a door, and if he manipulated things right, he'd get all the information he wanted from her.

Michael mounted the stairs to the second floor of the Johnson Engineering & Physical Sciences Building, known on campus by its acronym, the EPS.

Jacob Turner, long-time member of the faculty and chair of the Chemistry Department bore the reputation of being a rather peculiar old duck. If anyone could help Michael determine the chemical construction of his find, it would be Dr. Turner. Finding the door to the chemistry lab unlocked, he entered. The room appeared to be empty, until he noticed the professor bent over a microscope in the far corner.

"Dr. Turner."

Turner held up a finger of acknowledgement. "I'll be with you in a minute."

Michael ambled through the laboratory, shrugging out of his backpack as he walked. Life was much easier now that he had a cast on his arm.

"Look at this, young man." The professor stepped aside and let him look through the scope. "Do you know what that is?"

"No, sir. I'm afraid I don't have a clue. But it's very interesting. Look at the way the particles are expanding and multiplying so rapidly. What is it?"

"It's a new drug. You're seeing how it works in the blood stream to increase the volume and strength of white cells to fight infection. A pharmaceutical company in Pennsylvania sent it to me to do some off site testing before they apply for FDA approval."

"Wow. That's pretty amazing."

"Now, what can I do for you? Gant, isn't it?"

"Yes, sir. Michael Gant."

"Something about you different?" Turner peered at him, trying to determine what.

"Yes, I'm wearing contacts. That's probably it."

"Humpf. I suppose. Your hair looks different too. So, what brings you to my laboratory on a day when everyone else is out playing baseball?"

Michael pulled a bag of crystals from deep inside his backpack. "I found them at the dig up on Blaney's Mountain. I was intrigued by the way they move. I don't know how to explain it, other than to say the flakes seemed to drift on air currents as if they were alive, reminiscent of a butterfly in flight. Professor Blaney wasn't sure what they were either, so I collected samples to bring back. I thought we could run some through the mass spectrometer; maybe get an idea what the composition is."

Turner accepted the bag of crystals and opened it. He put his finger inside to touch them and a few small flakes adhered to his skin. When he withdrew it from the bag, the movement caused the particles to take flight, exhibiting the qualities Michael spoke of.

"Well, I'll be jiggered," he said in awe as he watched the spectacle for himself. "I've never seen the like."

"Yeah, it's amazing, isn't it?"

"Indeed it is, lad. Indeed it is." Snapping out of his reverie, he gave a giddy laugh and slapped Michael on the back. "This is the most interesting puzzle I've been presented with in years. Can't wait to get started." He rattled off instructions and seemed to be everywhere at once, gathering together equipment and through it all bursting into sporadic peals of laughter.

"So, Blaney saw these crystals, did he?"

"Yes, sir. He helped me scrape them from the rock. We planned to take a hammer and chisel to it to bring back a more solid sample for analysis, but the cave-in sort of cut things short."

"Yes, heard all about that. Such a tragedy. Glad you made it out safely. You and some young lady, if I recall."

"Yes, sir. Alesandra Davis was with me. We were fortunate to get out alive."

"Indeed. Well, if you don't mind, I'd like to keep these samples here at the lab. I'm sure I'll come up with experiments to run on them right through the summer. This is going to be the most fun I've had in years, my boy. Of course you're welcome to come in any time and give me a hand."

"Thank you, sir. I'd like to see the project through."

"Good, good. Well, let's quit jawing about it and get to work."

Michael thought of the solid rock specimen sitting in the bottom of his backpack, and said nothing. He intended to return to the mountain whenever feasible and collect additional samples. *Take nothing but pictures* was the spelunkers' unofficial motto. It was a rule he felt completely justified in breaking.

Michael logged on to check his email and found one asking him to come to Blaney's office in the EPS building at 4 p.m.. That gave him only fifteen minutes to get there. He noticed all the other member's of Blaney's Bunch were on the recipient list.

Grabbing his pack he headed across the campus. As he rounded the corner of the University Center, the entrance door swung open letting Alesandra and Susan spill out.

"Hey, girls. On your way to Blaney's meeting?"

"Yup. I wonder what's up?"

They congregated with the rest of the elite group and waited for their dauntless leader to tell them why they were gathered.

"The administrators may have located a suitable site for our field work. It's a lot closer to the university, so we won't have to travel as far."

There arose a resounding objection from everyone in the room, all of them defending their need to return to the original site.

"Please, Professor Blaney, we want to go back to the mountain. We're willing to make any compromise they ask of us. Don't let them do this to us."

The teacher rubbed his chin thoughtfully as he listened to their reasoning.

"All of our field notes and specimens were obtained there. Changing the site now means having to trash all that and start over again. It's going to jeopardize everything we've done and possibly keep us from graduating on time."

Blaney looked at each of the students and saw the determination on their faces. "I want to know how Michael and Alesandra feel about returning to the mountain. It's fine for the rest of you to be gung-ho, but these two went through quite an ordeal there. How about it?" He looked at the two in question.

"It's fine with me, sir," Alesandra confirmed. "I'll be really upset if we have to change locations at this point."

"Okay. Michael?"

He paused before answering the professor's question. "I agree that we should go back. Dr. Turner needs more crystal specimens before he can reach any conclusions."

"You aren't concerned about the danger of another cave accident?"

"We don't need to go back in the cave for anything. Our work was at the dig site, not in the cave. It's the archaeology aspect that we want to return for."

"All right, since everyone feels the same way, I'll speak to the Dean tomorrow."

When the students left the building, Max attached himself to Alesandra's side. She turned her head looking for Michael and saw him coming out of the building behind them. "Max, can you hang on a minute? I need to talk to Michael."

"Sure," he said, scowling when her back was turned.

Leaving Max, she jogged back to the steps to meet Michael. "Can we talk for a minute?"

"Yup. What's up?"

She grabbed his hand and led him off to the side so they could speak privately. "What about our trip? We are still going back together, aren't we?"

He quickly swallowed his surprise and assured her, "Of course we are, Sandy." He saw the determination in her eyes, and he meant every word. "Don't worry. We'll make plans soon."

"I've been thinking about those markings I found in that chamber. The more I think about it, the more convinced I am they were made by human hands. The lines were too regular to have been the result of erosion. They were too straight."

He watched her hands moving excitedly as she spoke and smiled at her enthusiasm. Yes, indeed. If she really wanted to make that journey with him, he'd arrange it in the near future.

"I could tell that much by touching them," she continued. "Also, those pillars were granite, and the only other granite on that mountain was the slab placed in front of the entrance. I think it was intentionally placed there to disguise the entrance by whoever those monoliths belong to. I'm just itching to get back there and investigate further. I'm going to take my camera this time."

He knew she was right. There was no other granite on the mountain. It stood out like a sore thumb to anyone who knew geology. "You're absolutely right. I can't believe I didn't recognize that fact at the time."

"Are you kidding? I'm amazed you did as well as you did considering your condition. You saved us and got us out of there. Identifying rocks was the furthest thing from our minds."

"We'll go back soon. I promise."

She squeezed his hand. "Thanks, Michael." With a smile, she let go and ran back to Max.

Michael watched her go, amazed that she had spoken to him in public, and even more so by her subject matter. Maybe he underestimated her character after all.

Her dreams that night were filled with ghostly spirits beckoning from within the cave, entreating her to return. She believed they offered her something, something both beautiful and terrifying. She felt a strange compassion for their absence from this place of their belonging.

Chemistry

The campus buzzed with talk about the cave incident. Classmates bombarded Michael and Alesandra with questions wherever they went, and the two found it difficult to speak privately with each other.

While Professor Turner was busily engaged with researching the crystals in his possession, Michael used the geology lab for tests of his own after regular class hours when everyone was gone for the day. The geology department was on the same floor of the EPS building as the chemistry classroom.

Having only given Turner a portion of the accumulated particles, Michael kept a sizable quantity for his own research. He avoided telling about the reflective properties witnessed in the chamber, leaving that avenue for his own exploration. Speculations regarding the crystals' importance played in his mind.

It was past ten o'clock at night when Alesandra and her friends left the UC after the weekly movie. She spotted Michael walking by himself in the opposite direction. "Michael, wait up." She ran across the lawn to close the distance between them.

"Hey, Sandy." He waited until she caught up with him, then fell into step alongside her. "Haven't seen much of you lately."

"I know. I feel awful about it. It's like we never seem to get five minutes alone together without someone interrupting. There's been a lot of homework this semester, too. But then, that's why I stayed for the summer, so I could get some of the heavy courses out of the way before cheerleading resumes."

"How've you been?"

"Good. How 'bout you? I notice you got contacts. Looks good."

"Thanks." He was glad she couldn't see him blush in the darkness. "Where you going at this time of night?"

"Just heading home after the movie. What about you?"

"On my way to the EPS. I figure if I wait until late at night like this, I can get into the lab without anyone else knowing what I'm doing there." He dropped his voice to a conspiratorial whisper. "Conducting a covert operation, you know." He shifted his gaze around the campus in an exaggerated manner, making her laugh. "Seriously, though, it's the only opportunity for absolute privacy. You know I can't take chances."

"Want some company?"

"I guess that depends on who the company would be. Now if it's Lewis and Brandon, I'd rather not. You want to come along?"

"Yeah, if you don't mind."

"I don't mind. You know how it feels creepy sometimes when you're the only one all alone in a big building like that at night?" He let his fingertips lightly creep up her back, sending a quivering sensation along her spine. "Muwahahaha."

Visibly jumping, she laughed. "Well, I'll come along and keep you safe from the boogey man."

He unlocked the geology lab with his card key. They entered, and the door automatically locked when he pulled it shut, keeping unwanted intruders from surprising them.

"How did you get a key?"

"The Prof gave it to me. I told him I kept a small portion of the crystals to do some experiments on my own. He has no idea about the rock. Only you and I know about that. You haven't told anyone, have you?"

"Of course not. We made a pact. Show me what you've been working on." She waited while he pulled out a small bag of particles scraped from the mountain and the rock from the cave. "I keep it with me at all times. I don't trust anybody. Too many people are asking questions, wanting details of what we saw and did. It may just be idle curiosity, but I'm not taking any chances. Brandon and Lewis keep harping at me, trying to get me to reveal the great secret of the entrance location."

"Val has asked me about it a few times, too. She's dating Brandon, so I guess that's her motivation."

"Look at these crystals." He poured them out onto a sheet of filter paper and held it under a lamp. "At first, I suspected their primary content was adamite, a fluorescent mineral. However, adamite is green, and these are definitely not green."

They worked together into the early hours of the morning. "There's something in this molecular structure I can't identify, but it seems to be exhibiting some strange magnetic properties."

"It seems like the more we learn, the bigger a mystery it becomes."

Michael glanced at the clock. "Look, it's almost three. We should probably pack this up for tonight. You've got an early class tomorrow morning, and you need to get some sleep."

She didn't ask how he knew her schedule, and it didn't bother her that he did. "Okay, but I want to come back with you again to work on this."

"Fine. I'll give you a call next time." He carefully packaged the specimens and tucked them into his backpack while she returned the equipment to the cupboards.

The campus stretched before them, evening shadows playing amidst the various buildings. The grounds were empty except for the two young scientists, walking together and talking animatedly like old friends. They dawdled in the cool breeze, discussing the results of their experiments. He was close to concluding that the crystals he found and the element discovered in concentrated quantities within the chamber were one and the same, and the excitement of the discovery gave them both a rush.

Days became an endless maze of classes and homework which the students faithfully plodded through. It was a late Thursday afternoon when Alesandra stopped at the front desk in the lobby of Cooper Hall to pick up any messages and found a letter in her mailbox. She waited until she was alone in her room before opening it.

Piglet,

I want to talk with you, but it's hard to find privacy here on campus. If you aren't going home for the weekend, why don't I pack a picnic lunch, and we can drive out into the country? Unless I hear otherwise, I'll meet you in the parking lot outside McCord Hall at nine o'clock. Hope to see you then.

Pooh Bear.

She lay on the bed and thought about it. A simple picnic somewhere near the river. They could be alone to rehash their adventure and talk about what they would do when they returned. It was a good idea.

The phone rang, pulling her back to the present. Picking up the cordless handset from the table by her bed, she answered it.

"Hello."

"Hi, Sandy. How are you?"

"Fine, thanks, Max. How 'bout yourself?"

"Great. Listen, I was wondering if you'd like to go to the ball game with me tomorrow afternoon?"

"Gee, I would have liked that, but I already have plans. Sorry."

"Oh, you and Valerie going somewhere?"

"No. I think she's going to the game with Brandon."

"Oh." Max paused, waiting for her to enlighten him regarding her plans, but she wasn't forthcoming.

"Maybe next time, Max. Thanks for asking, though. Talk to you later."

"Right. Okay. See ya around."

Max hung up the phone and stared at it. He was pretty sure she wasn't dating anyone but him, although they certainly weren't close enough yet to require exclusivity. Maybe he should keep an eye on things a little more closely on that front.

The first rays of the morning sun bathed the university in a promise of excitement as the two conspirators drove out of the campus area.

"You tell Max where you're going?"

"No. Why?"

"Because he's leaning against the building over there watching us. Has been since you came out of Cooper. Wondering where you're going, and why you're going with me, most likely."

"Really? I didn't even notice him."

"Sandy, it's kind of hard not to notice a guy in a bright red shirt with yellow flowers all over it. Doesn't it sort of embarrass you to be seen with that?"

"Not really. It's just Max. Don't think too much about it." She turned her head to the side to look out the window, not letting him see the smile as she thought of how different Michael's own appearance had been just a few weeks ago. And now he worried that she found Max's style embarrassing? How things changed. "Hey! You got your cast off."

"Yeah, yesterday afternoon. About time."

"How does your arm feel?"

"Good as new," he smiled.

The open highway stretched before them, luring them onward as they negotiated sharp curves and the rolling hills of the countryside. Content to listen to the wind rushing past and the humming of the engine, Alesandra remembered Sunday trips with her father behind the wheel and her mother sitting beside him while she and her sister played with their dolls in the back seat.

Telephone poles and gaudy billboards soon gave way to a picturesque pine forest and an unpaved road that ran alongside a river. Obion River was a small stream as rivers are measured. It branched off into various forks before meandering past Clifton College.

Pulling the Jeep off the road, they parked in the shade of a chestnut tree. She took a blanket from the back seat and spread it out in the sunshine on the grassy river bank while he lugged the food. Sitting down, she started unpacking to see what he brought.

Finding a bag of potato chips, she opened it. He handed her a can of 7-Up, and popped one open for himself. Stretching out, he let his gaze slowly roam over her, from top to toe.

"What are you looking at, Pooh?" she asked with her nose crinkled, a coy smile playing on her lips.

"Just thinking how pretty your red hair is with the sunlight shining on it like that, Piglet."

"Oh. Well, thanks." Her hand reached up to touch it automatically, smoothing it down and flipping it behind her shoulder.

"You're welcome."

"You managing to keep up with classes so far?"

"Sure, no problem. I simply eliminate sleep from my schedule, and I can fit everything in fine," he grinned.

"I know what you mean. I can't believe how much homework we get in Rubincam's class. I don't know where he finds the time to grade it all. I'll be glad when that one's over with."

"Yeah, it's pretty heavy." He closed his eyes and turned his face into the sun. "The guys have been talking."

"About what?"

"Going back to the mountain. The general consensus seems to be that everyone wants to return to the dig site to continue our work there."

"I know that. Everyone said as much in Blaney's office last week."

"Well, the thing is, they're determined to continue regardless of the university's sanction, or lack thereof. The only concern the guys have is whether or not to take Professor Blaney into our confidence. We certainly can't invite him along, because he's a member of the faculty."

"And we don't know when the Administrators will reach a decision about the dig site. By the time they decide, it could be too late for most of us to get our research done," she concluded.

"Exactly. So, how do you feel about it?"

She sat pondering the proposal for a few minutes before answering. "Well, I've been worried about getting my own project completed, so I guess I'm in agreement. What does this mean as far as you and me going back?" That was the question that had been monopolizing her thoughts ever since they made the pact.

"One has nothing to do with the other. If we went to the mountain with the group and suddenly disappeared, it would be too obvious. No, when Pooh and Piglet go to retrace the steps of their adventure, it has to be just the two of us. That way, we can stay as long as we want without being accountable to anybody else, and we won't have to worry about Lewis and Clark."

"Don't you mean Lewis and Brandon?"

"No, I meant Lewis and Clark, the exploring duo who are determined to blaze their trails into our cave."

She laughed at the play on names. The more time she spent alone with Michael Stanley Gant, the more comfortable she became and realized that maybe he wasn't such a bad guy after all. Although she didn't plan on making him her best friend on campus, she really didn't mind hanging out with him away from school. "What else did you bring to eat?" She reached for the other bags and continued unpacking the food. "Wow, you even remembered paper plates and plastic forks. You think of everything. I'm impressed."

He smiled as he scooped coleslaw from a plastic tub onto his plate. "Good planning is always important to a successful adventure."

"Well, you've chosen a beautiful spot. How did you know about this place?"

"I attended Clifton College, not far from here. This was sort of my place to come for solitude. I used to sit right here on the river bank with an open book in my hands and listen to the rippling water. It was peaceful here, and none of my classmates ever came around to torment me."

"Didn't you ever get lonesome?" She could not imagine living as isolated a life as he had. Not having anyone to talk to seemed such a bleak existence.

"Oh sure, sometimes, but I didn't mind. Being alone is not always a bad thing. I prefer my own company to people who feel that picking on someone they perceive to be different is an amusing pastime."

Ashamed, she turned her head, well aware that she was one of those people. When she felt she had control of her voice, she said, "I'm glad you wanted to share this place with me. I think it's lovely and serene, and I can see why you love it. Thank you."

"I'm glad you like it here."

"Well, Pooh, a picnic for two is much nicer than being alone. Besides, you said Piglet always accompanies Pooh on his adventures. This has been a nice change from the everyday routine at school." She bent to take off her runners, followed by her socks which she tucked into the discarded shoes.

"Cute piggies, Piglet."

Laughing, she stood and stepped to the water's edge, dipping a toe in to test the temperature. "Oh, this feels so good. I thought it would be too cold, but it's not. It's perfect. Come in with me." She reached her hand out to him in invitation.

Michael made short work of shucking off his own shoes and socks and rolling up his jeans, before going to the water's edge. She reached her hand out again from the center of the stream where she stood almost knee deep. He took hold of it as he boldly stepped into the water. The icy temperature came as a shock, and he jumped, trying to regain his perch on dry land. She refused to let him off so easily. Her gleeful peals of laughter filled the air as she pulled him in deeper. Losing her footing, the two ended up colliding together midstream, water splashing gloriously around them. They grabbed at each other, trying to find stable footing.

His hands clutched at her waist and she was soon in his arms, laughter on her lips as she lifted her eyes to look into his. He noticed the way her auburn hair glistened in the sunshine, and the way her eyes seemed bluer than ever. Before he knew it, he saw those same eyes closing as her mouth reached for his. Having never kissed a girl before, he tried to follow her lead. The only thing he knew for certain was his heart hammered so loudly in his ears he was sure she could hear it too. All too soon, he felt her lips closing as she pulled away.

"Wow, Piglet," he whispered.

She stared at him, as though really seeing him for the first time. "Yeah, wow!"

He placed his hands on her cheeks and pulled her back for more. Her arms wove around his neck, and she leaned into him. He couldn't believe he was standing here, kissing Alesandra Davis, the girl he lay in bed dreaming of every night. The girl he followed around like a devoted puppy since last fall. In his wildest dreams, he never imagined this moment would be real.

Numbness finally permeated his senses. "Piglet, I'm afraid I'm losing the feeling in my feet. This water is freezing."

She giggled, knowing her trembling had nothing to do with water temperature. Allowing him to pull her back onto the grassy slope, she remarked, "That's some magical river you have there, Pooh Bear."

"I'll say, and all these years I never had a clue."

They smiled at each other, both feeling surprisingly giddy. Talking easily, they ate more, then eventually began to pack up the leftovers.

"I'm glad you brought me here today, Michael. I've had a wonderful time." She sat and stared at him, unable to believe this was the same fellow that made her feel so squeamish just a few weeks earlier. It was like he was a whole different person, and she wasn't sure who had done the changing, him or her.

"I'm glad you're glad," he smiled. "Sandy, I've been thinking." He felt insecure about vocalizing his idea, but she had been receptive so far, so he plunged ahead. "You know, maybe we could make it a habit to do this, just so people get used to seeing us together. Then, when we take off for a few days to go to the cave, it won't seem so suspicious."

"People will eventually miss us, you know; especially if we don't return until the next day, or even a few days later."

"Sure they will, but," he hesitated, "maybe they'll think we spent the night together in a motel." He cringed inside as he waited for her verdict. She remained silent for several moments, her facial expression indefinable. Was she seething with indignation that he would even suggest such a thing? He stole a glance at her from the corner of his eye, anticipating a strong unfavorable response. Surprisingly enough, it didn't come.

"That's not bad," she finally said. "In fact, you're going to ruin the Pooh image if you continue to be so clever."

"Really! Uh...you don't mind what people will think?"

"Of course not. We're adults. We can do whatever we want, and it's nobody's business." She smiled at him.

The ride back seemed to take hardly any time at all. Neither felt awkward as they rode without talking. It was a comfortable silence, giving them a chance to examine each other and to reflect upon this relationship that started out so precariously on her part and so very adoringly for him.

The watcher looked out his dorm window and saw Gant's Jeep pulling into the parking lot. Alesandra got out, confirming his suspicions that they spent the day together. He checked his watch and did a quick calculation. There was no way they had time to get all the way to the mountain and back in the time they were away. And if it was not the mountain they went to, then where? And why? Something in the behavior of these two did not sit right with him at all. He determined to get answers to the questions that played havoc with his imagination.

Michael got out of the Jeep and walked her to her dorm. As they entered the lobby they were greeted by Jared with a coffee cup in his hand.

"Hey, you two! Enjoy your private little vacation off in the big wide world?"

She flashed him a smile. "We had a lovely time, thank you. Did you go to the game this afternoon?"

"Yup. We won, 12-8. By the way, Sandy, Max has been waiting for you."

"Hmm. I told him I was busy today."

"Yeah, he knows that. I think he's hoping you're available for a movie tonight."

"Okay, I guess I'll have to give him a call."

Michael's heart sank at the thought of her going out with Max after the wonderful afternoon they shared. A frown twitched at the corners of his mouth where the memory of her kiss still lingered.

Alesandra stood on tiptoe and kissed his cheek, thanking him for the wonderful day, and all other thoughts evaporated as though they never existed.

Rendered speechless, Jared watched the affectionate scenario before him. His eyebrows rose, and he quickly closed his mouth, aware he was openly gaping at the spectacle; the cheerleader kissing the nerd. He could not imagine anything more bizarre if he tried. Wait until Max found out. It would not be pretty.

Suspicions

Sunday morning made its appearance slowly, reluctantly. This was the one day of the week Michael claimed as his very own. He could leisurely do his laundry, hang out and watch television, or write letters, except there was no one with whom he regularly corresponded. A favorite option was sleeping late, which he was doing when the telephone interrupted his reverie.

"Yeah."

"Michael, Blaney here." His voice sounded strangely harsh. "Get dressed, and come to the EPS as quickly as you can. Dr. Turner and I are waiting for you."

"What's going on?" His question was met by a click and a dial tone. Hanging up, he sat on the side of his bed, stretched, rubbed his eyes, and lay back down. "No Michael, don't get some sleep, Michael. Don't enjoy your day off, Michael. Just be at our beck and call at all hours of the day and night," he muttered.

Without bothering to shower, he threw on a shirt and a pair of jeans, splashed his face with cold water and was out the door in five minutes. He ran a comb through his hair as he walked across the vacant campus. "Hope he at least has a doughnut waiting when I get there," he grumbled.

Low hanging clouds gave the impression of a gloomy day forming. A bad omen indeed. The fact that both Blaney and Turner awaited him, gave it an air of urgency. Surely if the chemical analysis resulted in a discovery, the news could have waited until sunup.

The door stood ajar as he entered the lab and found himself in the midst of chaos. Papers scattered everywhere. Shattered and overturned beakers lay on the floor alongside various other pieces of broken equipment. Both men worked on the far side of the laboratory sorting through the debris.

Stunned, Michael stood gaping. "Wow! What happened here?"

"We've had a break-in, as you can see for yourself," Dr. Turner told him. "By the marks on the doorframe, it looks like they used a crowbar to jimmy the door, then went wild smashing whatever they saw."

Professor Blaney straightened from his task, regarding Michael thoughtfully. "We thought you might have an interest in it."

"Me? I don't know anything about this," he protested.

"I don't mean to imply you did it, Michael. It's just that," Blaney cast his eyes in Dr. Turner's direction to include him in the opinion, "we believe whoever is responsible may have been looking for your crystals."

"What? You really think so?"

"It's only conjecture on our part, mind you, but it does seem the most probable hypothesis."

"Don't worry, my boy. I keep them in the safe in my office, and they're still there, intact as we speak," Dr. Turner assured him. "You see, your crystals are the only new objects being tested here. Although a few things are damaged, nothing seems to be missing, and some of the lab equipment is pretty expensive. It must have been the crystals they were after."

"What about that drug you were testing? Couldn't that be what they were searching for?"

"I finished the studies on it and returned it all to the pharmaceutical company three weeks ago."

"He's right, Michael. Someone evidently believes the crystals are very valuable."

"If that's true then they know more than I do." Michael shrugged his shoulders in a gesture of bewilderment. "Have you reached any conclusions to support that theory, Dr. Turner?"

"No, my studies are still ongoing, I'm afraid. That's a real puzzle you presented me with, Gant. Even the results of the mass spectrometer came up as inconclusive, and I've never seen that happen before. I doubt any answers will be forthcoming until more substantial specimens can be obtained. My supply is getting rather scant."

Michael wondered if the geology lab had also been ransacked in search of the crystals. Realizing Professor Blaney would be aware if it had happened, he relaxed. He only hoped whoever perpetrated the vandalism was unaware of the experiments he conducted late at night.

"Campus Security, or Public Safety, or whatever they're calling themselves these days, already finished with their investigation," Blaney said. "Now we're trying to assess the damages."

When a large portion of the mess was cleared away, Michael left the EPS building. Using his cell phone, he called Alesandra and invited her to breakfast. They met at the Skyhawk Cafeteria where they found a smattering of students eating and chatting.

Over Danish and orange juice, Michael told her of the break-in at the lab and the professors' speculations.

"I can't believe someone actually tried to steal them." She pushed her juice glass away and folded her arms. "Why would someone want them? What would they have done if they actually got hold of them?"

"I don't know. Maybe the culprit thinks they're more valuable than they actually are," he said. "The mineral content doesn't have a market value to make stealing them worth the risk. Either the person responsible didn't know what he was doing, or," he paused, considering the alternative, "he knew perfectly well what he was doing."

"Ooh, that's a sobering thought." She pursed her lips. "But how can anyone else understand the value of it, monetary or otherwise, when even Dr. Turner doesn't know? He's the one studying it."

"I don't know. None of it makes sense to me. I keep trying to put a face on the guy that did this and finding it hard. If the crystals were the goal of the break-in, who knew about them besides Blaney, Turner, and the Bunch?" Michael raised an eyebrow to emphasize his question.

"That's exactly what I'm wondering. The cave-in is pretty common knowledge. You'd have to be dead not to know about it, but the crystals haven't been discussed outside the group. At least not that I'm aware of. No one has mentioned them to me, or asked about them. The only questions have been about the 'great tragedy'."

"Same here. And if no one else knows, then it radically narrows down the suspect list, and I don't like the prospects that leaves us with."

"Right. And if it isn't you, and it isn't me, that only leaves six other possibilities. Of course, there's a chance somebody in the group mentioned it to someone else in conversation. It's not like it was a forbidden topic. I want us to consider other possible scenarios before we go blaming one of our group members. If someone outside the group is responsible, then the accusations are only going to cause hard feelings, and we don't want that either."

"Agreed. I guess we'll just have to keep our eyes and ears open, and in the meantime, not trust anyone."

Alesandra nodded. "I'm sure it's not the girls," she said in defense of her friends.

"I hope not. But we can't say the same about Brandon, and now that Val is tied up with him, that pretty much puts her off limits on this, Sandy. I'm sorry, but until we know for certain, you'll have to be very careful what you confide to your friends."

"I know you're right, but I don't have to like it." With lips pressed firmly together in resignation, she stood and gathered her garbage. "Want to walk me back to Cooper?"

"Of course." Rising to his feet, he walked her to her residence with his hand possessively planted on the small of her back, to which she did not object. Yesterday the kissing, and today she allowed him this public display of affection. Scholastic life was seemingly on a downward spiral, but his personal life had never been better.

He sat at his computer, watching and waiting. The campus webcam overlooked the walkways between the library and the Boling University Center where pedestrian traffic was heavy. Spotting the odd couple emerging from the UC together, he leaned forward with interest.

They were hiding something. Of that he felt certain. There was no other plausible explanation for the sudden closeness between the sexy cheerleader and the zero-charisma nerd. He had tried to pry answers out of both of them but to no avail. It must be something significant; something valuable for them to guard it so closely. Whatever it was, he determined to unravel the secret and cash in on it.

The foray into the chemistry lab the night before failed dismally. He did not find the crystals that had both Blaney and Turner so excited. He would bide his time for a while. Let the dust settle before his next search. He felt confident that one day the secret of Blaney's Mountain would be his, and it was going to make him a very wealthy man.

News of the burglary swept through the UTM rumor mill like an electric shock causing wild speculation. Immediate curiosity centered on who had been arrested and for what. Initial conjecture soon ballooned out of proportion until the campus was rife with fabrications by those who claimed they had been there and seen the whole thing for themselves.

A drunken brawl was the popular theory. A few dissenters spoke up in favor of a campus orgy; the only thing missing, being names and specific details. A general let-down occurred when it was learned that no fracas of any kind actually took place, and the so-called witnesses to the imbroglios silently hoped people would forget their contribution to the story. It was merely a trashing of the chemistry lab that brought the law.

"Not an orgy? Bummer!" one student was overheard. "We could sure use some excitement like that around here."

Michael walked Alesandra across the campus toward Cooper Hall after their structural geology class ended. They met Lewis coming out of the library.

"Hey, Lewis." Alesandra sounded less than thrilled to see him.

"S'up, Dude and Dudette?"

"Classes. That's about it."

"I'm heading over to the computer lab in the Humanities Building. A group of us are getting together to have a 24 hour marathon. A good game of Doom always clears my mind so I can concentrate on homework." Lewis took every opportunity to leave the world of academia for the free spirited universe of imagined space invaders and skillful contests of chance.

"I hear your abilities stretch far beyond games. One of my suitemates paid you a sizable sum to research and prepare a technical project for her," Sandy said.

"What can I say? I possess an enviable expertise in the complexities of computer usage. I have a profitable little business assisting fellow students. I'm no Bill Gates, but I'm on my way," he boasted. "Just give me a bit more time."

"You're an amazing man, Lewis," Michael agreed amiably.

Lewis smirked, knowing they were being condescending, but at this point in time he was happy to let them think his skills were no more than average. If they knew what he really did with his computer, they would be astounded. But he wasn't ready for anyone to find out those things yet. One day, in the not too distant future, they would all be eating out of his hand. Until then, he would deceptively continue to play the fool.

"Did you hear about Dr. Turner's playhouse getting busted up?"

"If you mean the chemistry lab, yes we know about it," Alesandra said, making no attempt to hide her growing impatience.

"I'll bet it was somebody from Murray State," Lewis complained. "Those guys from Kentucky will do anything to get even with us for that last football game."

"You may be right," Michael said as he turned to walk away.

"Hold up a sec. Either of you talked to Brandon?"

"Not for a few days. Why?"

"The mountain. We're heading up there next weekend. The whole group. Bring your gear and sleeping bag. We're going to camp out at the dig site. Meeting in the parking lot behind McCord Hall at seven a.m."

"Sounds great. We'll be there. Right, Sandy?"

"Of course. I'll make sure Susan and Val know about it."

"Great. Okay. Later."

"We'll see you round, dude," Michael affirmed, giving a brief wave of farewell before letting his arm settle around Alesandra's waist.

She giggled, "You called him dude."

"Yeah, I figured I owed him at least one for all those he's given me. You, on the other hand, seemed a bit miffed. What's up?"

"Lewis is okay, in small doses. His juvenile behavior and lack of language skills gets old very fast. He's sort of like Tigger. Everybody likes him, but they get tired of being bounced all the time."

Michael laughed at her analogy, and hooked his arm around her neck pulling her close. “You’re something else, Piglet.”

“Yes I am,” she smiled, “and don’t you forget it.”

They walked in silence for a few minutes before he issued an invitation. “Want to go to the geology lab with me and do some more experimenting on the rock?”

“Tonight?”

“No, not tonight. I think the security is still going to be tight. Even though we have Blaney’s permission to be there, I’d still like to remain as inconspicuous as possible. The end of the week; maybe Thursday night?”

“Sure that would be great.”

They sat on a bench in the lower courtyard at Cooper Hall. He kept his arm around her shoulders, content to leave it there so long as she was not objecting. He told her of his testing thus far.

She nodded in understanding. “We studied a mineral in class the other day called galena, and it’s very heavy with an opaque metallic luster. Maybe we should test for that.”

“Good idea. We’ll do that. What I need is more crystals to test with. We have to go back to the mountain and get some. At least I can get more of the surface samples when we return with the Blaney Bunch on the weekend, but I’ll have to wait until you and I go back on our own to get more rock specimens.”

“Well, we’ll just have to make that trip soon. I’m looking forward to it.”

“Me too.”

“I hate to cut this short, but I have things I have to get done this afternoon.” She stood reluctantly and paused. “Are you busy tomorrow, early evening?”

“I can be available. What do you have in mind?”

“I thought maybe we could grab some dinner together. Nothing fancy, maybe just at the caf.”

“Sure. Shall I pick you up here?”

“No, I’ll already be on that side of campus. I’ll meet you at the UC at 5:30. Is that good for you?”

He could not believe his luck. The girl of his dreams was asking him for a dinner date. Of course he was available. If he had to fly half way around the world and scale a mountain to be there, he was available.

She waited, but he did not reply right away. “Michael? Is that too early?”

He got to his feet and realized she was still waiting for an answer. Wanting to sound cool and confident, he replied, “Oh, sorry. I was just trying to remember what’s on my schedule for tomorrow. Yeah, I think I can make it for 5:30. I’ll meet you there.”

“Terrific. Okay, then.” Still she stood, as though waiting for something. “Okay. I’ll see you then, if not before.”

She lifted her eyes to gaze into his, and it hit him what she wanted. Slipping a hand behind her neck he pulled her closer and kissed her. Her response was not wild and passionate, but it was very...lingering.

"I'll see you later, Michael."

"Yes, you will, Sandy," he grinned in response. She backed away, and before he could warn her, she tripped over the ledge of the ornamental pond. A scream escaped as she landed with a splash in the middle of the pool.

He watched in stunned silence as the scene played out before him. He reached for her, but it was too late. Seeing her sitting like a wet kitten brought spontaneous laughter to his throat.

She stared at him in shock and, perceiving how comical she appeared, laughed with him. He walked to the edge of the water, extending his hands to help her out.

"Well, Piglet, it seems you have an affinity for water. I hope it's a little warmer this time."

"I'm a lot wetter this time," she proclaimed through her giggles.

"Do you need me to walk you to your room, or do you think you can make it without any further calamities?"

Slapping playfully at his shoulder, she blushed and assured him she could handle the remaining distance on her own. He helped gather her scattered books and handed them to her.

"See you later, Piglet." He bent and gave her a quick kiss on the lips and then headed for McCord Hall, chuckling to himself all the way.

Valerie and Alesandra roomed together while Susan shared a room in the same suite with a nursing student. The girls, until now, always confided intimate secrets of their lives and loves. Their camaraderie on the surface, continued as before but Alesandra kept mum regarding her cave adventure, and Susan hugged her affair with Carl Blaney to herself.

"Have you got everything packed and ready, Val?"

"Just finished. I'm all set. Is Susan waiting or meeting us down at the parking lot?"

"She's in the living room."

The suitemates collected their gear and headed to McCord Hall where they met the other members of the Bunch. The group divided themselves into two vehicles for the trip to Blaney's Mountain.

Max busied himself cramming things into the trunk of his 4X4 while Brandon loaded up his Honda with the rest of it.

"Do you girls really need all this stuff? We're only going 'til Sunday, you know. You don't need steamer trunks," Max complained. "How are we supposed to fit all this in and still have room for passengers?"

"Sorry, Max. It's all 'must have' stuff," Susan insisted.

With all the various paraphernalia finally wedged in, the students climbed into the vehicles. Before they could pull out, a red van materialized behind them, effectively blocking their way.

"Who the hell is that?" Jared stormed as he leaped out of the passenger door. "Move it, jerk," he hollered, advancing toward the offending vehicle.

The driver's door opened, and Carl Blaney stepped out. "Hold that thought, Jared," he warned. "Everybody out of the cars."

The members of the Blaney Bunch did as their leader demanded, pouring out of the automobiles and gathering around him.

"I know what you kids are up to, and I've come to stop you."

"But, Professor," Brandon started.

"No buts. I'm telling you flat out. Don't go there."

"We need to finish our projects," they cried in unison. "It's not fair to make us start all over again somewhere else."

"I know that. Now listen, I told you I would try to get the Board's approval to go back to the dig site, and it's in the works. I promise you. If you go there now, and word gets out, it's going to make us look bad, and we'll never get the ban rescinded. Please, guys. Let's do this the right way."

"But it could take them forever to change their minds," Valerie complained. "We can't wait that long."

He raised his hands in a calming gesture. "I'm well aware of what you're up against, and I've made that perfectly clear to the Dean. I think the orders will change within the next week or two. Please, let it run through the proper channels. If you go now, they'll interpret it as defying their authority, and I'll be hard pressed to get co-operation for anything like this again in the future."

Clearly disappointed, the students shifted around and looked at each other, trying to discern one another's thoughts on the matter.

Jared spoke for the group. "All right, Professor. Two weeks. After that, we go."

"That's all I'm asking. Thanks, gang. This really is the only way." Blaney's shoulders sagged with relief, and his gaze strayed to Susan, whose eyes shifted guiltily away. "Okay. I'm going to trust you on this," he told them before departing, "and I'll see you in classes on Monday."

As Blaney drove away, Brandon opened his trunk and started unloading the gear.

Jared halted him. "Okay, everybody. We have a problem here."

"What's that?" Max asked.

"How did Blaney find out about our little trip? Everyone was sworn to secrecy. No one outside the eight of us knew of our plans. So, who here is the snitch?" He stared accusingly at each member of the group, and with suspicion aroused they began to doubt one another.

The seed of mistrust was planted. For Michael and Alesandra, even more so, because they knew the lab break-in made this the second breach of confidentiality.

University administrators debated Professor Blaney's appeal. Their final decision permitted limited archaeological activities, provided no exploration was conducted within the mountain itself.

The caves remained off-limits.

Blaney summoned the group to his lab late Wednesday afternoon to deliver the news. Considering how adamant they had all been about wanting to resume their work, their subdued elation surprised him. While each member was personally pleased, he noted a deterioration in the group spirit.

"Come on, guys. You have the green light to pick up where you left off."

"That's great, Professor. Thanks for all your help."

"Yeah, thanks."

The lackadaisical attitudes puzzled him.

"Okay, what's going on here? You should be thrilled with this news."

"We are. Honest."

"You just let us know when we're going, and we'll be ready."

They gathered their things and filed out of the room, leaving the professor staring at the empty doorway. Something was wrong in Blaneyville, and he determined to learn the reason.

"Sandy, can we talk?"

She looked up from the tome on mineralogy she was reading at her study corral in the library. "Sure, what's up?"

Susan looked around, making sure they were alone. "I've been wanting to talk to you for awhile now. I just needed to wait until the time was right." She pulled up a chair and sat so they were almost touching.

"Is something wrong?"

"No. Everything is right. I must tell someone. I just can't keep it in any longer. But first, you have to promise you won't tell Valerie."

Alesandra's eyebrows knit together, and she studied Susan's face. "All right, I promise. But why? We've never left her out of anything before."

"Because I think she tells Brandon everything. They spend so much time together now, and this secret it too important to take a chance."

"Susan, you're driving me crazy. What is it?"

"I'm in love. And he loves me. He told me so last week."

Lighting up with excitement, Alesandra grabbed her friend's hands and squeezed them. "This is so wonderful, but why is it such a secret? Who is the lucky guy?"

"He's not a 'guy' guy. He's a man."

"Okay, so who's the man?"

"Promise me on your life that you won't tell. I know I shouldn't tell anyone, but if I don't have someone to share it with, I'm going to burst."

"Susan, if you don't tell me now, I'm going to hit you."

"It's Carl."

"Carl. Carl, Carl, Carl…okay, I'm drawing a blank. Carl who?"

"Blaney."

Alesandra could not have been more shocked if she had said the president of the United States. "Oh My Glory! You are kidding me."

"No, actually, it's very serious."

"Susan, Wow! When did this happen? Tell me everything, and don't you leave out one single sigh. I want the whole story from the beginning."

With their heads tucked together, Susan shared the details of her romance with her beloved professor, right down to the minutest tremble when they kissed. In her world, everything was blooming roses.

It required a series of steps to prepare for their solo return to Blaney's Mountain. Michael made several trips to his Jeep carrying items he stored out of sight. He did this casually and as unobtrusively as he could manage, mostly in the late evening, imparting an odd sensation of guilt that quickly dissipated into the shadows.

Alesandra worried about slipping away without telling either Valerie or Susan, especially since Susan had entrusted her with such an important confidence. She felt guilty about not trusting her friend in return, but she kept her pact with Michael and stayed silent.

On the other hand, there was still the question of who sold out the group to Blaney last weekend. Since Susan's revelation, Sandy believed she knew. The problem was, she did not like the answer. It meant she could no longer trust her best friend.

At five thirty Friday morning, she climbed into the passenger seat next to Michael.

"Hey, pretty girl. I'll bet most girls can't look half that good this early in the morning. You ready to go?"

"Thanks. Yes, I have everything." Her manner seemed quieter than usual, and he picked up on it right away.

"Something's bothering you."

"The girls."

"Don't be concerned. Val will probably be busy with Brandon, and no doubt Susan has plans for the long weekend already. I'm sure they have better things to do than sit around the dorm wondering where you are." He reached for her hand, offering reassurance. "You know we wouldn't be able to re-enter the cave if we waited for everyone else. This is our only chance of doing it without the whole group tagging along."

The campus still slept when they strapped themselves in and headed for their destination.

Blaney's Mountain.

Interlopers

"We have a lot of extras this time, and it's going to make the climb more difficult. Now that my cast is off, I can pull my own weight. Are you sure you can handle all that stuff?" Michael asked.

"Well, it's all necessary, so we don't have any other options. You just lead on," she said, readjusting her burden. "I'm stronger than I look. I can probably outlast you. Don't worry about me. I'll manage all right."

Progress was arduous. Heat blazed down reflecting from barren rock facings, and perspiration drenched their clothing within the first half hour.

Nothing looked familiar to Alesandra. "Do you really know the way back to the cave opening? I haven't seen any of the landmarks we put on the map."

He turned to look at her. "I was a boy scout, you know, and we learned not to get lost in the woods. I have my trusty GPS to guide us. I've the track saved from the time we came out of the cave until we met up with the rescue team."

"Oh, I thought you just held up one finger to see which direction the wind was blowing and followed that."

He chuckled. "Save your breath. You're gonna need it when the climb starts to get tough."

"No problem." In spite of her bravado, her eyes burned from sweat trickling down her face, and there was a particularly uncomfortable object knifing into her back.

He noticed her attempts to shift her load. "Let's take a break for a few minutes." He dropped his own pack to the ground, then maneuvered behind her to lift hers from her shoulders. "Let me see if I can adjust some things in here to make it more comfortable for you."

She welcomed the respite, allowing him to rearrange the contents of her knapsack. Glad to be free of the heavy weight, she leaned against a tree and bit into an apple. Juice squirted as her teeth sunk through the red skin, and she wiped it from her cheek with a finger. "Mmm. This is good."

"Why didn't you say you were hungry? I guess we should have

stopped for something before we started."

"It's okay. I brought along some munchies, and I'm willing to share if you're nice to me." She dug through a side pouch and extracted another apple, offering it to him.

"Look, you had the corner of this halogen lamp digging into your back," he told her as he moved it. "The climb is challenging enough without you being uncomfortable like this, Sandy. Next time, say something." He took the proffered fruit and sat next to her.

"I'm not a sissy."

"It's got nothing to do with being a sissy. You don't have to suffer in order to make the climb. We've been planning this trip for weeks. I want us to enjoy it, not act like it's a test of stamina, for crying out loud. I already know you're tenacious."

They resumed the climb, and his longer legs forced her to double her steps to keep up with him. "Why do guys always have to show off like this?" she muttered.

"You all right?"

"Yes, I'm fine." She lied, refusing to let him hear her complain.

They crossed a ridge line, and he carefully selected the best pathway on the precipitous footing, reaching back to take her hand.

Knowing that in spite of her protests, she found the journey demanding, Michael made frequent stops to ease the burdens on their backs. When their destination finally came into view, he pointed it out to her. Smiling, she recognized the trail sign left behind on their previous visit; the circle of stones with one slightly larger rock in the center, symbolizing *I have gone home.*

From where they stood, it was difficult to differentiate between the granite slab and the rest of the rock facing.

"It really is impossible to know there's an entrance there," she remarked. "It's so well camouflaged."

"If we hadn't located it from the inside, it would still be unknown. We never would have found it from this vantage point. I guess that's why the caverns have stayed undisturbed all these years." Michael studied the disguised threshold and mused, "You know, it makes me wonder about the people who left the markings inside the chamber. Did they use some other way to get in, and if so, why hasn't it been discovered before this?"

"I've thought about that, too. Maybe we'll find answers once we get back inside. Do you want to go first, Pooh, or shall I?"

They unloaded their backpacks, sleeping bags, and utility pouches while Michael studied the configuration of the wall cavity. Getting out the last time had been a tight fit. Digging into his pack, he retrieved a rock hammer and began chopping at overhanging outcroppings to make the opening easier to pass through.

"There, that should do it," he stepped back to admire his handiwork. "I'll go in first. You can pass the gear through to me." He started to work his way through the crevice, then turned to look back at her. "Don't forget to strap your helmet on this time," he reminded before disappearing into the dark hole.

One by one she passed the parcels to him and quickly penetrated the cave herself.

Shortly after lunch, Susan found Valerie in the lobby of Cooper Hall waiting for Brandon. "Hey, Val, have you seen Sandy?"

"Nope. She was gone when I got up this morning. It's a weekend though. She probably went off with the geek on one of their picnics."

"Yeah, what's that about anyway? One day she can't stand the guy, and the next she's running away on 'little picnics' with him. I've asked her, but she's not spilling anything."

"Well, that makes two of us. I was hoping she told you what's going on. She did a sudden one-eighty where Michael Stanley Gant is concerned, and I can't believe there isn't something behind it. I wish she would trust us enough to share it. In the meantime, it is a beautiful day for a picnic," Valerie noted. "Why don't we do something like that? We have four whole days before classes resume."

"We should plan a day in the country. Why don't we get a group together?"

"I'll mention it to Brandon. He'll gather up a party in no time. Where should we go? Too bad we don't know where Sandy and Michael went. We could have picnicked with them."

"Let's plan it for tomorrow. Sandy should be back tonight and can go with us."

"Good point. All right, we'll have everybody meet here at ten o'clock tomorrow morning. Sandy's going to be happy that we've planned it so she can come. There's no way she's having as good a time with Michael as we'll have. I mean really, how could he possibly compete?"

"No kidding. Okay, I'll go and make a few phone calls and see who hasn't gone home for the long weekend. Talk to you later, Val." With that, Susan headed upstairs to their suite to invite her roommate to join them for guys, grub, and a good time.

Max dropped into Cooper Hall late in the afternoon with plans to ask Alesandra to the picnic as his date. He found it extremely unsettling to learn she was off skylarking somewhere with Gant, and not for the first time. He turned away greatly disappointed. He had been looking forward to playing touch football with her; more touching than football.

Passing the parking lot, he noticed Gant's Jeep missing from its usual space. Sharp pangs of jealousy stabbed at him. He never played second fiddle to another man when it came to wooing a woman. To do so now to Gant, of all people, was demoralizing. He cringed as he thought of her being with the nerdy weasel instead of him.

Like everyone else who knew her, he could not fathom what the fascination was. Surely she was not attracted to Gant. The very idea was ludicrous. It likely revolved around their mutual interest in the cave. What did they find that was so intriguing as to demand their constant companionship? They must have stumbled onto something they shouldn't have, and he knew they could be unwittingly walking into danger. He tried unsuccessfully several times to sound her out regarding their cave experience. She simply was not obliging.

His gaze wandered to his 4X4 Tracker, and he toyed with the idea of going after her. The thought was tempting, but where would he look? Thinking about it, he walked back to his campus apartment. Not being in control of a situation, any situation, made him uneasy. Perhaps it was time to resort to other measures. Using his cell phone, he dialed a number and waited.

"Hello. Max here." He listened attentively. "No. Nothing yet." There was a pause. "I know, but I'm still on top of it. I'm keeping close tabs on Blaney, so don't worry about him. No one else seems to suspect anything yet, but I'll let you know if something new develops." He hung up and made a notation on his Palm Pilot before returning it to his pocket.

Several hours later, when Michael and Alesandra failed to return, he made another telephone call.

"Grubbs, this is Max. I'm calling to warn you. You might have two little birdies returning to the nest."

The other man spoke briefly before Max responded. "No, nothing drastic at this time. Just be careful, that's all."

"Oh no, not this slope again." Alesandra stood at the top, her brows knit together as she looked with distaste at the path ahead.

"Wow! This is amazing."

"Well, it's not like you haven't been here before."

"Yeah, but don't forget, I didn't have my glasses. Couldn't see anything. This is sort of like my first time all over again."

"The aragonite is beautiful to look at, but it sliced my hands to pieces the last time."

"I remember, so I came prepared." He pulled a long length of nylon rope from his backpack and tethered it to a boulder at the top of the slope, complete with knots at regular intervals as hand holds. "Have you got your gloves on? It should be a whole lot easier this time."

Grabbing hold of the rope, he started to descend backwards into the narrow chasm, with Alesandra above so if she slipped she would fall back into him.

Upon reaching the bottom, she smiled. "My tender body parts thank you. I've made it uninjured."

"Glad to hear it." He returned her grin and noticed she already had dirt streaks on her nose. "Now for the mousehole." Pushing his gear ahead, he wormed through the low passageway. In the tunnel on the other side, he took her gloved hand to keep her at his side.

In addition to the usual carbide lamps on their helmets, they carried 6-volt halogen lanterns attached to their utility belts.

"We'll be able to see much better this time." Darkness was the biggest obstacle underground, and he did not want them groping blindly.

A short time later, she felt a reverence settle upon her as they entered the Chamber of Gods. She hurried to the praying figures to examine the markings, running her fingers over them tenderly, almost devoutly.

"Michael, I never noticed before but now in the light, they appear to be some sort of symbols."

His gaze wandered around the chamber in wonder before focussing on the pillars. "This place is pretty cool, but don't let your imagination fool you, Sandy. I think they're probably too indistinct to identify them as anything other than random lines."

"Oh no, they're much more than that. Max explained some of this to me when we were in that small cavern with the professor." She grabbed his arm and dragged him closer. "Look how these horizontal lines intersect with the vertical lines right here, almost resembling a ladder, or perhaps a gate." Another thought occurred, and her voice softened. "Maybe even a tomb. Imagine if an ancient tomb was somewhere here in this cave. Think of the research we could do with the skeletons. Oh, Michael, we could learn so much."

The light from his helmet lit her face, and he smiled as he watched awe and fascination flutter across her features. "Why don't you get out the camera and start shooting?"

"Oh, right. I'm so excited I almost forgot I had it with me." She scrambled to retrieve it from her pouch while he situated the lanterns, giving her optimum lighting as she snapped the shutter.

She moved along to the second column. "Hey, did you notice this? Two of these pillars are in raised relief rather than engraved. This is so cool."

Freed from assisting her, he directed the light of his hand-held lantern around the chamber. The walls, as before, radiated whenever the rays touched upon embedded mineral veins. He moved forward for a closer examination. Taking a rock pick from his pouch, he started chipping away.

Two hours passed before she pulled back from the stone etchings. Letting her gaze roam around the room in search of her companion, she saw nothing but utter darkness. "Hey! Where'd you go? Michael?"

"I'm over here." He appeared around a corner, shining the lantern at her.

"A fine protector you are. You left me here all by myself."

"You're not by yourself. I'm right here with you."

"No, I'm here, and you're clear over there. What are you doing?" She crossed the room to join him.

He handed her a Ziploc bag containing fragments he'd chipped from the wall. "These look like the crystals we found at the dig site, except they're larger and not as fragile. I wanted some more of them."

"Right. Dr. Turner said he needed more too, didn't he?"

"Yes, but he'll have to wait until I can get his crystals from the site when we return as a group. Couldn't explain having these."

"Want to take a break, have something to eat, and maybe explore a little bit?"

"Sure. Sounds like a good idea." He rubbed his hand over his stomach. "I'm starting to get hungry."

"I've brought some nice ham and cheese on Kaiser buns. That should help." They sat down near the spot where they slept on their previous visit.

Two large buns were short work for him, and he smiled when she handed him a package of Twinkies. "You're a good ole girl, Sandy."

"Why thank you," she grinned at the compliment.

When the remnants of the meal were gathered together and packed away, he shined the lamp around the large chamber. "We have a lot of rooms and tunnels branching off from this one. Which would you like to explore first?"

She spun around in the center of the room with her eyes closed and her arm extended. Stopping, she opened her eyes. "This way, Pooh," she said, and headed toward the doorway ahead of her.

The corridor was narrow but high enough to permit walking without stooping. Using only the light from their helmets, they proceeded until a quick gasp from Alesandra brought them to a halt. She clutched his arm and pointed.

The skeletal remains of a human protruded from beneath a ledge not ten feet in front of them. Lying on its side, the body was clothed in a ragged uniform, tattered and decaying, bearing the markings of a soldier; a Confederate soldier, judging from the CSA insignia on his wide-brimmed, gray Stetson.

"Well," Michael said, "there goes your theory that we're the first humans in this cave."

Reaching out to grip his hand, she ventured a few steps closer. "How do you suppose he got here?"

"He was probably hiding from the Union army and couldn't find his way out again. Doesn't look like he had anything with him for light; no lantern or anything. He must have gotten lost in the dark."

"What are we going to do about him, Michael?"

"We're gonna leave him right here," was his short answer. He knelt by the soldier and took a closer look at the yellow braid on the uniform hat. "The man was an officer. A cavalry officer, I think." Lifting the edge of the uniform a few inches from it's resting place, he uncovered a heavy-duty black holster with a snap flap covering a 7-inch Colt .44 revolver.

"Not much we can do about it. We're not supposed to be here either, you know."

"We should tell somebody about him. He probably had a family who never knew what happened to him." She thought how she would feel if he had been one of her ancestors. "Don't you think he deserves a proper burial after all these years?"

"Let's see if he has any identification on him."

She held the light while he nervously swallowed to overcome a natural aversion to touching a dead body. In the soldier's bony right hand was a brown message pouch marked "U.S.". Michael slid it from the fingers that no longer clutched it tightly. Opening the flap, he shined his light inside and gingerly extracted a yellowed paper, under which lay a single metal bar. Although the writing was faded and almost unreadable, they could make out a reference to "G" Company, 6th Infantry Regiment, Jefferson Barracks, Missouri.

"Now, here's a puzzle," he said. "This Johnny Reb is carrying a Yankee message packet, and if I'm not mistaken, that's a gold bar he has there!"

Max kept a lookout all day for their return. As the late evening shadows descended on the campus, he felt certain they returned to the mountain. Propelled by the searing mental picture of Alesandra lying in the arms of Michael Gant at this very moment, he strode to Michael's dorm. He waited in the stairwell for someone to leave, so he could access the floor without a card key. Standing at Gant's door, he removed a small case containing lock-picking tools from his pocket and opened the door.

Thinking Michael must have smuggled something out of the cave, he intended to search the room to identify what it was. Gant had one of the few private rooms in the dormitory, so Max was not worried about being discovered. Flicking on the wall switch, the room flooded with light, and he stood astounded.

The room had clearly been ransacked. Drawers were pulled free from the dresser and desk and were tossed haphazardly, their contents scattered everywhere. The sheets were pulled off the bed and the mattress turned over. No doubt about it--someone else had speculated the same thing and beat him to the punch, blustering through the room like a southern windstorm.

The question was, did they find what they were looking for?

Eternal Stones

Night came without warning inside the cave. Within the dark world, the only way to distinguish day from night was by the tiredness in their bones and the time on their luminous watches.

Alesandra lifted a hand to her mouth, trying to stifle a yawn.

"Geez, you must be tired. I say we've found gold, and you yawn? Man, Sandy." He hefted the metal bar, surprised by the weight of it. It wasn't much bigger than a chocolate bar, but it took two hands to hold. "This sucker is heavy."

"Well, remember the periodic table. Gold is heavier than lead."

"It sure is."

"What are we going to do with it?"

"At the moment, I don't have a clue. Listen, you're tired, and so am I. It's not like we're going anywhere with it tonight. And, neither is our friend here. Let's go back and get some sleep."

Returning to the Chamber of Gods, they dug their yellow- capped plastic bottles from their packs, and after taking separate journeys to fill them, unrolled their sleeping bags.

The residual fluorescent effect kept the chamber from being immersed in total darkness. Alesandra was able to perceive the shadowy shapes of the praying figures as she lay awake next to Michael, listening to water dripping from somewhere and thinking.

"Michael," she whispered. "Michael," this time a little louder. She nudged him. "Are you awake?"

"Uh, I am now. What's the matter?"

"Why are you sleeping?"

"I thought that's what we were supposed to be doing."

"Well, I'm still awake."

"Oh. Is this how it's always gonna be, Sandy? I'm not allowed to fall asleep if you're still awake?" He waited for her to give him some sassy attitude, telling him they were not going to be spending their nights together, but she did not.

"Well, it's nicer for two to think together, sometimes."

Realizing sleep was not in the cards, he adjusted the pack beneath his head. "Okay, I'm listening. What's on your mind?"

"I can't help thinking about that soldier and the gold."

"He may have been wounded by Yankee soldiers and crawled into the cave to hide, and then he just died."

"That's possible, but it doesn't explain his possession of the gold bar. I wonder what we should do with it. I wonder how much it's worth. I wonder where he got it. Think of all the things we could do with that money." Her words tumbled out in quick succession as her excitement bubbled within.

"That's a lot of wondering. No wonder you can't sleep."

"Well, what do you think?"

"About which question?"

"Take your pick."

"I think a gold bar like that on today's market would probably be in the neighborhood of maybe $50,000."

"Is that all?"

"Have you ever had that much money before?"

"No."

"Then don't say 'is that all'."

"True." Her imagination kept running full tilt. "Think of all the things we could buy with $50,000."

"You might have a problem spending it, you know."

"What do you mean? I'm a girl. I know all about shopping."

"Where do you think you're going to sell it to get the money? And don't you think people would have questions? It's not like we've found a suitcase of cash here."

"Oh. I guess I never thought about that. Surely there must be a way."

"Well, let's sleep on it."

She lay quiet for a moment. "I wish you would turn around and face me."

He chuckled into the darkness. "Sandy, we can't see each other."

"I just want to know you're looking at me, because I feel a bit uneasy in here." She hated herself for sounding like a scared little girl. "I feel as if someone is watching us." There was a tiny quiver in her voice.

"Sandy, no one is here but us. We're all alone. The soldier sure can't come after us if that's what you're worried about."

"No, it's not that. I don't know, Michael. I sense a strong presence all around us, like somebody, or something, is observing everything we do."

"That's silly," he said, but he rolled over to face her and reached his arms out to pull her snugly against him. "Better?"

"Yes, thank you."

He placed a gentle kiss on her forehead and tightened his arms around her. "Okay, now let's go to sleep."

It was the cave sounds that eventually lulled her into slumber—the dripping water, whistling air currents, the soft snores of her partner now snuggled against her.

They lay together, sated, sweaty, and trying to catch their breath. Susan rested her head on his chest, their bodies entwined as she sensuously ran her foot up and down his leg.

Carl brushed a strand of hair from her face and broached the subject that had been on his mind for the past few days. "Susan, there's something I've been meaning to ask you."

"What is it?"

"The other day when I gave the group the news that the university was letting us go ahead with our trips to the mountain, I expected they'd be thrilled about it. It's what they said they all wanted. I have to say, I was surprised and disappointed by their unenthusiastic response, unlike the response you just gave me a minute ago." He grinned and kissed her.

She giggled and ran a finger over his chin. "So what's the question?"

"What's up with them? Why weren't they happy about it?"

"Oh, they were happy. The problem is we have some dissension in the ranks."

"What does that mean?"

"No one was supposed to tell about the trip we were going to make back to the mountain last week. We were all sworn to secrecy. Yet, you showed up and stopped us. Nobody is admitting to breaking the pact, so now everyone is eyeing each other with suspicion, wanting to know who sold us out."

"Speaking of which, why the hell didn't you tell me about it? I couldn't believe you would involve yourself in something like that, let the group put themselves in that kind of jeopardy, and not tell me about it. I thought what we had outweighed some pact made with a bunch of kids."

Susan tried to piece her thoughts together. She knew this moment would come, that he would expect her to justify her silence.

"I couldn't tell you for two reasons," she started. "First of all, if it ever came out that I was the one who told you, it could cast suspicion on our relationship. I can't do anything that might bring our association into question."

"Okay, I can appreciate that. I'm not saying I agree with it, but I understand your motivation. What's the second reason?"

She lifted her head and kissed him before moving to lay next to him. "If you knew we were going, and it came out, you could be held accountable. I wanted you to be blameless if the feces hit the fan."

"So, you believed, yet again, that you were protecting me."

"Yes."

"Susan, I'm not a little boy. I don't need you safeguarding me. I would rather have heard it from you. If this is going to work between us, we can't be having secrets from one another. I want us to be able to trust each other. Understood?" he asked softly as he rolled onto his side and caressed her cheek. "I want this to work out, Susan."

"I love you, Carl. I'm sorry."

"It's okay, this time. I love you too, honey." He kissed her lips softly and ran his fingers through her blonde hair, admiring it in the moonlight that streamed through his second floor bedroom window.

Smiling, she folded her arms around him, and they soon fell asleep together.

Alesandra came fully awake in Michael's arms. Opening her eyes, she saw he was already awake, watching her. "Good morning."

"Morning. Get enough sleep?"

"Mmm. I think so." She stretched then relaxed back into his embrace.

"Much as I hate having to move from this position, I could do with something to eat."

"I'm hungry too." Digging into her backpack, she brought out two oranges and a Tupperware container with a few oatmeal muffins in it. "I made these late Thursday night, so they're still fresh. I hope you like dates."

"I like dates with you," he bantered.

"Thanks, but I meant dates in your muffins," she smiled.

"Well, I like them, too, but not as much."

"Have a couple of juice boxes." She tossed him a tetra pack of fruit juice and settled to peel the paper off her muffin. When their appetites had been satisfied, she cleared away the remnants and they geared up for work.

"You know, Michael, I had the strangest dream last night. There were eerie spirits all around me, wanting me to join in their ghostly dance. They led me to a secret cavern lit by two bright lights overhead that shone like beacons. I watched the lights disappear as if swallowed up in the darkness. The spirits were once again illuminated as a row of rocks on the ground began to glow, brightening until they rose suddenly from the earth like balls of fire. They continued to rise until they left the cave and found their rightful place in the sky, where they became stars."

He listened intently before confessing his own dream. “Now that you mention it, I had a rather strange one too. At least I think it was a dream.

"What happened? Tell me about it.”

“It’s still kinda fuzzy. I was staring into the darkness beyond where the soldier lies, and I saw a mound of rocks in the center of the room. The thing that caught my attention was another group of stones. There were several of them, white and translucent, arranged in a straight line, each glowing like the sun. I saw them, but I couldn’t touch them.”

“Ooh, this is spooky! You had glowing rocks, too.”

“It’s strange that we should have similar dreams, but that’s all they were, you know.”

“Yes, of course,” she agreed, but her mind would not let go of it. It was clear he was not going to indulge in flights of fancy, so she changed the subject.

“I want more time to study the markings on the statues this morning. Maybe the photographs will reveal clues when I enlarge them on the computer. They’ll probably show things that are hard to see here in the cave.”

“Sounds like you’re on to something positive. Take as much time as you want with it. In the meantime, I think I’ll photograph the soldier.”

Michael carried the halogen lantern, illuminating the corridor. Positioning the lamp near the body for proper lighting, he snapped several photos.

Satisfied he had catalogued everything regarding the body in his PDA, he wandered the last few feet toward the end of the tunnel. The opening only stood about two feet tall, and from a crouched position he could look through to see what lay beyond.

An eerie glow radiated from the far wall of the adjoining cavern. Curious, he went inside to investigate. Although the room was the size of a large gymnasium, it was nearly devoid of standing formations, only boasting three tall pillars. Being part of the dry cave system, no stalactites hung precariously overhead.

The only access he could find to the odd light was a sharp, narrow fissure. Peering through the crack revealed an ante-chamber with a raised central area. Excitement gripped him and his first calls to Alesandra came out as mere whispers before he managed to acquire volume.

“Sandy, come here, quick. Sandy.”

She heard him calling, and reluctantly left her work. As she made her way through the connecting corridor, she saw him pressed up against a wall in the glow of a light shining from yet another room. “What is it?”

“Come see this. You not going to believe it.”

She crowded against him to look through the wall cleft. The sight of nine round glowing stones, in a single line just as he described in his dream, astounded her.

"What are they?" she asked in wonder.

"I'm not certain, but they seem to be radiating from within and independently of each other. I don't understand how that's possible if they've been isolated here for, who knows how long?"

"This is amazing. These rocks seem to be glowing internally rather than reflectively like the other rocks. They must be something different."

"Yes, the question is, what? I don't see another opening to the chamber, so it isn't like I can nab one to take back to the lab. We don't have the time or the proper tools, and it'll take a long time to break down the wall."

"So what do you want to do about it?"

"I guess we'll have to plan another trip back here to get hold of one of them." He rubbed his hand across the back of his neck in frustration. "I really would like to examine them closely and figure out what makes them radiate like that."

"We'll come back." Setting her hand on his arm as a gesture of reassurance, she spoke soothingly. "You'll get the chance, Michael. I promise I'll come back with you, as many times as it takes to get one of those rocks for your research."

"Thanks, Sandy." He leaned down and kissed her. "I suppose I'd better get started chipping away at this, but I also want to collect some more specimens from the chamber for testing reflective properties."

"Okay, I'll go back to work, too. See you in a little while." Rising on her toes, she kissed him one more time before returning to the Chamber of Gods.

Hunger finally caused him to check his Indiglo watch and he wandered back to the main chamber. "Hey, Sandy. It's past lunch time. You ready to take a break?"

"Yeah, matter of fact, I'm starving." She stood and stretched. "My back is starting to get sore. One of the liabilities of the trade, I fear." Sitting beside him, she sifted through her backpack. "You know, since I carried all the food, my pack is going to be a lot lighter on the way back down."

"On the way back down, we'll be redistributing some of the gear. Your pack will still weigh less, but not as much as you think it will."

"At least we don't have to catch any fish for dinner. You have some of those nifty little fire starters with you again, don't you?"

"Sure do."

"Good. I was counting on that. If you'll dig them out and light a couple, we can cook lunch." With a manual can opener in her hand, she removed the lids from two cans of Chunky Soup. "I brought tongs to hold the cans over the flames."

"Smart girl. I knew there was a reason I brought you along." He smiled, thinking again of watching her in her cheerleading outfit with the little skirt flipping in the breeze, knowing the reason for his attraction had nothing to do with soup.

"I've got pudding cups for dessert. Chocolate and vanilla."

Michael lit the egg carton cups, and soon they sat eating hot soup and crusty bread rolls with cheese.

"What have you been doing all morning?" he asked between bites.

"I made a bunch of relief impressions of the markings on the statues to corroborate the photographs I took yesterday."

"That's a clever idea. What made you think of it?"

"I did brass rubbings on a trip to England when I was in high school. I figured it might pick up any stray marks that don't come out clearly on the photos."

"Good thinking."

"That's what I'll be doing for a while this afternoon. I'm enjoying it."

"Why don't I put away the lunch things, so you can get back to it?" he offered.

"Thanks, Michael. I appreciate that, and I'll take you up on it. I'm just getting started on the third statue."

"Then get to it, Piglet. Have fun."

With a grin, she scooted back across the room to the statues. He watched with interest as she placed a thin tissue paper over the characteristic markings on the figures. Gently, she ran a soft charcoal pencil over them. By this method, she was able to lift impressions which she then inserted into protective plastic covers for safekeeping. In spite of the tedium of the task, she was happy with what was accomplished. The hours passed slowly while they worked until twilight loomed outside the cave.

"Sandy, I think we've accomplished what we came for. I have my rock specimens, and you have your pictures. Let's get out of here first thing in the morning."

"Well, if you're ready to go, I'd rather we spent tonight outside. I still feel like someone is watching, and it makes me uncomfortable."

In the oral incantations and traditions of the Cherokee, lives a vague but persistent image of a race of men who preceded them. The stories tell how they came from a land far distant, bringing their religion and their magic with them. This was their home, this range of mountains and hills called Tennessee.

Not many folks visited the mountain. Perhaps a few hikers or a troop of boy scouts earning merit badges. Then there were the students from the university who regularly came to sift through the old sacred mounds. Bubba Grubbs watched in amusement as they unearthed old bones and artifact treasures left behind by the "others."

Like everyone else who lived near the mountain, he tolerated the periodic excavations. Yet, he made it a point to keep a watchful eye on these activities, especially when it resulted in unfavorable publicity such as the recent rockslide involving two students. Frequent unique finds, however, kept the Cherokee traditions alive in the minds of scholars and historians alike.

Bubba delighted in telling the stories of his supposed ancestors to anyone who tarried long enough to listen. He was careful to regale his audience with many tales about the Tsaga'si, unseen mischievous fairy spirits who often helped hunters. The Cherokee worshipped them, but outsiders feared the Tsaga'si because they did not understand.

It suited his purpose that strangers found the mountain harsh, rugged and inhospitable. The professor was an exception. Local folklore interested him, and he enhanced the university's reputation with the accumulation of recovered Indian relics. For Bubba, Blaney's archaeological group served as a smoke screen to mask certain nefarious activities, enterprises branded as somewhat outside the law.

Bubba's telephone conversation with Max alerted him to the possible return of the two young students who previously managed to escape from the cave-in. It would not do for them to stumble onto something that was none of their business.

Southern Hospitality

The splendor of the cavern held them in its grasp even as they prepared to leave. Drooping stalactites, curved and tapered, mingled with tall spindly "broomsticks" and ornate flowing formations to create an underground fairyland.

Despite the absence of creepy crawlies and swooping bats, Alesandra felt a persistent uneasiness in the murky confines of the mountain cave. She could not assuage her fears with logic. They were feelings more than thoughts and not subject to the arguments of rationality.

She wandered once more through the tunnel to the body of the rebel soldier, lying serenely in the place where he took his final breath.

"I hope we can find out who you were," she told him. She crouched next to him, her fingers brushing across the gray fabric of the sleeve. A play of light on the walls caught her attention, and she turned to see Michael approaching.

"You ready to go?" he asked.

"Yes, I just wanted to say goodbye first. I hate leaving him here like this."

"He's been here for over a hundred years. I don't think he'll mind staying awhile longer. We'll come back."

"I need to find a way to get him a proper burial, even if it means we have to wait until we're no longer a part of the university so we can make his presence known."

"Don't worry, we'll figure it out."

"What about the gold bar?"

"We'll figure that out, too." He offered his hand to help her to her feet. "Come on. Let's get out of here."

Back in the Chamber of Gods, he lifted her heavy backpack to help her into it. But even as they donned their gear, the mountain uttered an objection. From somewhere behind them came an all too familiar sound.

Recognizing it as a cascade of falling rocks, Alesandra grabbed his arm, her eyes large with alarm. "It can't be. Not again."

"Sandy, stay here and don't move."

Her clutch tightened. "You're not going to leave me here. Whatever is happening affects me too."

"I'm just going to see what happened. You'll be all right."

She was adamant. "You're darn right I will, cause I'm going with you. We aren't going to get separated now."

Accepting the inevitable, he surrendered to her demand, and they retraced their steps toward the upward slope that led to the cave opening. The passage became suddenly narrower with large rocks littering their way.

"Michael, we're trapped again!"

"Maybe not. I think we can still crawl through." He removed a trenching tool from his gear and shoveled the smaller rock fragments to one side, creating a pathway. When the dust settled, they made their way through and pulled themselves up the incline aided by the knotted rope.

Finding the portal to the outer world uncluttered, they squeezed through, eager to breathe fresh air again. "Hey! We're pretty good at getting out of caves," she facetiously remarked as she wiggled her shoulders out.

"That's because we keep getting ourselves in trouble. We're very good at that."

"Yeah. I suppose we'll just have to stop meeting like this."

Stepping out from behind the rock facing, they were greeted by the pinks and purples of the setting sun. "Oh, Michael, look at it. You don't get a view like this every day. It's glorious." She dropped her gear to the ground and stepped further into the softening shadows of dusk, feeling the essence of the panorama in front of her. A sense of freedom washed through her as she drank in the sight.

He slipped his arms around her waist, letting her lean back into him. "It is magnificent."

"I started remembering how it felt when we were lost in there the first time, when I thought I'd never see natural light again. It was such an empty feeling."

His embrace tightened, and he tipped his head closer to her ear. "I remember when I thought I'd never hold you in my arms like this, and it was such an empty feeling."

She gazed into his face and whispered, "I'm here now."

The small, grassy meadow provided an ideal place to enjoy a light meal and spend the night. They welcomed the woodland scent on a cool refreshing night breeze, and sleep came almost immediately.

The morning sun rose brightly, shining in Alesandra's eyes. "Val, turn the light out," she muttered as she pulled the cover over her head.

Masculine chuckles answered her. The sound of someone bustling around dragged her further from the arms of slumber, and she slowly oriented herself to her surroundings.

"Michael, is that you making all that noise?"

"I think it's me. Just a minute, and I'll check," he teased. "Good morning, sleepyhead."

"Is it morning already?" Her voice sounded strange, even to herself. "I don't want morning yet." She tried to burrow deeper into her sleeping bag.

"Suck it up, buttercup. Time to get up. I have breakfast ready for you."

With a sigh of resignation, she crawled out of the bag and stood. He watched as she stretched, the sunlight gleaming on her hair. Wandering toward him, she asked, "Why didn't you wake me? I could have done that."

"Too late, it's already done. All you have to do is sit with me."

"Okay, I'll be with you in a minute." Lifting her backpack she lugged it with her into the nearby woods, thankful the bushes were lush with greenery. When she returned she washed her face and hands, then stood looking at the summery countryside filled with bright flowers and leafy green shelters. It presented a stark contrast to the colorless cave.

"I want to take some pictures before we start back. This place is so pretty."

"That's a good idea. I wrapped the camera inside a shirt and tucked it in the top of your pack so it wouldn't get broken being shoved through the tunnels."

When breakfast was finished she rolled up her sleeping bag, and they repacked the gear. He redistributed the weight between them, keeping the heavier items in his own pack. Still several hours from where their Jeep was parked, they began the descent.

This time, rather than being consumed with worry about rejoining the rest of the Blaney Bunch, they enjoyed the beauty of the woodlands. Taking their time, they paused to examine stands of trees and the irregular exposure of rock layers emerging above ground; evidence of primordial upheavals. In this manner, the day glided past until they rediscovered a small waterfall dropping into a rock-lined basin.

"This is a perfect place to have lunch," she suggested, shrugging off her pack. "I want to take some pictures here, too. Wouldn't this make a lovely postcard?"

"It's a great spot. We've been going at a pretty steady pace. We can use a break."

He located their Jeep quickly enough but failed to find a campsite after reconnoitering the area. Bubba had no idea what those two kids were doing on his mountain. It was important that he find out. He was not always guided by conscience when it came to the protection of his assets.

His search centered around the vicinity where his rescue group found the lost students. They might have re-entered the cave through their undisclosed escape route. In that case, things could get sticky fast.

With two of his special employees, he scoured the area looking for the trespassers. They spent the better part of two days searching, unable to cut their sign anywhere.

Bubba began to lose patience. Climbing over ridges and crossing animal trails, many freshly made, he alternately cursed the mountain for luring the college kids back, then himself for associating with Blaney in the first place.

Bubba's companions exchanged knowing glances as they listened to his mumbles but wisely remained silent. The last thing they wanted was to direct his wrath toward themselves.

Temper rising, he finally found Michael and Alesandra casually dangling their feet in the catch basin of a waterfall, laughing and dining on peanut butter crackers. A broad smile broke across his face as he greeted them with a false show of surprise.

"Well, if it isn't my two little lost birdies," he called.

She waved at him. "Hi, Mister Grubbs. Bet you didn't think to see us again so soon."

"I sure didn't." He turned to his associates and made introductions all around. "I didn't know your group was back out here."

"No, it's just us this time," Michael said.

"You mean you came out here all alone? The others didn't come with you? I'da thought you got enough of this old mountain the last time you were here."

"On the contrary, we wanted to see more of it so we decided to come camping."

Bubba looked around but failed to see any evidence of a camp site. "I don't blame you for that. She is a fine old mountain with many great qualities." A brief pause. "I hope you found your way back into that cave without any difficulty?"

Sidestepping the question, Michael answered. "Actually, we're all packed up and ready to head back to the university."

"You don't have to rush off on our account." Bubba needed to probe them for information about their activities. "We've been on the trail ourselves, and this looks like a nice place to rest a spell. Why don't y'all tell us about your camping trip? Such as where you've been, what you've seen...."

Michael and Alesandra both suspected he wanted to draw them out about the cave, but they remained wary and mute on the subject.

Alesandra glanced at her partner. "It's a very large mountain. We could walk it for days and not see all of it," she snuggled up against Michael and lay her head on his shoulder, "but we've spent all weekend right here at the waterfall. It's so private." She batted her eyelashes flirtatiously for emphasis.

"Yes, she is a big mountain, although not as big as she used to be."

"What do you mean?"

Bubba settled himself. "The Cherokee speak of the 'old ones', the others who were here before them. The land was fairly new then, and the Earth still trembled occasionally. The mountain was home to the fierce panther and the brown bear, and they roamed freely in search of food. Tribal hunters made every effort to avoid them.

"One day the mountain rumbled and shook so hard that huge boulders tumbled down and smashed everything in their way. Whole villages were destroyed. One in particular suffered so much damage to its lodges, the people decided to move and build a new village.

"The panther and the bear escaped the anger of the gods because they lived deep inside the mountain. The mountain continued to shake off its rocks, eventually reducing itself to its present size."

Alesandra listened raptly but with disbelief. "So, the people in the village moved away. What about the panther and the bear? What happened to them?"

Bubba was silent for a long time before giving an answer. "Nobody knows for sure and certain what happened to them. Folks never saw them again. The Cherokee insist they stayed deep inside the mountain, probably in the very cave you two got yourselves trapped in. And there they remain to this day."

"But, Mister Grubbs, that can't be true. How could they still be alive after all these years?"

"Hard to say, little lady. But the Cherokee believe it, and who are we to question. This mountain is their home."

"Well, we certainly didn't see any evidence of that."

"That's good. I'd say you were mighty lucky, but iffen I was you, I'd make it a point never to go back inside that old mountain. The panther and the bear just might still be hungry."

Michael laughed. "Are you saying the mountain wouldn't welcome us back?"

Bubba rubbed a hand over the stubble on his chin. "Not at all, young fella. This old mountain welcomes you with open arms, and so would the panther and the bear. It's what folks around here call southern hospitality."

Michael found it hard to get a good read on this man who claimed to be part Cherokee. At first glance, he appeared to be just what he said, a

Tennessean with an uncanny gift of gab. He thought he detected more than that. Was the legend some sort of warning? And what about the other two men? Neither of them said a word, merely nodding occasionally, their steely eyes fixed on him and Alesandra. As he sized them up, the word “henchman” came to mind.

Michael reached a hand to help Alesandra to her feet. “It's been nice seeing you again, Mr. Grubbs, but we should start heading back now. We still have a long drive ahead of us, and we want to be home in time for dinner.”

Hiding his disappointment, Bubba assisted them in shouldering their gear and watched with narrowing eyes as they pushed off, homeward bound.

It reminded him of his own youthful adventures on the mountain. He, too, discovered a cave, plus a secret cache of gold bullion buried in a collapsed chamber undisturbed for more than a hundred years, its origin a mystery. The bulk of the treasure remained under a blanket of fallen rock, and he determined to hang onto it at any cost. He smartly managed to build an empire from it, one bar at a time.

Assault

They stopped for dinner on the way home and drove at a leisurely pace, discussing their new discoveries. After dropping Alesandra at her dormitory, Michael pulled the Jeep into the parking lot next to McCord Hall.

Looking over the gear stashed in the back, he pulled out his personal items and sleeping bag. He decided to leave the lanterns and caving equipment until he could discreetly transport them after dark.

The dormitory foyer was deserted with the exception of the desk clerk. Michael climbed the stairs to the fourth floor, and used his card key to gain entrance to the hallway. Exhaustion wove its magic as his feet plodded closer to home. Thoughts of a soft mattress and a plump feather pillow beckoned him.

He flicked the keys on his key chain and snatched hold of the one that would open the door to his private room. Inserting it into the lock, he felt no tension when he turned the key.

With eyebrows drawn together in puzzlement, he pushed the door open and saw the mass destruction that had been his home when he'd left three days before. Scanning the room, he found nothing left untouched. He picked his footing across the floor in an effort to uncover his telephone. When he located the base, he hit the pager button and listened for the telltale beeping that would guide him to the handset. Finding it buried under an overturned drawer covered by a heap of textbooks, he pushed the on button and was glad to learn the battery was not dead. He placed a call to the front desk switchboard.

"McCord Hall," a voice responded

"This is Michael Gant in 414. Call Public Safety."

The aftermath of a four-day holiday exhibited itself in students and faculty alike trying to re-adapt to the pace of university life. The day before classes resumed, Alesandra sat at her computer searching for websites pertaining to ancient alphabets and writings. A knock at her bedroom door interrupted her train of thought, and she minimized the screen to keep prying eyes away.

"It's open." She turned to face the door as Susan poked her head in.

"Hi, Sandy. Mind if I come in?"

"Course not. Make yourself at home."

"Val's not around?"

"Not very often. She's always off with Brandon these days. Haven't seen too much of her all term, actually." Alesandra twirled on her chair to face the bed where Susan sat. Sensing tension in her friend, she asked, "Everything okay, Susan? You seem a bit, I don't know, nervous."

"I guess that's what I came to find out. Is everything okay?"

"I'm fine. Shouldn't I be?"

"That's not what I mean. I'm trying to ask, are things all right between us?"

Alesandra scrutinized Susan's face, trying to discern a hidden meaning. "Of course. I don't understand what you're getting at."

"Well, about you and Michael."

"Michael? What does he have to do with anything?"

"Well, you just went away for a long weekend with him, didn't you?"

"Yeah, so?"

"In the past, something like that wouldn't have come as a surprise. We used to talk about everything. We've been best friends forever, and I don't know what's changed, but you don't talk to me anymore. Sandy, I entrusted the biggest, most important secret of my life to you, and you don't talk to me at all. I thought you and Max had something going and the next thing I hear, you and Michael turn up missing for a full weekend."

"I'm sorry, Susan. I didn't think I needed a note from my mommy to date somebody different. Nor did I think we kept score to make sure we're sharing an equal number of secrets."

Susan, visibly stung by her friend's sarcasm, blinked at the tears welling in her eyes. "Stop it. That's not what I'm saying, and you know it. I just sense a distance between us that was never there before. I don't know how it got there, but I want it gone. I miss you, Sandy. I miss the friend that I've always shared confidences with."

"Maybe you shouldn't have betrayed that trust then."

Susan stared in astonishment as the hurt rippled through her. "Alesandra, I have never, never revealed anything you have entrusted to me. What are you talking about?"

"Gee, I don't know, Susan. You tell me how 'Carl Darling' discovered our plans to go back to the mountain as a group. Somebody obviously told him, because he came peeling into the parking lot to stop us. Nobody but the group knew the plan, so how did he find out? Seems logical to me his little songbird sang. As your 'friend' I haven't told the rest of the group who his source is."

"You think I told him?" she asked in disbelief.

"Well, duh, Susan. Who else could it possibly be? And that's why I can no longer confide in you regarding my personal life. Anything I say to you goes back to him."

"I don't know how to prove it to you, but I'm not his source. In fact, he was angry with me for not telling him. I promise you on a stack of bibles, it wasn't me." She reached forward and clasped Alesandra's arm as tears started to spill. "I didn't tell him. Cross my heart," she said, drawing an X over her heart with her free hand.

Alesandra wanted to believe her. Susan had always been trustworthy in the past, but she knew devotion to boyfriends often superseded loyalty to friends. She valued the friendship they shared and hated to see it end like this.

Reluctantly she conceded, "All right, Susan. I'm sorry I doubted you."

Susan smiled through her tears, relieved the friendship was reconciled. Reaching her arms out, the girls embraced.

As Susan hugged her, Alesandra stared over the girl's shoulder out the window as she made her decision. She would continue to be Susan's friend, telling her about her romance with Michael to mollify her. Yes, even down to the smallest sigh. But the real secrets, the secrets of Blaney's Mountain, were hers and Michael's alone.

Max couldn't shake the thought of Gant cozying up to the girl who, for some reason, preferred his company while keeping Max at arms length. Aware that his jealousy could possibly jeopardize his mission, he strove diligently to keep his personal feelings under control. Too much was at stake to allow the situation to adversely affect any decisions he would have to make.

Loud banging on the door of his dorm room roused Michael from sleep. After a late night answering questions for Public Safety, he reluctantly crawled out of bed to answer the summons.

"Michael, hey man, what happened here?" Max, Lewis, and Jared filed into his small quarters to observe the destruction first hand.

"Why don't you come on in?" Michael invited facetiously.

"Wow, Gant. You got yourself a real mess here." Jared flopped himself down on the recently vacated bed.

"We heard the cops were here last night." Lewis picked up a drawer off the floor and inserted it back into the dresser. "Thought we'd come by and see if you needed a hand, which you obviously do. Jared, get off the dude's bed. We're here to help clean up, not lounge around."

Max bent to pick up the scattered text books. "Any idea who did this, Gant?"

"Not a clue who or why. Found it like this last night when I got home."

Jared said what they were all thinking. "Everyone knows about the crystals. Probably somebody looking for them."

"Sure," said Michael, "but I turned them all over to Dr. Turner for testing. I don't keep them around here."

"Maybe somebody thinks you've got some dough hidden." Lewis raised an eyebrow at Michael. "You don't, do you?"

Jared interrupted. "Of course he does. Can't you see this room is actually Fort Knox in disguise?"

Michael had a twinge of conscience at the mention of Fort Knox, knowing the gold bar clutched in that Confederate soldier's hand was now resting in Michael's backpack.

When order was somewhat restored to the room, he was eager to be rid of his helpers and get to the lab. "Thanks guys, but I can manage now," he hinted.

"Okay. Say, you want to come to the game room over at the UC and play some air hockey with me and the Bran Man? Jared's coming too."

Lewis' invitation took him by surprise. It was the first time he had ever been invited to fraternize with any of the fellows. The possibility of social acceptance outweighed his immediate need to research.

"Thanks for the invite. I've got a few things to take care of, but I can join you in about half an hour if that's not too late."

"Great. See you there, dude." Lewis gave Jared a shove out of the room, and their voices trailed down the hall.

Max hesitated at the door. "It sure looks to me like they were searching for something, Gant. If not the crystals, do you have any idea what it might be?"

"Wish I did."

"Well, I think you should be careful from now on."

"Thanks, Max. I intend to."

Michael pulled open the stairwell door on the second floor of the Johnson EPS building and saw his favorite professor down the hall.

"Professor Blaney," he called as he jogged the distance, trying to catch the man's attention.

Carl heard his name and turned. “Mr. Gant, how are you this morning?”

“Fine, sir. But I wanted to talk to you about something.”

“Sure. Shoot.”

Michael followed him into the classroom and sat on the end of a lab table. “My room was broken into.”

Blaney looked startled. “What?”

“Yeah. When I got home late last night, I found the place had been ransacked. Somebody went through everything I own.”

“So you’re okay? You weren’t there when it happened?”

“No, I’m fine. My place was sure trashed though.”

“Hmm.” Carl leaned back against his desk with his legs crossed and his arms folded, thinking. “First the chem lab, now your room. I don’t like the sound of this at all. You called Public Safety, didn’t you?”

“Yeah. The front desk at McCord Hall said nobody came into the building last night who wasn’t a student. So I guess that means it’s got to be someone on campus.”

“That would make sense.” He rubbed his chin thoughtfully. “Dr. Turner is convinced someone is after your crystals but neither of us can figure out why. It stands to reason that our vandal is someone privy to campus gossip in order to know about your discovery.”

Michael kept his mouth shut about the new batch of specimens. Plenty of time for that later. He did not feel up to defending his reasons for going back to the mountain.

“My advice to you, Michael, is to be careful.”

Michael nodded. “Thanks, Professor.” The door opened, and students drifted in. “I guess you’ve got a class in a few minutes, so I’ll talk to you later.”

He slid off the table and headed across the hall to the chemistry lab, pleased to find it still empty except for his mentor.

“Hey, Dr. Turner.”

The older man did not look up right away, not easily distracted from his task at hand. Michael strode across the room to stand in front of his desk.

“Dr. Turner?”

“Huh, what?” Leaving a finger to hold his place in his textbook, he lifted his eyes to see who was demanding his attention. “Oh, young Gant. What can I do for you?”

Lifting his shirt tail, Michael revealed a belly bag around his waist. He pulled out a Ziploc bag filled with larger rock samples of the crystals.

"I brought you these."

"What have you got there?"

Michael averted his eyes, hoping to evade the question. "I thought you might be able to use some consolidated samples."

Deciding it might be better not to know how the lad acquired the specimens, he refrained from pressing Michael for details. "Rest assured. They will be safe with me." He opened the bag and lifted out a rock the size of a golf ball. Holding it up to the light, his eyes danced at the possibilities it presented. "These look good, Gant. I'll be able to run more varied tests with them. Thanks for bringing them in." He dropped it back into the bag and resealed it. Winking, he gave a sly grin. "We'll just keep them our little secret, shall we?"

Michael grinned back. "I think that would be a good idea."

Alesandra juggled her books as she ran across the campus not wanting to be late for squad practice. A large percentage of the team had gone home for the summer, but those that remained still got together to practice and work on creating new routines.

"Hey, Sandy."

Hearing Michael, she changed her course and headed toward him. After hugging him tightly, she panted, "You are in so much trouble with me."

"Mmm. I could tell that from the hug," he teased. He pulled her closer and kissed her, sensing her instant acquiescence as she relaxed in his arms.

"Wait a minute," she pulled back. "You don't get out of it that easily."

"Okay, why am I in trouble?"

"I heard your room was broken into while we were gone."

"Yeah. So why does that get me in trouble? I didn't do it to myself, Sandy."

"You didn't tell me about it. I had to hear about it from other people. You should have called me last night when you got home."

"Couldn't find the phone, hon. It was buried."

"Smarten up, Michael. You know what I mean."

"Yes, I do. I'm sorry for not telling you myself, but there was nothing you could do about it. There was no sense in getting you all upset."

"What happened? Do they know who did it?"

"Come sit on the bench." He led her across the quad to the benches at Centennial Court. "You know what happened. Somebody broke in and wreaked havoc. We'll probably never know who did it. But I do need to talk to you about it."

"I think it's terrible. I'm so upset by the whole thing."

"I know, honey, but listen. I think, and the Prof agrees with me, they were after the crystals. First the break-in at the chem lab, and now my room. It's the connecting factor. Now, here's what worries me. Since they didn't manage to get hold of the specimens yet, they might try to break into your dorm too."

"Oh, I don't think so. I have suitemates, remember? It would be difficult not to find one of us there at any given time."

He still worried. "Just the same...."

She answered him soberly. "I know, Michael. I'll be careful." Looking down at her hands entwined in his, she noticed her watch. "I'm running late. I have to get going." She pulled him to his feet.

He watched her run to practice in her lycra outfit, admiring her figure and the way she moved. For the twentieth time that day he said a prayer of gratitude that she was his. He still hadn't told her about keeping the gold bar and knew that would bring another tongue lashing when she learned of it.

Feeling the weight of it pulling in his backpack, he decided he couldn't carry it with him forever. Various ways to safeguard it had played on his mind since taking possession of it. The antiquities vault in the Geo Lab might be the safest place, but he wasn't yet ready to take either Blaney or Turner fully into his confidence.

Strolling nonchalantly to the parking lot, he got into his Jeep and drove out into the countryside. Finding a side road, he drove two miles before pulling over to the shoulder. Confident he couldn't be spied on in the middle of nowhere, he turned off the ignition and got out.

The vehicle was designed with a small receptacle for tools under the floor board. It was cleverly concealed by a factory-installed mat and secured by a thin metal strip. No tools were in it now, and it provided the perfect hiding place. He wrapped the bar in an extra tee-shirt from his backpack to prevent a telltale rattle. Using his Swiss army knife, he removed the few screws and tucked it inside the cavity before tightening the mat back in place. The Jeep normally sat open to public perusal in the University parking lot. If anyone thought to search it, they would overlook the floor compartment.

Satisfied he had provided the best security he could manage for the time being, he drove back into town with one less thing to worry about.

Dinner with Alesandra provided relaxation at the end of a hectic day. They walked to Pacer Pond afterward and sat on the bridge talking until the stars blinked their presence in the twilight sky.

Finally tired, he walked her home then headed back to McCord Hall where he showered and got ready for bed. A quick check on his computer displayed an email waiting for him. The sender's name, Jacatom, meant nothing to him. Curiosity won, and he opened it.

Michael,

You are still not safe. Don't let down your guard. You are being watched and followed.

Jacatom

He sat back in his chair. The hackles on the back of his neck rose as he considered his situation. The warning served its desired purpose, leaving him uncomfortable enough to stay cautious.

Keeping up with homework and term papers caused several days to elapse before Michael could sneak back to the EPS building at night to commence his own experiments with the new crystal specimens.

Standing to stretch his back and shoulder muscles after being hunched over the work table, he caught sight of the clock on the wall. It was almost two in the morning. Time to pack his things away and get some sleep. Luckily, his first class the next morning wasn't until ten o'clock.

As he stashed his notes and the crystal samples in his small locker within the Geology lab, a sudden creaking noise from the hall made him freeze. It sounded like the door at the end of the corridor leading to the stairwell. The quiet thud of the door settling back into place against the doorjamb followed. He leaped to the light panel on the wall and flicked the switch off, plunging the room into darkness.

He waited in silence, afraid to move a muscle, for over ten minutes. No footsteps could be heard, and he finally decided recent events were making him paranoid. If someone else was in the building, what he heard could have been them leaving, or it might have been a wind gust in the stairwell caused by a door opening and closing on another floor. The whole thing was probably nothing more than nervous imagination.

Stepping into the hall, he locked the door behind him and quickly covered the distance to the stairs. Part way down the first flight the door opened behind him. He looked over his shoulder. The light from a window gleamed onto the lower steps, leaving the top of the staircase in shadow. A meaty fist knocked him down the remaining steps to the ground level.

He tried to clamber to his feet but earned another jab to his jaw and a hard boot to his stomach for his trouble. As he drifted into unconsciousness, he felt someone roll him over and yank his backpack from his shoulders. His eyelids fluttered, catching only a brief glimpse of his assailant rushing out of the building.

A deep throbbing in his head penetrated his senses, dragging him from the mind-numbing darkness. With pain radiating in his side, he felt nauseous and struggled to his feet, stumbling to vomit in the bushes outside the entrance. Clamping a hand to his head trying to hold it steady, he staggered away from the building, hoping to make it back to the dormitory before he passed out again.

A Public Safety patrol car cruised along Pat Head Summit Drive stopping at the corner to turn onto Mt. Pelia Road. Officer Doug Milroy caught sight of a figure emerging from the shadows with an unstable gait. He drove across the intersection and pulled into the parking lot behind the Johnson EPS building. Leaving the engine running, he got out, prepared to make an alcohol-related arrest.

“A little too much partying, buddy?” he asked in a friendly manner. Working in a college town, he was accustomed to students who drank too much and needed to be escorted home.

Michael saw the approaching officer and swayed precariously. Milroy’s arm shot out to steady him. As the street lamp cast its glow across Michael’s face, the blood streaking down his cheek became obvious.

“Are you all right? What happened here?”

“I was attacked in the stairwell.” Michael’s voice came out slurred, and his knees began to buckle under him.

The officer scanned the area quickly but saw no one else. “Let’s get you over to the hospital. You need medical attention.” Wrapping an arm around the injured student, Milroy helped him to the vehicle and deposited him in the back seat. A short drive took them to the hospital emergency room next to the campus.

The doctor on call diagnosed Michael with a concussion and two broken ribs. It required three stitches to close the deep gash under his eye.

The policeman entered into the cubicle to gather information for his report. “Any idea who did this to you?”

"I didn't really see him. He hit me from behind. I only caught a fleeting glimpse as he ran away." In spite of his denial, Michael couldn't help feeling there was something familiar about his attacker.

"You say he took your backpack. What was in it?"

"Just some books and school stuff; nothing valuable." Muttering under his breath, he added, "Thank goodness." He was grateful he had the foresight to rid himself of both the crystals and the gold bar before the attack occurred.

The officer looked at him with an eyebrow raised, as though waiting for further explanation. Michael gave him a blank expression.

When the doctor finished his ministrations, he wrote a prescription for pain. "Take it easy with those ribs. We don't bandage them any more so you're just going to have to be careful. No strenuous activity. They're going to be pretty tender for awhile."

"No worries there. I won't be playing football any time soon." Michael gave a half-hearted grin, hurting in spite of the pain medication. "Thanks, Dr. Murphy."

The officer drove him back to McCord Hall. Micheal trudged up to his room, glad that at this unholy hour of the morning, no one was around to witness his decrepit state of being.

Collapsing into bed, he immediately fell into a deep sleep.

Lewis saw Michael the next day and immediately called a meeting of the Blaney Bunch. By noon hour the group was gathered in the lounge at Browning Hall where Lewis roomed.

"Dudes and dudettes," he looked at each one of them. "We've got a problem. It seems pretty apparent that our man here is being targeted by somebody with an axe to grind. We can't be certain, but obviously we're all speculating it has something to do with those crystals he found up the mountain."

Heads nodded in agreement while Max studied Gant through narrowed eyes. Seeing Alesandra curled up next to the subject of their conversation rankled him.

"I think we should consider what's happened to Gant as an attack upon us as a group," Lewis continued.

Jared spoke. "I don't know about that. We don't have a clue who's responsible. This could be a personal matter. I don't see that it involves any of the rest of us."

"Wait a minute." All eyes turned to Alesandra. "Of course it's a personal matter, but Lewis is right. Michael is one of us, and we should stand with him against whoever is causing trouble."

"Spoken like a true love-sick little puppy, Sandy. Fine for you, but he's not my boyfriend," Jared retorted.

"Don't be an idiot, Jared. That has nothing to do with this." Alesandra leaped forward in anger, sending pain shooting through Michael's ribs. Hearing his sudden gasp, she quickly sat back and turned to him, worried. "I'm sorry, Michael. I didn't mean to hurt you. Are you okay?"

"Fine," he winced. Embarrassed at being the center of contention and as much as he hated public speaking, he decided to make his feelings known. "If, as you say, someone doesn't like me for whatever reason, that's no excuse for anyone else to suffer. I appreciate your concern, but I can take care of myself."

Max snorted in derision. "Yeah, we can see that, Gant."

Susan interrupted with conviction. "Are we supposed to turn away and say, 'Oh well, good thing he's not after my discoveries'? I don't think so. It's the principle of the thing. One for all and all for one."

"Exactly," Alesandra affirmed, folding her arms across her chest and staring at Jared.

Susan's anger continued to intensify. "As scientists, we need to stand together in this. Being members of the Blaney Bunch should make that bond even stronger. We aren't going to stand aside and let someone else walk off with something a member of our group has reaped. It's unconscionable."

Max stood with his hands on his hips. His anger was kindled and he strove to control it. As much as he detested having to defend Gant, his integrity demanded it. "If we don't stand for Gant now, then what's to stop someone from stealing some mind-boggling relic that you find, Jared? Or something that Susan or Brandon discovers?"

"Thanks guys, but let's not get carried away," Michael mumbled, a blush rising steadily in his cheeks.

Max pointed a finger at Michael's bandage, "I know you think we're being overly concerned, but it won't hurt for all of us to be more vigilant. Try not to be alone at any time, and pay particular attention to people who seem to be lurking around that we don't really know."

"Well, uh..." Brandon was heard for the first time. "I don't think the rest of us are actually in any danger, since we don't have any stellar discoveries to speak of."

Lewis agreed with Max. "Let's assume we're all in danger, and be careful."

Each of them considered Lewis' comment. Brandon sat back and draped his arm around Valerie. "Since we all think this has to do with Gant's crystals, why don't we ask Blaney to take us back to the dig so he can gather more of them?"

"What good would that do?" Max asked.

Susan shook her head, disagreeing. "I don't know if that's a good idea."

"But don't you see," insisted Brandon, "if the crystals are the objective of our unknown stalker, then the more crystals that are discovered, the less valuable they are," he rationalized.

Alesandra's nose crinkled and her brows knit together as she tried to fathom the logic of the statement. "That doesn't even make sense. It would only make them more available to be stolen."

"No, it doesn't." Jared looked at Brandon suspiciously. "You seem pretty eager to go back for more crystals, Bran. Makes me wonder what your interest in them could possibly be. Hoping to grab a few for yourself since you didn't manage to snatch any from the lab or Gant's room?"

Brandon's eyes bulged at the implication and the only words he could think of were a faint denial. "I don't care about Gant's crystals."

All eyes watched him, and he knew he had to offer more. "I didn't do it. Listen, I figured we all want to go back to the mountain anyway. Honestly, I was thinking more about the caves."

Lewis jumped to support his friend. "I'd like to have another chance at that cave. Of course, we know the prof would never allow us back in, but it sure tickles my mind."

Michael, deep in his own thoughts, ignored the nonsense. "You know what keeps coming back to me? I can't figure why anyone would be interested in the crystals. Outside of our group, why would anyone even know or care about the find? The cave-in was the big event of the trip. That's what everyone talked about. Heck, even I almost forgot about the crystals in all the ruckus."

"He's right," Valerie agreed. "After the circus that created around here, the crystals discovery seemed insignificant in comparison. The only thing I heard people talking about around campus was the cave-in, not a word about the crystals. I didn't think anybody outside of our group and Turner even knew about them."

Heads around the room nodded in agreement. If she was right, if word had not spread, then who was so desperate to get their hands on the specimens that they would resort to criminal activities to do so?

Uneasiness settled on the group as they pondered the question. Eight pairs of eyes slid around the room, glancing at one another as mistrust once again flourished.

Captured

Professor Blaney prepared to take his Bunch back to the mountain to resume their studies. He worried about Michael, but Max suggested it might be advantageous to get everyone away from the campus and from the unknown culprit.

"It's worth it if we can take the heat off the university, and let us get back to our projects."

"I guess it is a good idea. All right, Max. Let's make plans to go Friday morning. I'll email the rest of the Bunch."

Max headed back to his dorm room with purpose. The trip required more planning and strategy for him than it did for the others in the group. He placed a call to Bubba Grubbs. "The group is returning, and I will be with them." Grubbs made his displeasure readily apparent, and Max warned him, "Don't send any of your goons to frighten them. They're scared as it is."

"Well, you just see that they stay out of the caves. I don't want 'em snooping where they don't belong."

"I told you, they're only working on school projects. They won't be leaving the dig site." Max slammed the receiver down in anger.

The group found it necessary to travel in two vehicles due to the increasing tension in their midst. Suspicion and unspoken accusations continued to stir, and in the forefront of each mind lingered the idea that Michael's recent problems could be the work of someone in their own crowd.

The mountain itself seemed unchanged upon their arrival, and they began their long trek, their packs heavier than the last time they made the trip. One thing they did agree on was setting up camp at the dig site instead of hiking up and back down to the motel every day.

Summertime on the mountain exhibited an aura of serenity with the fertile presence of spruce and pine, laurel and Queen Anne's Lace. In single file the Blaney Bunch, with their namesake leading the way, headed up the trail over a moss-covered blanket, roaming past fallen trees and patches of wild flowers.

Alesandra felt the mountain greet her with its very own personal welcome. She glanced back at Michael, and he smiled as if he knew what she was thinking.

At the campsite they pitched their tents, eating as they set up their home for the next few days. They would have hot food later in the evening, but the sandwiches they brought along would suffice for the moment.

"I've brought yogurt for anyone who wants some," Susan announced, holding up a container with a dozen individual cups and a bag of plastic spoons.

"Yogurt! I think I love you, dudette! You're not spoken for, are you?" Lewis teased as he tore open the cardboard container and helped himself.

"Oh, I don't know about that," Susan replied, trying to keep her eyes from straying to Carl. "Just because my fellow isn't on campus doesn't mean I don't have one."

Blaney knew they wanted a break after their long climb, but if they sat down now, they would never get up again, so he hurried them along. "You're losing daylight the longer you dawdle. Unless you want to dig in the dark, you'd better get moving." He served as their overseer and motivator, but this was their undertaking. Their grades greatly depended on their individual accomplishments here, not to mention the experience gained for future careers.

Brandon and Lewis needed no prodding. They scampered off to reclaim their areas without waiting for the rest. The others made their way more casually to previous tasks while the professor hovered nearby.

Michael located the rock facing where the butterfly flakes were imbedded and worked at scraping additional samples. His concentration, however, wandered from the fragile crystals to the discoveries made inside the mountain on his last trip. The mystery of the glowing rocks and curiosity about the Confederate soldier with the gold bar dominated his thoughts.

The following day found them back at their individual labors, occasionally calling out to one another regarding their progress, except for Brandon and Lewis. When Blaney's email concerning the trip arrived, they decided to take advantage of the opportunity and do some exploring.

Michael and Alesandra had wandered inside for a long time after the cave-in, meaning there must be some great tunnels in the mountain. The boys determined to find the cave exit and explore it themselves.

Together, they edged away from the dig site, quickly ducked into their tent to grab their caving apparatus, and wound their way to the other side of the mountain. After traversing a grassy slope leading to a rocky ridge, they found themselves on a well-traveled path.

"People have used this trail," said Lewis, "and recently, judging from the looks of it."

"I didn't think anyone lived on this mountain." Brandon remembered one of the rescuers saying this area was deserted with the exception of wild animals. "Hey, remember that Bubba guy? Hope we don't meet up with any bears."

His friend grunted. "If that happens, we'll see which one of us can run the fastest."

Half an hour later, they stumbled onto a steep sliding grade leading straight to a sheer rock wall and a partial crevice opening. Excited, they surged forward to discover a passageway with a low ceiling that slanted downward.

"Come on," Lewis spouted, "this is what we've been looking for." He led the way, lured underground by a strong desire to explore unknown regions within the Earth.

Shedding some of their gear, they pushed it in ahead of them. The passageway they entered was large enough to walk upright with plenty of elbow room. Brandon pushed ahead rapidly, guided by his power light. Not far from the entrance, it expanded into a wider open area with a high ceiling and an array of calcite formations.

Unearthly growls and guttural utterances traveled through underground caves and echoed across wide caverns. With plenty of caving experience under their belts, the boys were accustomed to such sounds. Brandon, ever the cautious one, halted and motioned for his companion to stop. "Listen, I think I hear men talking."

Laughing, Lewis teased him. "You're beginning to sound like an old woman. You know it's only the wind playing tricks."

"Oh yeah? Well it sounds like several voices to me."

Lewis cupped a hand to his ear and listened intently. "Wait a minute. I think you're right. I hear them too."

"It sounds like they're up ahead around the corner."

"They're close all right. Douse the light, and take cover. I think they're coming."

Hardly daring to breathe, they crouched together in the darkness and listened to indistinct voices drawing nearer. They watched as beams of light reflected off the rock walls from flashlights in the hands of two men, their feet splashing through puddles as they passed in front of them. The voices were loud, as if the men were angry, but only a few words were discernible.

"Damn college kids…not allow 'em here at all."

"…leave 'em to us…"

"…take care of all of 'em. Just like…"

"Lewis, they're talking about the Blaney Bunch."

"Sure sounds like it. Wonder who they are?"

"I don't know, but I don't think they like our being here."

"Thank you, Captain Obvious."

"We need to warn the others."

"Yeah, but we can't go back the way we came. That's the direction they took. Listen, we're here. We might as well take a look around before we go back to tell the group. That should give those guys a chance to clear out of here so we don't get caught."

Reluctantly, Brandon agreed. It was, after all, why they came. He convinced himself that an extra hour to explore wouldn't put the group back at the site in any danger.

When the sound of the men's voices died away, the two youthful adventurers headed deeper into the cave system. The first hundred yards was wide enough to move quickly before it branched into two tunnels, both narrower. Leading, Lewis arbitrarily selected the one to the right.

Minutes later the tunnel opened onto a ledge winding around a chasm, deep and dark. They felt their way with only their hand-held lights to guide them.

"Be careful here, dude."

The words were scarcely spoken when a chunk of limestone gave way under Brandon. He lost his balance and slid down the cave wall, wedging his right leg at an awkward angle in a narrow groove a few feet below the circular ledge.

"Hold on, Bran. I'll try to get to you."

"My foot is crammed in pretty tightly. Geez, my ankle feels like its already swelling."

"Be glad. As long as it's wedged it'll stop you from falling further down." He lowered a rope for Brandon to tie around his waist and secured it around himself. Leaning over as far as he could, he struck the sides of the fissure with a short-handled rock pick, breaking off pieces and widening it so the leg could be loosened and pulled free. Finally, Lewis pulled him to safety, and Brandon sat on the ledge rubbing his ankle.

"How does it feel? Can you walk on it?"

"It hurts, but I can make it. Let's keep going."

The ledge continued several yards farther before descending to a lower level. They untethered themselves from one another, and Brandon limped along, anxious to get a good look around before returning to the surface.

During one of the rest stops noises behind them increased in volume as the seconds ticked by. The two men they encountered earlier were coming back, and this time there was nowhere to hide.

Flattening themselves against the nearest rock wall they tried to remain absolutely silent, hoping they wouldn't be noticed.

Brandon's ankle hurt, and his heart pounded. Lewis put a finger to his mouth motioning to remain silent. The men were very close, their voices now clear and resonant.

"I tell you, Jack, somebody is in here. I heard them using a hammer."

"I know, I know. I heard it too." They shined their light around the cave but passed the boys without seeing them.

Lewis whispered, "They didn't see us. Now's our chance to backtrack where we came in." They retraced their steps to the circular ledge where Brandon had fallen.

"Hey, you!" They were spotted.

"Run, Brandon!" Lewis surged ahead through the cave's semi-darkness, the thin beam from his light showing the way. Running with a hitched limp, Brandon struggled to keep up.

"Come back here!" The men were gaining on them.

"Yeah, like we're that stupid," Lewis muttered.

They raced through the tunnel until a Y junction loomed ahead. Which direction should they take? Making a quick decision, Lewis turned into the first tunnel with Brandon close on his heels. They entered a chamber inhabited by a colony of bats roosting high overhead. The bats began fluttering at the interruption, and the boys discovered there was no other way out of the chamber.

"It's a dead end," wailed Brandon. "We're trapped!" They were indeed. A fact brought home by the arrival of their two pursuers who kept up the chase until they stood three feet in front of them. The boys stood motionless and nervous as they faced their trackers.

"What do we got here?" asked the one named Jack. "I believe we have some trespassers." He shined his light in their faces. "What are you fellas doin' in our cave?"

Lewis glared at them and spoke with a bravado that belied his tension. "It isn't your cave. It belongs to the State of Tennessee, and we have permission to be here."

"Yeah," echoed Brandon. "Who are you guys anyway?"

"They want to know who we are, Red. I'll tell you who we are," he sneered. "We work for the overseer of this mountain, and we're gonna take you to meet him right now."

The disappearance of both Brandon and Lewis from their work stations disturbed Professor Blaney. He had no doubt they were actively pursuing their caving interest at this very moment in spite of the university ban.

More concerned than Blaney, however, was Max. He knew those two could get themselves in real trouble without half trying. He saw the professor standing at the edge of the dig site, overlooking the mountain, concern etched on his features.

"If you don't mind, Prof, I'll go find them and bring them back."

"Thanks, Max. I appreciate it. There's no need to tell the others what's going on." He wanted to avoid a panic over two students being lost in the caves. Again.

"Get moving, you two. We'll see what the boss wants to do with you." Brandon and Lewis were herded once again around the circular ledge. "If I had my way," Jack said, "I'd toss you both down there into the Devil's Chasm." He pointed to the deep, dark hole far below the ledge. "That's what we do with wise guys who come looking for trouble."

His words crawled over Brandon's nerves, making him break into a sweat. "We didn't come looking for trouble."

"Stop sniveling, dude." Lewis muttered, refusing to cower before the captors. He knew a show of fear would put them at a bigger disadvantage. Refusing to be intimidated, he told Jack, "We have as much right to be in this cave as you do, and I'll tell that to your boss, whoever he is."

"You're gonna get that chance," the man called Red chimed in. "Just don't get smart with him or it's the Devil's Chasm for your trouble." His evil laugh emphasized the warning.

The boys stumbled forward as they were pushed and threatened along the passageway. Jack led the way, leaving Red as the rear anchor man. The tunnel began to gradually slant upward. Too narrow for an escape attempt, they were forced to bide their time until they could meet this "boss" and take it up with him. Lewis mentally rehearsed his speech while furtively fingering the short-handled rock pick on his belt in case they had to physically defend themselves.

They were each lost in private thought when their little troop suddenly rounded a corner entering a large dimly lit but obviously well-used chamber. Jack led them to a smaller alcove, unkindly ushering them inside with orders to "cool it here, while we check if the boss wants to see you now. And don't go gettin' any funny ideas about escaping. We'll be right outside."

With nothing to do except wait, they sat on the cold clay floor just inside the open doorway and examined their prison cell. "I don't like this place," Brandon complained.

"Well, it's not exactly the Hilton."

"The Hilton! This place isn't even the Holiday Inn. What's over there, Lewis?" He pointed to a heap in the far corner.

Lewis walked to the corner to investigate. "It's just a pile of old rags." Kicking them aside, he uncovered a crumpled canvas backpack. Something was still in it, adding a small bit of weight. Lewis unzipped the bag and looked inside. "Brandon, there's a name stenciled here." The beam from his flashlight illuminated the letters M. GANT. "This is Gant's pack! I wonder if it got left behind when they were lost." He pulled a notebook out and leafed through it. "Wait a minute, there's stuff in here dated only three weeks ago. This is his pack that got stolen the night he was attacked. It must have been one of the Boss' goons that mugged him outside the lab."

"I'll bet it was that guy, Red, who did it. He looks the meanest."

Lewis tucked Michael's backpack inside his own. The discovery escalated their desire to escape. "Hey, I've got an idea. I'll send a message for help."

"How are you going to do that?"

Smirking, Lewis reached into his coveralls and extracted his palm pilot from his shirt pocket. "With this. I'll send a text message." He began tapping the keys, then hit the send button. "Max should get this, and we'll be out of here in no time."

The electronic gadget in his hand beeped. Lewis looked down and read the message. “Damn, I can’t get a signal. We’re too deep in the mountain.”

They stood together near the open doorway, peering into the outer chamber, trying to see their jailers. From their vantage point they noted several recessed areas containing discarded wooden crates.

“Looks like a trashy, disorganized operation of some sort going on in there,” Lewis remarked.

“I don’t like it. I don’t like it at all.” The other continued to grumble, his anxiety escalating.

“You think I do? Hang in there, dude. Stop worrying.”

“What do you think they’re gonna do with us?”

“Oh, they’ll probably yell at us for trespassing or some silly thing. I don’t imagine they plan to eat us.”

“Well, you can joke all you want, but I think we’re in deep trouble this time.”

Lewis was more concerned about Jack and Red than about the “boss.” Those two were hard cases, no doubt about it. Their tough demeanor, scraggly beards and torn, unwashed clothing undeniably exhibited the sort of men they were.

Tsuneguñ-y

"Those idiots have no idea what they're getting into. This stupid little spelunking adventure of theirs could destroy everything," Max mumbled as he followed the trail of his younger classmates.

In spite of the university's ban, they remained dead set on exploring inside the mountain. Even the close brush with death faced by Alesandra and Michael in the rockslide had not deterred them. Max knew his bargain with Bubba included a promise to keep the group out of the caves. "Well, I'm not my brother's keeper; especially those two. I can't tie them to a tree."

Reaching into his shirt pocket, he retrieved his cell phone and dialed Bubba's private line.

"Yeah, this is Max. Two of my kids wandered off and are probably looking for a way into the mountain. I just thought you should know."

"They're already here. My boys picked them up a while ago."

"They don't know anything, so they'll be no problem."

"Let me be the judge of that, my friend. I haven't talked to 'em yet."

Max chose his words carefully. "Listen, Brandon and Lewis are only interested in exploring caves. They don't suspect anything else, and they aren't looking for anything else."

"So, it's Brandon and Lewis, is it? Somehow I'm not surprised it's those two goof-balls." Bubba heaved a sigh. "Well, if they're innocent lambs as you say, you can come and get 'em. But I still wanna word with 'em."

"I don't want them finding out we're connected. Just point them in the right direction, and let them go. They'll find their way home."

"They can leave after our talk." He needed to find out what they discovered on their little quest.

Lewis nudged his friend and pointed to the outer room. "I think we can slip out of here. No one's in sight, and we can probably make it if we keep close to the wall."

Brandon whispered. "Are you sure they aren't still out there? They said they would be. Maybe they want us to think it's safe to leave so they can shoot us in the back."

"You watch too many movies, Bran. Come on. Just move easy, and don't make any noise."

"Won't they be angry if we leave?"

"What's wrong with you? They don't like us now; that's why we gotta get out of here."

He helped Brandon to his feet and without another word slipped through the alcove, creeping past several tall columns that rose to the ceiling. A pile of bones lay stacked in the center of a blackened circle, a ring made by fire. Lewis recalled seeing a similar set of bones earlier. It puzzled him, but he dared not pause to satisfy any curiosity.

Once across the large room they sprinted through the nearest tunnel, guided by the thin ray of Lewis' flashlight. The desire for survival made Brandon ignore his pain and push on, moving quickly. Driven by the need to put as much distance as possible between them and the bad guys, they ran helter-skelter, challenged by uneven inclines and loose stones underfoot with no knowledge of where they were or how to exit.

The tunnel was broken at intervals by partial wall cavities leading to other chambers, but they no longer took the time to explore. Lewis relied on his amateurish perception of cave systems to keep moving in the direction he hoped would set them free.

They surmised that the "boss" knew of their escape by now. His men were undoubtedly searching for them at this very moment. Their hearts pounded and muscles ached as they endeavored to elude their certain pursuers.

Max's pocket played a short melody, and he pulled out his cell phone. "Max, here."

"Your two numbskulls are on the loose, and I don't have the time or manpower to go huntin' for 'em."

"Did you talk to them?"

"No. They skedaddled before I got the chance. You'll have to question 'em if and when you find 'em."

Max fumed. All they had to do was stay put. But no, not those two. They had to make things difficult. Now he had to enter the caves himself and try to find them.

Out of breath and blowing like race horses finishing in a dead heat, they paused for a breather and to ease the pain in Brandon's foot. A gurgling sound directed their attention to an underground stream, so they knelt to drink from the cold mountain water. Brandon quickly removed his shoe and sock and immersed his injured ankle in the frigid stream to reduce the swelling and ease the throbbing.

"We can't stay here for long," Lewis cautioned. "Those guys know these caves better than we do, so we have to keep moving." A chill raced through both at the thought of what might happen if they were recaptured.

After allowing Brandon several minutes of soaking, they resumed their search for an escape route. Despite their dire situation, they experienced a thrill at being so far underground.

Lewis felt particularly gratified by their adventure. He looked back at his friend. "Whatever happens, dude, we did what we wanted to do."

Brandon cracked a sly grin. "Yeah, but under the circumstances I'll be happy to see daylight again."

Resuming their journey, they crawled on their bellies through a tunnel of about seventy feet before spilling into a larger cavity where they could walk again, rising upward at first and then slanting in a steep descent. They continued into a low-ceiling chamber resembling a maze featuring bluish white drapery and stone water basins.

Working through the network of twists and turns, they were eventually rewarded with a thin, dust-laden shaft of sunlight, originating from a small fissure overhead. At the same time, fear returned with the sound of approaching footsteps. A figure outside moved, blocking the sunlight from filtering through. Dousing their lamps, they dove for cover.

Susan knelt to put the last of the foil wrapped dinners into the fire. The rest of the students were still at work, all of them disgruntled. The professor had offered to help Susan in putting the dinners together.

"I can't believe those two would do something so stupid," he exclaimed for the umpteenth time. "Of all the irresponsible...."

"Well, Carl, it is Lewis and Brandon we're talking about here. Not exactly Einstein and Edison."

"Yeah, you're right but still, I can't believe they'd be so incredibly stupid. We fought so hard to come back here." He ran his hand through his dark brown hair as he stared into the flames. His anger increased as the day wore on, and the recalcitrant students failed to return. "If we can keep it quiet, we might get away with it, but if anybody finds out what they've done, our digs will be permanently prohibited. The university isn't going to accept excuses. Hell, there is no excuse for this."

Susan stood next to him, the urge to touch him creating havoc in her. Struggling to keep her hands to herself she commiserated with him. "All of us have something at stake here. I'm sure the rest will agree to keep the idiots' escapade confidential, if they come out of it alive." She heard the words as they left her mouth and mentally kicked herself. Turning to Carl, she placed a hand on his arm. "I'm sorry. Of course they'll come back in one piece. Lewis isn't the type to be taken down by a mere mountain. At least they have experience at caving. Brandon has albums full of pictures he's taken on caving expeditions."

"Yes, I suppose that's a small comfort. They may not be alive when I'm done with them, however. I could kick their asses into next year for this."

"Yes, and you have six others in line behind you to take a turn. We're all royally furious with them."

A shout from Max caught their attention. Carl turned and saw him helping a hobbling Brandon as Lewis brought up the rear. The other students stopped their digging and tucked their tools away for the day. Anger which simmered all day was kept in check as the group individually debated the options of giving the rebels hell or the cold shoulder.

The group congregated at the firepit, all staring intently at the crackling blaze. Max and his foundlings joined them. Brandon moved next to Valerie and dropped an arm around her shoulders. Shrugging him off, she walked around the fire to stand next to Alesandra, refusing to look at him.

"I think dinner's ready," Susan said to no one in particular. She pulled a packet from the coals and used a fork and an oven mitt to open it. Poking into the chicken breast, she found it cooked all the way through. "Let's eat."

Jared knelt next to her. "Let me get them out Susan. You go ahead and get your plate."

"Thanks, Jared.

He used a pair of sticks to pull the dinners to the edge of the cooking fire and lift them onto a log the kids had set close by. They were quickly snatched up, and the group sat around the fire to eat.

Feeling the stifling silence close in on him like a shroud, Lewis spoke. "That was a foolish thing we did, and I'm..." "Foolish! You're the biggest jerks I've ever known. What's wrong with you." Jared's anger emerged in full force. He set his plate on the ground in front of him and jammed a finger in Lewis' face. "Every person here wants you two off the dig team for what you've done. You've put this entire project into jeopardy because you're a couple of morons."

"I hope you enjoyed your little escapade," the professor added. "The rest of us didn't appreciate it at all, especially after all the trouble we had getting permission to come back here."

"I'm sorry. I'm afraid the temptation was just too much. You don't understand, because you're not cavers."

"We understand two imbeciles when we see them," Alesandra reproached them, glaring first at Brandon, then at Lewis. "Michael and I told you we found nothing special inside the cave. You should have listened to us."

"Next time you feel the need to create a crisis, do it on your own time, not ours." Valerie still couldn't bring herself to look at Brandon, feeling betrayed by his actions.

Brandon looked at his cohort for mutual consolation, but there was none there. Lewis was busy trying to think of a way to abate the anger. Maybe telling of their adventure would get everyone so interested, they'd forget how mad they were. But the professor wasn't finished with them yet.

"You displayed poor judgment by leaving the dig site without notice and by entering the caves. I have a lot of thinking to do, but as of this moment, if the group is permitted to return for future digs, you won't be accompanying us, so you'd better finish up your projects in the next few days. Now, that said, why is Brandon limping? Are you two all right?"

Brandon told about sliding down the ledge and injuring his ankle. He played up the danger of his situation, hoping for pity. Instead, it created more ire.

"Great. Just go get yourself killed while on a U trip. How much more clever can you be?" Jared felt nothing but disgust for the spelunkers.

"It could have been a lot worse," the professor remarked. "It's a good thing you had someone right there to help you."

Valerie went to her tent and returned with an Ace bandage for Brandon's ankle. It was her only concession. Still not speaking to him, she tossed the dressing at him, leaving him to wrap the injury himself.

Everyone listened as Lewis regaled them with tales of their imprisonment by "bad guys", how they escaped and were chased before being rescued.

"We finally saw a beacon of light and thought we were out of there, home free. Then something moved and blocked it off. We thought those creeps caught us again. Dudes, we were scared. Then I tried to look through the crevice, and I saw a flash of red. I told Bran, 'There's only two things I know of that are that shade of red--the Canadian flag and Max's shirt.' I took my chances."

"Max, did you see any 'bad guys'?" Michael asked, looking to corroborate their story.

"I never saw anybody but these two goofs. I think they're full of it," Max answered before turning his attention to the reckless twosome. "You were lucky I found you or you two idiots would have wandered around lost for days. And what have you learned from your caving experience?" He got little information from them on the trek back to the dig, other than their relief at seeing daylight again. What he really wanted to know was whether they observed anything unusual during their sojourn.

Lewis replied carefully, "We learned two things. First of all, there's no place like home, Toto. We won't be stupid enough to go off like that again."

"Perfect twenty-twenty hindsight. What's the second thing?" Susan asked.

"Well, uh...we think those guys are up to something in that cave."

"What do you mean?" the professor asked.

Brandon joined the conversation. "We saw bones in two separate places."

"Bones? What bones?"

"Don't know what kind they were, animal bones most likely. We didn't have time to examine them."

"Why was that a strange thing?"

Lewis warmed to the telling. "They weren't scattered around on the ground like a wild animal would have done with them. It looked like they were purposely placed in a pile."

"Some predators do that," Blaney said. "They often bring the kills into their den, eventually gathering the aged and dried bones together."

"Why do they do that, Prof?"

"Perhaps to make room for other prey. I don't really know."

The group, still aloof to the cavers, dispersed to take care of individual tasks before settling for the night.

Bedded down in their tent, the girls talked about the day.

"Do you believe all that stuff about them being taken prisoner and having to escape," Valerie asked. She wanted it to be true. Her anger towards Brandon started to melt.

"No, I think they made it up so we'd become intrigued and forget about being mad at them. I don't believe any of it," Susan told them. "What about you, Sandy?"

"Sounded pretty far fetched to me, too. I always thought Lewis had one foot in fantasy land. This pretty much clinches it, I'd say."

Michael stayed outside waiting for the others to settle into their tents for the night. His last trip to the mountain planted questions in his mind that plagued him all day. When at last they were alone together, he sat poking at the fire with a stick. "Professor, can I ask you a hypothetical question?"

"Of course. That's why I'm here. To impart wisdom and encourage possibilities. What's on your mind?"

"If you saw rocks that seemed to glow on their own, what could cause that?"

"Probably a concentration of phosphorous. You know how it works. It would absorb any light and then radiate it for a period of time afterwards."

"But if it wasn't phosphorous. What if the rock didn't need another light source to instigate the glow? What if it glowed independent of its environment?"

"Can't imagine too many possible scenarios for that. I suppose, given some thought, I could come up with a few ideas."

"I was thinking, if such a thing existed it could possibly provide answers for a new energy source, if it could be contained."

"Possibly so." He looked more intently at his student. "I've never heard of such a phenomenon before. This is purely hypothetical, right?"

"Of course it is, sir. Just one of those little thoughts that rambled through my brain. Sometimes I like to play 'what if' is all."

"Well, it's an interesting concept. But I doubt very much you'll ever run into such a thing in reality."

"I know." Michael stirred the coals around and swatted at a mosquito on the back of his neck. "I suppose I ought to hit the hay. The sun'll be up before ya know it, and it'll be time to get back to work. Thanks, Prof."

"No problem." Carl picked up a bucket of water and doused the fire.

He lay in his sleeping bag listening to the geek and the professor talking. They obviously didn't realize how easily their voices carried in the calm night air. They probably thought out of sight meant out of earshot as well, and didn't try to hush their conversation.

His curiosity was aroused when he heard Michael asking something about glowing rocks and a new energy source. A light bulb clicked on in his head, and unlimited prospects abounded. What if it wasn't hypothetical? What if Gant's description was in fact based on reality?

He listened intently, determined to hear every word until he heard Michael go to his own tent. It had been a very long eventful day, and he was tired. Dollar signs floated before his eyes as he fell asleep.

The following day found each student concentrating on individual projects, trying to get as much completed as possible. They were well aware this could be their last trip to the mountain if the school decided to take action.

At the end of the day they sat in silence eating supper. Carl Blaney watched his students, unhappy with the tension they exhibited. "I have a surprise for everybody tonight." They lifted their eyes in unison, waiting. "Some of you may remember Mr. Grubbs. He was part of the rescue party that found Michael and Sandy. I've invited him to join us tonight for campfire because of everybody's apparent interest in this mountain. He'll tell you something about it and answer any questions you have."

Michael and Alesandra exchanged worried glances and knew they were thinking the same thing. Mr. Grubbs was the only other person aware of their second trip back to the mountain, and they hoped he wouldn't give them away.

Grubbs presented a friendly appearance, a broad smile and wave of his hand to Michael and Alesandra as he arrived. "I am happy to see my two friends who loved my mountain so much, they arranged to get themselves trapped inside her."

A long breath escaped Alesandra's lips, and she smiled tremulously.

Sitting down, he let the chuckles die before continuing. "The Cherokee name for this mountain is Tsuneguñ-y. Your fascination for her is understandable. Long before the Cherokee were driven from here, this was also home to the Cree, to the Delaware, Wyandotte, Seneca and other ancient tribes before them. It is said the voices of invisible spirits once warned of wars and misfortunes ahead in the future. Believers were invited to come and live with the Nuñne'hi, the Immortals, under the mountain where they would be safe and prosper.

"People listened and entire villages came to live on the mountain. So many showed up that there was little room remaining for anyone else. The spirits caused a roar of thunder and lightening, shaking the mountain from its very foundation. A darkness such as they had never known before fell upon the land for three days. Those who weren't killed, were scared and ran away, but when it finally was over, they returned to find the mountain had created enough caves for everyone to live in.

"And then the white man came, preaching about peace and an Almighty God. Then they forced the Cherokee away, leaving only the invisible spirits to preserve their memories in the many underground chambers."

As he paused, Alesandra posed a question. "You told us before that the mountain welcomes us with open arms. Did it also welcome the white men who drove the Cherokee away?"

Bubba was taken aback at the meaning behind her question, and Michael himself was surprised.

"Sshhh!" he cautioned her under his breath.

"No, no. It's a good question." Bubba took his time answering her. "You must keep in mind, the spirits that watch over this mountain are also vengeful. Folks who intend no disrespect toward the honored ones don't have to be afraid, but all others risk pain and retaliation."

Brandon raised a hand. "Uh, Mister Grubbs, Lewis and I were in the caves yesterday, and we saw several piles of bones. Can you tell us about them?"

Bubba rubbed his gristled chin. "Probably the bones of animals. However, it reminds me of a story."

Jared and Max glanced at each other and discreetly rolled their eyes, resigned to hearing another old Indian tale. Bubba knew so many.

"One of the ancient tribes living here was called the Anāda'dùñtāskĭ, or simply 'Roasters'. If they caught you, they put you in a pot and feasted on you.

"The story goes, two boys went huntin'. The Roasters saw 'em and called out to each other, 'Here are two nice fat strangers!' They caught the boys and dragged 'em into their cave, making a great fire and boiling water inside a large pot. The younger boy was placed in the pot, but the other was unafraid and knelt beside the fire. When the Roasters thought the meat was about ready, they lifted the pot from the fire, and at that instant a blinding light filled the cave. Lightning darted from one side to the other, striking down the Roasters until not one of them was left alive. The next moment, the older boy found himself standing outside the cave as though nothing happened. When he went looking for his friend, all he saw was a pile of dried bones beside the pot."

Brandon nearly choked, his eyes large. "Uh, I don't think that explains the bones we saw."

Bubba's teeth gleamed in the firelight as he smiled. "Well, there is a Cherokee tradition that might satisfy you about the bones. When a person died his body was placed high on a funeral pyre where it lay exposed to the elements and wild animals for several weeks."

Bubba paused for emphasis, making sure he held their rapt attention. Using his hands to illustrate the significance of his words, he continued. "Within the tribe was a group known as the bone-pickers. They grew very long fingernails for the purpose of removing any remaining flesh from the bones when the body was taken down. The stripped bones were boiled, then given to the surviving family. Some of them buried the bones. Others may have left them in the caves, and that may be what you saw."

"Picking the flesh off the bones?" Valerie cried out and covered her ears. "Eww, that's gross."

"He's pulling your leg, dudette," said Lewis. He took two marshmallows from the bag before passing it on to Susan. Poking his stick through the first one, he tossed the second at Brandon hitting him between the eyes. Alesandra burst out laughing, breaking the tension created by Grubbs' tale.

The kids sat around with their sticks in the fire, talking as they watched their treats turn golden brown. "Dang, mine's on fire again," Brandon complained. "Every single one has turned to charcoal."

One by one, the group melted into the darkness and prepared themselves for sleep. Bubba and the professor were curious to know how Max located the boys so easily in the cave.

"I just followed the sounds of Brandon's griping. They made so much noise running and scrambling, it was a simple matter to track them."

Blaney retired for the night, giving Bubba and Max a chance to rehash recent events in hushed tones.

"I hope your people are finished running through the caves."

"Like I told you, Lewis and Brandon only wanted to look around. I have a feeling, though, that Michael and Sandy aren't finished yet. He discovered some crystals they're testing at the university, and he might want to gather more condensed samples."

"Why can't he get 'em here at the dig site, instead of traipsin' through the caves?"

"I'm not sure." Max suspected another reason for their interest in returning to the cave but did not hint of it to Bubba. "There's one more thing," he said.

"Go on."

"Someone ransacked Gant's dorm room and a few nights ago he was attacked and his backpack stolen. You wouldn't know anything about that, would you?"

"Really!" Bubba feigned surprise. "I didn't know college was such a mean place."

Max noted the absence of a denial. "I don't want any of these kids hurt."

"Why don't you worry about yourself, and let me tend to everythin' else?"

He watched as the older man turned and sauntered off. Max knew the two of them would have a showdown eventually, but that time had not yet arrived.

Morgan's Raiders

"Mister Secretary, our man is still working undetected although there are no additional developments to report."

The man behind the desk sat ramrod straight, his eyes locked onto those of his senior agent. "Let me get this straight," he said. "Since this operation began, we have made only three recoveries. Is that correct?"

"Yes, sir."

"How do we know our informant isn't holding out on us and keeping some of the goods for himself?"

Special Agent in Charge Lanahan nodded knowingly. "Of course, there is always that possibility. But we have no reason at this juncture to distrust him. We're watching his activities closely, and any deviation from normal will be noticed immediately."

"How are we as far as appropriations are concerned? Are we still under budget?" Money was always a concern for these types of undercover projects.

"I think we are in good shape on that score, Mister Secretary. We've only paid out $150,000 so far, discounted of course. I don't anticipate any problem on future purchases at this time."

The Secretary pondered the information. "Tell me about your Special Agent. I don't know much about him."

"He's a good man. Not married. Looks younger than his age. An experienced police officer. He can hold his own with the bad guys."

"Good. I don't need to tell you the military is extremely interested in this operation, so if you need anything, anything at all, just let me know."

Well aware of the army's interest, the SAC had studied the archived records of an armed military escort column bushwhacked early during the

Civil War. The Rebs waited in concealment with a Gatling gun killing all 21 troopers, and made off with three wagons carrying gold bullion enroute to the Denver Mint. The government doesn't forget something like that, and both federal departments were cognizant of the absence of a statute of limitations involved in this particular instance.

The 7th Kentucky Cavalry, known as Morgan's Confederate Raiders, had perpetrated the ambush. Afterwards, in accordance with their usual habit, they scattered without a trace. Now, more than a hundred years later, two gold bars surfaced in Knoxville, identifiable by engraved markings as part of that missing army shipment.

Lanahan contemplated how much of the stolen bullion remained unaccounted for. His agency established the primary goal of their undercover mission to be its recovery, and the apprehension of all individuals responsible for currently marketing the gold.

Silence dominated the ride back from the mountain in the professor's van. Lewis and Brandon still felt the air of animosity from the others. Jared's SUV provided the only other transportation option, and the air was just as frigid there. They knew they had a disciplinary speech due, and waiting for it kept them on edge.

Blaney let them worry.

That evening as Lewis unpacked his belongings, he came upon something he had completely forgotten. Clutching it in his hand, he left his residence and ran to McCord Hall where he found Michael sitting on a couch in the study lounge, a binder open on his lap.

"Hey, Gant. You won't believe this. Guess what I found?" he blurted as he held out the missing backpack.

"Where did you find that?" a voice asked from behind him.

Lewis turned to see Max sitting nearby.

"We found it crumpled up in the corner of the cave. I picked it up and saw your name stenciled on the inside flap. Is this the one that guy stole when you were attacked?"

The news stunned them both. Michael was first to recover and stammered, "Yeah, this is it." He took the bag and opened it, finding his science notes still tucked inside. "Why...how did it get in that cave?"

"Whoa! Dude, you must have been attacked by those same bad guys that captured me and the Bran Man. I told you they were mean."

"Indubitably," Max confirmed. He knew beyond a doubt Michael's mugging was the work of one of Bubba's stupid stooges. He confronted

Bubba with this bit of information, expecting an apology or even a denial from that particular southern gentleman but instead received a bitter telephonic tongue lashing.

"Let me remind you, my fine college friend," Bubba ranted at him, "I don't work for you. It's the other way around, and if you wanna continue to share in this partnership we got goin' here, then butt out of my business. Your science pals don't mean a blessed thing to me, and I'll do whatever I want, make no mistake about it. Now, if you cain't handle that, then bug out."

Max let the man rave on without argument. "I don't want to bug out of anything," he told him. "Campus security patrols are on the alert for strangers, and we don't want policemen getting wind of what we're doing, now do we?"

"All right," Bubba calmed down with an effort. "Your precious school will be off limits to my people. But I still think that girl and boy went back inside the mountain and found something. Your job is to find out what."

Eyes monitored the university webcam, observing Michael and Alesandra as they left the library, arm in arm. The watcher knew they were hiding something, and was determined to learn what it was. If they weren't willing to share it of their own free will, then extreme force might be necessary to pry it out of them.

A warm summer rain bathed the campus, the kind that brings a thin mist rising from the ground and ripples rustling through the trees. Students attended classes and gazed wistfully out dorm windows as the sultry morning slowly creeped onward.

Alesandra felt the gentle sprinkle of raindrops on her face, and she breathed in the honey-fresh aroma. A soft rumble of distant thunder greeted her as she walked across campus.

Sharing her dorm meant she was seldom alone. With no classes on Wednesdays, she seized the opportunity for privacy and spent the next few hours glued to her laptop, magnifying, highlighting and cropping the photographs taken in the Chamber of Gods. Enraptured, she watched as images emerged on her monitor. Most remarkable were the raised etchings indicating a culture far in advance of their suspected time period.

Digging the charcoal rubbings of the same raised characters from where she had hidden them, she spread them out and studied them intently. To her, they indicated thought patterns rather than an alphabetic form. However, she needed corroboration from either Jared or Max, both of whom studied extinct languages. Leaning back against her pillow, she weighed her options.

Jared's generally calm demeanor urged her to approach him. He manifested an air of competence and an impartial view where scientific projects were concerned. Max, on the other hand, although equally qualified as a semanticist, was interested in her personally, and might be inclined to use this as an opportunity to get closer to her. The choice seemed clear.

Grabbing an empty notebook, she made drawings from the samples in front of her. With several pages completed, she folded her large sheets of charcoal drawings and lifted the mattress off her bed, sliding them securely underneath to conceal them.

Security at the front desk at McCord Hall called upstairs to Jared's room, and he agreed to meet with her. She climbed the stairs to the third floor, and he met her there, using his card key to allow her into the corridor.

Once inside his room, he sat at his desk while she sat on a beat up stuffed chair in the corner. The springs had seen better days, and she sank down into it. She noticed the bulletin board had so many things tacked to it, she did not think he would be able to find anything on it. The sheets on his bed lay in a twisted heap, and clothing remained wherever it was discarded. Jared was definitely not a neat freak.

"So, what brings you, Sandy? Want a Kit Kat?" He pulled open a drawer, and she saw it loaded with chocolate bars and other sugar highs.

"No, thanks. I've brought something I was hoping you could take a look at. I'm afraid I need your expertise." She pulled a large manila envelope from her bag and offered it to him. "What do you think? Can you read it?"

"Well, not off the top of my head. But with some study I might be able to make out something. What is this stuff? Where did you get it?"

"I went home on the weekend to see my parents. My sister and I found an antique book store. I came across it when I was browsing there. I copied this stuff down, 'cause I thought it was interesting. I know they aren't that good. I drew them rather quickly. It reminded me of the writing Max was showing me in the cave at the dig site, so I just sort of wondered...you know."

He stared at the pages, his interest piqued the moment he saw the drawings. As he studied the papers, not answering her, she continued. "I made some penciled copies of the symbols, thinking they might have a native Indio origin. But I can't read them. I would have bought the book, but they wanted a couple hundred bucks for it."

"I'll be glad to go over them, Sandy. Languages can usually tell us a lot about ancient cultures." He examined several pages of characters, letting his gaze linger on each drawing before turning to the next. She leaned over his shoulder, watching with avid interest while waiting for a verdict.

"Where did you say you got these?"

"Um. An old bookstore," she lied. "Well, really an antique store that had a section in it of old books. I thought it quite interesting." Coming up with her story on the spur of the moment, she hoped it was plausible. She scratched her arm absently as she spoke, unwilling to divulge the truth. She should have realized he would want to know her source and prepared a better story.

"At first, I thought they were hieroglyphics, but I've changed my mind. These writings contain more straight lines and compact blocklike forms."

"Yes, that rules out an Egyptian influence." His fingers scanned the drawings while his eyes followed their trail. "Is there a particular order they should be in?"

"Oh, I'm not really sure. They're from various pages throughout the book."

Knowing she was lying about the origin of the drawings, he pressed further. "What's the name of the book you found them in?"

"Gosh, Jared. I'm sorry, but I didn't make a note of it." She turned her head away and winced. It was a bald-faced lie, and he knew it. One of the first things a scientist learns is to document everything down to the most minute detail. She held her breath as he continued to inspect the drawings.

Finally, he looked up. "I suggest they are Mayan or possibly Olmec, but I need to study them at leisure before giving you any definitive answers." He smiled at her. "It would be helpful if I had that book for reference."

She shrugged lamely and collected her purse from the bed where she had dropped it. She placed a quick call to Michael asking him to meet her on the floor above.

"Thanks for your help, Jared. I realize it's not for a class or anything, but I really am interested in whatever you learn from them."

Jared stepped to the door and opened it. "Not a problem, Sandy. I'll be in touch." He smiled and closed the door behind her before pulling out his magnifying glass and looking over the pages in greater detail.

In spite of the intrigue the images provided, he could not shake her lies from his mind. Where did she really get the drawings, and what was she hiding?

Michael waited at the top of the staircase. “Hey, Sandy.”

She wrapped her arms around his waist and kissed him before they headed to his room. “I've been missing you today.”

“Good. Me too.” He dipped his head and kissed her again. “What have you been up to?” He unlocked his door and drew her inside where they sat on the edge of the bed next to each other.

“I made some drawings of the writings we found in the cave and took them to Jared. That's his area of study, so I figured chances are he'll do better with them than I will.”

“I think you're right. It was a good idea.”

“Well, it was either him or Max.”

“I'm glad you chose, Jared,” he said with an edge in his voice, and she smiled.

“You don't want me taking my problems to Max?”

He raised an eyebrow and glared. “I don't want you taking anything to Max.”

Giggling, she drew her finger across his frowning brow. “Is my man jealous of Max?”

“I don't know. Am I your man?”

“You know you are.” She smiled as she looked into his eyes, and his heart hammered.

“Then I guess I don't have to be jealous, do I?”

“Want to make out?”

“Yeah, but first I have something to tell you.” Reaching over to his desk, he twitched the second drawer open and pulled out a file. Inside the cover, photos he had taken of the soldier in the cave were attached with paper clips. “These photos show he was a Cavalry officer. Not only that, but his collar insignia identifies his unit as the 7th Kentucky Cavalry.”

“Michael, that is terrific!”

“Wait, there's more. I looked it up on the Internet. The 7th Kentucky Cavalry was Colonel John Hunt Morgan's outfit. They rode into Missouri and Ohio, destroying Yankee supplies and killing as they went.”

“Okay, but what were they doing here in Tennessee?”

"Probably stationed here while planning other raiding operations up north, but never mind about that. I read up on them and learned they came here after destroying a Union army wagon train, and guess what was in the wagons."

"I have no idea. What was it?"

He grinned and whispered mysteriously. "Gold, Sandy! It was gold, and the Rebels took it all! That isn't all I found out."

"What else?"

"The Rebs were ordered to transport the gold to the Confederate treasury, but the war ended, and the gold simply disappeared."

She gasped. "That soldier in the cave…"

"Just what I'm thinking."

"He carried a gold bar in his pouch. He must have been one of Morgan's men. We have to tell someone about him now."

Michael hesitated. "Well, not just yet. You see, I brought that gold bar out of the cave in my knapsack. I'm wondering if the rest of the bullion is stashed somewhere in that mountain, and if so, who do we tell about it?"

"I didn't know you picked up that bar."

"Yes, I meant to tell you earlier but with everything else that's been happening, it kinda slipped my mind. It's in a safe place for the moment, but I think that's what the mugger was really looking for. Oh, and here's another piece of news. Remember my school bag being stolen when I got attacked?"

"Yes, of course."

"Lewis found it. In the cave where he and Brandon were held."

Her eyes grew large as she realized the implications. "They really were captured and held prisoner, weren't they?"

"Yup. Obviously the same guy who came after me. Something's going on at that mountain, and I'm afraid it's a dangerous game."

Michael felt torn between finding a new and safer place to hide the gold bar or leaving it where it was. He finally decided the old adage of "hide it in plain site" seemed to be working.

"About that soldier, Michael, I made him a promise. I want him to have a proper burial, and with the things you've learned, we certainly have a better chance of finding out who he really is."

"That will mean another journey on our own back to the cave. With what we know now, you know it could be risky."

"I understand that. But it's something I have to do."

"All right then. We'll go back. It'll give me another chance to look at those glowing rocks. I sort of questioned Blaney about them, rather vaguely of course, and he's never heard of anything like it. Makes me all the more curious."

Big Bear Walking

Wilbur "Bubba" Grubbs was not the easiest man to get along with, having learned at an early age to make good use of his most valuable assets; a devious mind and two quick fists.

The proud descendants of the Cherokee, who once claimed this land as their own and who miraculously escaped the infamous Trail of Tears, accepted this white man in their midst, teaching him their traditions. They called him Yaw-e'gwa-gi', or Big Bear Walking. Bubba backed down from no man, let alone invisible spirits of bygone days.

His quick temper landed him in Brushy Mountain State Prison on various charges, including manslaughter. Prison reinforced his desire for the easy life, but it took a fortunate accident to achieve it.

In a wild stroke of luck, a cave-in deep within his mountain knocked down a partition revealing a stash of refined bars of gold. For Bubba, it was lust at first site.

He drove his battered old Chevy pick-up into Memphis to find Linus Dawkins, a small-time fence to whom he occasionally sold items of questionable ownership.

Linus examined and weighed the bar. "Where'd you get this, Bubba?"

"Don't ask me no foolish questions. I didn't steal it, if that's what you're gettin' at."

"Do you know what you got here?"

"There you go askin' questions again."

"Well, I'll tell you," Linus ignored the interruption. "This is a genuine United States minted gold bar. It'll be hard to find a buyer for it."

Bubba suspected the man was preparing to cheat him with a ridiculous low price. "I want a decent return from it, and if I don't get it, I'm gonna bash your face in. But if you treat me fair, I'll bring you more just like this one."

They struck a deal and over a period of time exchanged several more gold bars, making Bubba a wealthy man. He chose not to spend his money on a lot of obvious luxuries. Instead, he felt it better spent buying people and power.

His new financial status caused several old cronies to gravitate around him seeking a bit of gravy for themselves. They found him generous when he wanted something, and they never refused his bidding.

Townsmen and community leaders pointedly included Bubba in their deliberations and political affairs. The Governor himself appointed him to the State Forestry Commission for the perpetual conservation of timberlands.

Now a man of importance, he acquired the family homestead following his father's untimely passing. The old man died late one evening while sitting on his porch. He suffered a heart attack and fell from his rocker, breaking his neck from the impact. Bubba failed to mention it was his foot that kicked the rocker out from under his sire.

He was a familiar sight throughout the county, delivering moonshine with impunity and surrounded by the music of Charlie Daniels on the radio while two hound dogs rode in the bed of his brand new black pick-up.

Finding it expedient to further conceal the gold bars still in the cave, he called on Jack and Red to do the job.

"Yessir, boss." They readily accepted whatever task he gave them. Bubba led them into the mountain and ordered them to remove evidence of the earlier cave-in. He then supervised their construction of a wall around his new vault, built to deceptively appear like natural rock walls.

His orders were explicit. "I want you to make sure nobody meddles with the caves. Keep a good watch, and let me know if there's any trouble."

"Yessir, boss," they agreed in unison. "We'll keep our eyes peeled. Don't give it another thought."

Familiar with the natural curiosity of man, Bubba knew it wouldn't be long before they would question the contents of his mountain vault. Well acquainted with subterfuge, he set up a moonshine still in the upper cave, allowing his workers to believe that operating it was their true vocation.

A ruthless man, Bubba soon developed a distrust for his gold trader, Dawkins, suspecting the man pocketed a good portion of the money received from fencing the gold bars. Lying in wait one night as Dawkins closed his office, Bubba struck him from behind, dragged him into a nearby alley and garroted him with piano wire.

Forced to find another go-between, he remembered a name from his time in prison. An investment banker in Knoxville by the name of Allan Cornelius dabbled in precious gems on the side and dealt with an extensive listing of international clients. Bubba decided to make the trip to Knoxville.

After introductions, Cornelius informed him, "Let me say up front my mediating fee is twenty-five percent."

"Ain't that a little steep, friend?"

"I'm not your friend," was the curt reply. "Let's get that straight, too. But no, it's my going price. I'm in business to make a profit, and I earn my commission."

A handshake finalized the arrangement. In reality, however, Cornelius was a paid government informant. He recognized the mint markings on the initial gold bar offered to him and immediately notified his contact in the U. S. Treasury Department.

In keeping with his position with the Forestry Commission, Bubba inherited the responsibility of encouraging historical studies of the state's acreage inventory. His predecessor authorized Carl Blaney's classes to conduct excursions within the forested areas. This included the mountain, and although Bubba wasn't fond of college kids digging and poking around, he had no choice.

"I think it would be safer," he told Blaney, "for your people to stay on this side of the mountain." He watched the budding scientists closely, leery of them wandering into the caves.

Evenings usually found him looking for fun in various beer joints featuring country music and short-skirted women. The pulsating bass guitars and drums, mixed with the aroma of spilled liquor and sweaty dancers rubbing against each other, created the atmosphere he sought. The noisier and rowdier, the better he liked it.

He knew everyone in the bar scene from the plowboys and wise asses to the perverts and hookers, and he generally dismissed them all with a casual wave of his hand. It was on such a night, that a stranger claimed his attention.

Bubba sat at a table with his arms around two buxom beauties when the young man entered. He spoke with the bartender who nodded in Bubba's direction, and the newcomer approached.

"Mister, is that your black pick-up out front?"

Bubba started to rise but the other smiled and said quickly, "It's all right, just a scrape. I kinda backed into it when I was parking. Don't worry, it isn't bad, and I'll gladly pay to have it fixed."

"Maybe I'd better take a look at it." Bubba led the way outside, and the young man followed. A small scratch was visible on the front left fender. "Aw hell, boy. I expected somethin' worse than that."

"Well, I feel bad about it. I want to make it right with you."

"No, but I'll tell you what. Come back inside with me, and I'll let you buy me a beer."

Together, they returned to the bar, and when Bubba started introducing the newcomer around he realized he didn't know the man's name. "Folks around here call me Bubba," he said.

They shook hands. "My name is Max. Max Dugan."

"You're not from around here, are you Max?"

"Just passing through, looking for work."

They drank their beer while Bubba appraised his new friend. "Times are hard right now. What kinda work you lookin' for?"

Max paused before answering. "Nothing fancy. I'm not particular. Just something I can make a lot of money at."

"I might have a job for a man who can take orders and keep his mouth shut."

"I'm used to doing both, if the pay is good."

Bubba leaned closer. "You ever been to college, Max?"

"Hah! Yeah, I graduated from Georgia Tech. That's why I'm roaming the country looking for a job," Max said, his voice dripping with sarcasm.

"Okay, I'll let that go. You look smart enough to pass for a college guy. Suppose I fix it up for you to enroll at the University of Tennessee."

"What do you have in mind?"

"I want you to keep tabs on a Professor Blaney and his group of geology students. They do a lot of diggin', lookin' for fossils and stuff. I don't trust this professor, and I wanna make sure they stay away from certain places, if you know what I mean. The job pays a thousand bucks a week."

"Just how do I keep them away from…certain places?"

"That'll be up to you. Think you can handle it?"

"Oh, I can do it, but I'm not used to hassling a bunch of school kids."

"You don't have to get tough with 'em." Bubba wrote a name on a slip of paper and handed it to Max along with ten one hundred dollar bills.

"See this man at the university. He'll set you up there, and I want you to check in with me regularly by phone. Here's my number."

A sense of satisfaction swept through Bubba at having this special young man on his payroll. Max was the kind of guy he always wanted to be, intelligent and self-confident to the point of being cocky. But Bubba had one thing Max did not...money. And that made all the difference in the world.

Bubba slept that night, content with his beer-filled belly and confident his empire was even more secure. A minimum of hard work and a lot of good luck brought him to his present station in life. Now he could afford to lay back and enjoy those simple pleasures for which every man desired.

The gold made it all possible.

Voices From The Past

Alesandra sat cross-legged on the hard ground. Her shoulders slumped, and her muscles ached from prolonged inactivity. She felt the cool, moist mountain air brush against her face like an old familiar friend. Time passed slowly since the two of them returned to the Chamber of Gods, but where was Michael? It was unlike him to abandon her there in the subdued light of the cavern.

In reality, however, she was not entirely alone.

She watched fascinated as seven human figures twirled and gyrated about her wildly, sensuously. Their glistening bodies, indistinct but clearly unclothed, writhed in movements unlike any she had ever seen. They danced in ever narrowing circles inviting her to join them. A reddish hue reflected in their eyes, emphasizing the fiery passion of the ancient rite they were performing. Drums hammered a resounding rhythm in tune to the beating of her heart, and a strange desire enticed her to share in their ritual.

Yet, she hesitated.

The chamber itself seemed larger than she remembered. A constant hollow sound reverberated throughout as shadows flitted across the far walls, growing larger and then retreating, only to resume the pattern again and again. The dancers with painted faces continued to spin and pirouette, now calling her name and uttering words she did not understand. They held their arms high, hands waving in the air, and occasionally reached down to scoop up a handful of loose clay.

She grew fearful. "What do you want with me? Why am I here?"

They responded first as whispers, then repeated louder until they seemed to roar. "*Kotzuk Naka Shee! Kotzuk Naka Shee!*"

Her flesh trembled. She felt a touch on her arm, and her scream tapered to a gurgle as she recognized the face of her roommate.

Valerie, alarmed at hearing her whimpering and thrashing about, crept to Alesandra's side to awaken her. "It's all right, Sandy. It's just a bad dream."

She sat upright, eyes opened wide, her hands covering her face. "Oh! But it was so real. There were people, at least I think they were people, dancing all around me. I was scared and..." She let her voice trail off, deciding not to say anything more.

Valerie sat on the edge of the bed as her friend shook the fantasy cobwebs from her brain. "I guess it was just a dream after all," Alesandra admitted with a sheepish grin.

Valerie rubbed her arm gently, feeling the goosebumps, and consoled her, "Sure, that's all it was." Heading back to her own bed, she reassured her friend, "If you need me, I'm right here."

Alesandra recalled a previous illusion in which similar cave spirits appeared, also attempting to include her in their performance. Light from the lamp outside in the courtyard splayed across her ceiling, and she lay staring at it as she tried to rationalize the two visitations. She considered the possibility they were signals of some sort, possibly influenced by age-old primitive auras yet present in the mountain chamber.

Memories of sitting around the campfire with the others, listening to Bubba Grubbs' tales of ancient Cherokee ghosts flitted across her mind. She lay wondering if his tales triggered the nightmare.

The mysterious phonetic sound of "Kotzuk Naka Shee" continued to ring in her ears, remaining with her long beyond the normal fading time for dreams. She understood the words clearly, but not their meaning. However, a strong impression convinced her more than ever, that they were of Indio origin.

As Alesandra exited the stairwell and stepped onto the carpeting of the university library's third floor, she scanned the room for signs of Jared. Walking toward the maze of individual work stations, she caught sight of his black hair above the melamine covered partitions, and redirected her footsteps. She slid into a chair of the work station cubicle next to his.

"Did you learn anything about my writing samples?"

Jared looked up from his books, his brown eyes glinting in the light from the station lamp. "Fine thanks, Sandy. How 'bout you?"

She flushed with embarrassment. "Sorry. Hi, Jared. You're looking well today. I got your message."

He chuckled at her discomfort, and leaned back in his chair. "I probably don't have anything as concrete as you were hoping for. But I might be able to tell you a bit about it."

"Great. I appreciate whatever light you can shed on it for me. What have you got?"

He flipped a notebook open to pages filled with diagrams and symbols. "I think the relief drawings you gave me are from a culture dating from about 1200 BC to 600 BC. I'm not certain these features actually identify specific words in a spoken language. I think your symbols belong to the early Mayan period."

The young scholars became engrossed in their subject matter. They discussed various possibilities presented by the drawings, including contemporary American Indians.

Her eyes sparkled with animation, and she leaned forward on her seat with her foot tucked beneath her, as though subconsciously trying to propel herself into the realm of aboriginal civilizations. She yearned to know and understand the peoples of the ancient societies they discussed.

When Jared averted his gaze toward the windows at one point, he noticed for the first time that dusk was setting. "Holy crap, what time is it?"

Alesandra looked at her watch, and her eyes grew in alarm. "Oh, no! It's almost eight thirty. I was supposed to meet Michael for dinner two hours ago. I can't believe it's this late."

"It's all a part of the time warp that surrounds this library, Sandy. Come in for ten minutes, and hours roll by unnoticed. Happens every time."

"I've noticed that." She gathered her things together and tossed them haphazardly into her book bag.

"What is it with you and Gant anyway?" Jared asked.

Her eyebrows knit together. "What do you mean?"

"I mean you being with him. He's not exactly in your league."

"Just what are you trying to say?"

"Come off it, Sandy. Smart, pretty, cheerleader; you could have any guy you wanted. So why are you hanging out with him?"

"Why shouldn't I? Maybe I'm not superficial like the rest of you. I got to know him, Jared, and found out what a great person he is."

"Get real, Sandy. You can do so much better, and you know it."

"I guess that's where we differ. I don't think I've ever met anyone better. I think I'm damned lucky to have him," she snapped. Hiking her book bag onto her shoulder, she considered the discussion closed. "Thanks for your help, Jared. I appreciate it."

He watched her hips swing the little denim skirt back and forth as she walked away. He still did not understand what she saw in the goof that appealed to her, but he wished he had some of it, even for just one night.

Turning back to collect his own materials, he let his eyes play over the copied pages she had given him, easily recognizing the syllabic system of writing used prior to the Mayan period. "You're lying, Sandy," he muttered. "There's no way you found this stuff in a book store. I'll bet you found it in that cave with Gant. I just hope I did a better selling job than you, cuz I just fed you a load of crap."

He considered the ramifications of such a find to the anthropological world, and knew he wanted to personally contribute to that prize.

Alesandra ran from the library to McCord Hall. She used the telephone at the front desk to let Michael know of her arrival, and he met her at the stairwell door.

"I'm sorry, Pooh," she breathed in his ear as she hugged him close. "I didn't forget you. Time just got away from me."

"I figured it was something like that. Don't worry your pretty head about it, Piglet. Want to get something now?"

"Didn't you eat?"

"Not really. I just grabbed a bag of chips to tide me over. Let's go to Ryan's for smorgasborg."

Holding hands they walked to the Jeep and drove to the restaurant in nearby Union City. After filling their plates from the varied selections of meats and vegetables, they sat comfortably in a booth. The waitress brought their drinks and left them alone to talk.

"I got a message from Jared to meet him at the library. We started talking, and I just lost all track of time. I was shocked when I learned what time it was."

"You got caught in the library time warp, huh?"

She looked at him, and her eyes grew large. "You know about that, too?"

"Sure. It hangs over that building like a shroud. So what did you talk about?"

Alesandra told him of the things she and Jared discussed concerning the glyphs. "He knows a lot about this kind of thing, and it was interesting, but I don't think he was absolutely open with me."

"What do you mean?"

"Well, he completely neglected the Olmec's development of a 'mother culture' which they passed on to civilizations following their own. I personally believe our cave glyphs are more Olmec than Mayan because, and I didn't tell Jared this, I learned the word they used to identify themselves was Xi, pronounced 'shee.'"

Michael sat forward with interest. "And that's one of the words you heard in your dream?"

She stopped fingering her spoon and reached out to tangle her fingers with his. "Yes. I know it seems far-fetched, but I have a feeling about this, Michael."

"I don't think it's far-fetched at all. I think you should follow your instinct, and run with it. Go where it takes you. I think you're on to something, girl."

His encouragement and support meant a great deal to her. He never doubted or belittled her instincts.

When they returned to the campus that evening, she threw her arms around his neck and kissed him deeply before bounding off to her dorm room.

As she sat on her bed reviewing documents printed from the Internet regarding the Olmecs, she compared similarities between their sophisticated concepts and modern language structures. The more she studied their culture, the more convinced she became that Jared's knowledge was far greater than he admitted.

Sitting back and chewing on the end of her pen, she wondered if she made a mistake consulting with him instead of Max.

Before turning in for the night, Michael booted his computer to check his emails. He did not expect there to be any from home. There never was. A name in the sender list caught his attention– *Jacatom.*

With a click of his mouse, he opened the letter.

Michael,

Please stay alert. With a new semester starting and all the students returning, it's easy to be distracted. You can't allow that to happen. You are still in danger. You are still being followed. Also, keep a close watch on her. Evil has it's eye upon her, too.

Shutting down the computer, Michael got into his bed and turned out the light, but sleep did not come easily.

A week of excitement dominated the campus as people flocked to Martin for Homecoming Week. The UTM Student Government Association kicked off the event with a bonfire and a fireworks display at Pacer Pond. Days that followed included a cook-off competition and other similar activities. The Homecoming Queen and her court were honored by the ladies of Alpha Delta Pi Sorority in a special program, and the campus buzzed in a flurry of fun things.

For Michael, the highlight of the week was a meeting of the West Tennessee Historical Society in the Seminar Room of the Paul Meek Library. Dr. Wilson Castleberry, history professor, lectured on the subject of Tennessee's role during the Civil War. He described the decisive battles at Shiloh and Fort Donelson as possible turning points, and also mentioned several Confederate regiments operating near the present-day university grounds. The 7th Kentucky Cavalry was one of those units.

"This particular military element included many of our local citizens in its ranks," he said. "Some of those who were too young to enlist when the War Between the States began, came of age in time to participate and were assigned to the 7th Kentucky."

"Colonel Morgan commanded and led them on raiding forays into northern areas previously untouched by the ravages of war. Upon Lee's surrender, all southern soldiers either returned to their homes or disbanded and vanished into the hills."

Michael leaned forward at the cursory mention of Morgan's Raiders, and listened intently. When the meeting ended, he waited until the majority of the attendees left the room before approaching the Professor.

"Thank you, sir. I enjoyed your lecture very much. I took plenty of notes." Michael briefly held up his notebook as though offering proof.

"You're welcome. Glad you found it interesting." Castleberry gathered his papers together as he prepared to leave.

"Sir, you mentioned Morgan's Raiders in your talk. I read an article about an action in Missouri in which Morgan's men attacked and confiscated a gold shipment from the Union army. Supposedly, it was never recovered, and I was wondering if the 7th Kentucky divided it up among themselves."

The professor stopped his packing for a moment and looked up, pleased to have an enlightened query. “I heard the same rumors about that gold, but I'm certain Colonel Morgan, an honorable southern gentleman, presented it to the Confederacy as spoils of war. At any rate,” he added with emphasis, “he did not bring it back here.” He stuffed the remaining pages in his brown, leather briefcase and snapped it shut.

“Just one more question, sir.”

“One more, and then I really must go.” He picked up his case and sauntered toward the door, letting Michael know his time was short.

“I appreciate it. Can you tell me where I might find the names of Confederate soldiers in the 7th Kentucky?”

Dr. Castleberry spoke over his shoulder as he stepped out the door. “The best place would be the State Archives in Nashville. They maintain rosters of many military units, Union and Confederate.”

Michael smiled as he devised his strategy. The archives might also have a list of the names of rebel soldiers missing in action. One of them might be the soldier they found in the cave, and Nashville was only a few hours away.

Alesandra skipped up the stairs and followed a small cluster of girls into Boling University Center. She found Michael waiting for her in a booth at the food court. In front of him sat a tray with two pepperoni pizzas from the Pizza Hut, and two Smoothies.

“Thanks for ordering for me. We were a bit late getting out of cheerleading practice today.”

“I've been meaning to talk to you about this cheerleading business, Sandy.” Michael kept his eyes on his food as he spoke, hoping she did not see his smirk.

“What about it?”

“I don't think I like it. Guys having their hands on your gluteus maximus all the time. I think you should quit.”

“Is that right?”

He looked up and met her sparkling eyes. “Yeah, that's right.”

“Well, as long as they aren't touching it the same way you do, I wouldn't be too worried.”

He held out a slice of pepperoni, and she bit into it, grinning. “Sounds like a deal, Piglet.” He touched his fingertip to the end of her nose affectionately. “Did you have a good practice?”

"Yeah. I think we're good enough to compete at State this year."

"That's great. I must say I'm not surprised. You've got a terrific squad this year."

"We do. We're lucky to have Breonia and Katie this year. They've been great additions to the team, and we've come up with a new routine to feature the Vaughn twins." Reaching across the table with her napkin, she wiped tomato sauce from the corner of his mouth. "What's the news from Dr. Turner on your crystals?"

Michael shrugged. "He hasn't said anything about them lately. I don't think there's anything fascinating to learn from them, or he would have told me by now."

She bit into her pizza and gazed out the window as she chewed, silently brooding. He looked at her expectantly, wondering what weighed on her mind. After thoroughly masticating the food in her mouth, she swallowed, then took a long drink of her Smoothie before finally sharing her thoughts.

"You know, Michael, everyone seems very curious about us, me and you. They suspect we discovered something unusual inside the mountain."

"They sure do." He leaned toward her, tucking her auburn hair behind her ear and lowering his voice. "And of course, we did. I found my Piglet."

She wrinkled her nose. "Yes, we discovered each other, but people have a hard time believing that."

"I know, we're considered an odd couple. You're the prettiest girl on campus, and I'm just a dork."

Having heard these same thoughts voiced almost verbatim by Jared the previous week, she frowned. "You're not a dork." She pursed her lips and blew him a kiss before resuming her train of thought. "No, I meant something else."

"They're just guessing, Sandy."

"Maybe, but think about this." She held up her hand and began counting on her fingers. "Number one; Dr. Turner's lab was broken into; two, you were attacked outside the Geo Lab; three and four, your backpack was stolen and recovered *from inside the cave*, and five, someone searched your room looking for something."

"I know what you're saying, but–"

"All these things are not coincidences. Somebody is more than just a little curious about you, and us."

"None of this is news, Sandy. What's really on your mind?"

She leaned closer and murmured. "I believe someone has been in my room, too."

He reached for her hand and clasped it tightly, instantly concerned. "What! When did this happen?"

"It's nothing radical like yours was. The place wasn't ransacked or anything, but some of my dresser drawers seem disheveled; clothing mussed up, stuff like that. Finding things in odd places."

"How about your suitemates?"

"I haven't mentioned it to them. I can't see why they would be that interested in us. After Lewis found your stuff in the cave, I sort of absolved members of the Blaney Bunch from involvement in any of this. Now, I'm not so sure any more."

Michael was quiet. "I think we can discount Brandon from having an ulterior motive. He is way too rattlebrained. I do have another prospect, though. One we never considered before. The professor. He could easily know something we don't."

"Yes, and he is a personal friend of Dr. Turner, so they might be working together on the crystals."

"There is that possibility." He looked over her shoulder and whispered a hurried shush before pulling back.

"Hello, troops." Max approached, carrying a yogurt sundae. "Okay if I join you?"

"Sure, Max." Michael scooted over in the booth to make room, but Max wedged himself next to Alesandra instead. Michael frowned.

She smiled as he sat. "Are you enjoying the wild festivities of the day, Max?" She watched with an inward chuckle as Michael fought against a pique of jealousy.

"Oh, things are pretty wild all right," he joked. "That bonfire almost got out of control, and I dropped a strawberry tart down the front of my shirt. Gotta love Homecoming Week, though. What have you two been doing?"

"Believe it or not," she said, "I've been taking a bit of a breather now that exams are over. Getting myself geared up for the new semester. Not too exciting, I admit."

Max looked at Michael. "I noticed you at Dr. Castleberry's lecture earlier today. It was great, wasn't it? History is one of my personal interests, particularly where the Civil War is concerned. What about you?"

"I didn't know that." Michael replied with raised eyebrows, surprised by the revelation. "I thought your historical interests were focused on ancient history."

"Oh, sure, but not exclusively. As I was leaving, I heard you ask about the 7th Kentucky Cavalry, a notable regiment, and one comparable with Mosby's Rangers of Virginia. Although they were both guerilla units, the Rangers were better known for the harassment and havoc they created." Max spooned his sundae and noticed the quick, furtive glances when he asked, "What made you mention that particular outfit, Michael?"

"Well, uh...actually, Dr. Castleberry brought it up in his seminar, and it aroused my curiosity."

"You mean about the federal gold? A very interesting tale, and I'll bet a lot of folks have been looking for it."

"You know about the gold? The professor said Colonel Morgan turned all of it over to the Confederacy."

"I've read about it, and I've heard others say the same as the professor." Max finished his yogurt and pushed the empty dish away, standing to leave. "Still, the rumors continue to circulate, don't they? Makes you stop and think what somebody could do with all that gold if they found it today. I think I'll say goodnight on that note. Thanks for the company."

As they watched him walk away, she turned to Michael with a questioning gaze. "Do you think he knows about the gold bar?"

"I think Max is one of those curious folks you spoke of earlier, where we're concerned. I made a mistake approaching Castleberry like I did. I didn't notice Max there, and now he is probably more than just a bit curious."

"What do you think we should do?"

"I'm planning a trip to Nashville to look up old Confederate unit rosters. Maybe I should make that trip tomorrow and talk to someone in the Treasury Department instead."

Spirit Dancers

"No, Michael! You can't do that."

He stared at her in surprise. "Why not? It's not ours to keep. We have to turn it in."

She shook her head. "That's not what I mean. I'm talking about the cave."

His brows drew together, and he leaned forward. "You've completely lost me, girl. Explain."

"If you hand it over, they're going to ask where you found it. And then they'll want to see it. You can't let them go into the cave. They don't care about scientific preservation. They'll destroy the place. There are too many artifacts in there, too much history, to let them invade and destroy." She clutched his hand. "Please, Michael. For me."

He saw the pleading in those sparkling green eyes and knew he would probably do whatever she asked of him. "I understand your concern, but we'll have to figure something out because I have to turn the gold in. It's probably a federal offense or something to have it."

Her lips pursed as she thought. "Let's walk back to the dorm and think about it." She gathered up the remains of their meal to toss in the garbage, and Michael stacked the tray in the ever growing pile as they left the Boling Center.

Darkness crept up earlier each night as autumn approached. In the evening shadows, they walked to Cooper Hall and settled on a bench in the courtyard. He sat close against her and hooked an arm around her neck, drawing her head onto his shoulder.

"Any brilliant ideas yet?" he prompted.

"Only one." She raised her head to look in his eyes. "We have to move the body."

He pulled back and stared at her. "You didn't just say what I heard you say."

"I probably did. We have to move the soldier's body. It's the only way. The feds will want to see where we found him so they can search the vicinity for more gold. We can't let them in our cave. I can't explain it, but I feel very protective of it. So, the only other option we have is to move the body."

"I know I'm going to regret asking this. How and where?"

"Why do I have to come up with all the answers? Why aren't you helping?"

"All right. Let's consider the possibilities."

Laying her head back on his shoulder, she sighed heavily and thought.

After a few minutes of silence, he suggested, "We can get a body bag from the anthropology department. We'll have to sneak it out though, since we can't give them any reasonable justification for borrowing it." He felt her lips press against his neck for his trouble.

She lifted her head again, and looked into his eyes. "You know, it doesn't have to be radically far from where he is now. It can still be on the mountain. We can place him in one of the other caves. One of the false caves that only goes in for a distance before hitting a dead end. That way we wouldn't have to lug him all the way down the mountain. And it would rationally explain why his body wasn't discovered before this." Her eyes sparkled in the courtyard lights glow, reflecting her desire for his approval in the whole escapade.

He brushed a lock of hair from her face and confirmed, "Yes, that does seem like the best solution. All right, I won't contact the government until after we move him. But we'll have to do it soon. The longer I hang onto that gold, the more nervous I get. I think we're involved in something bigger than either of us knows, Sandy, and I want out. I'm tired of looking over my shoulder all the time, and worrying whether you're safe from one minute to the next."

She lay her hand on his cheek. "Oh, Michael. I love you for worrying about me, but I'll be fine. Thank you for indulging me in this. It means a great deal to me."

"I know. The more I think about it, I believe you're right. Those guys would go trampling in there and destroy thousands of years of preservation. Too much at risk. We'll do it your way."

She wove her arms around his neck and lifted her lips to his, knowing that the true treasure she discovered in Blaney's Mountain was in her arms.

The University of Tennessee at Martin, founded in 1900 as Hall-Moody Institute, exuded a peaceful atmosphere. Alesandra walked beneath the spreading arches of maples and oaks along the pathways of the school's grassy quad, her hand firmly tucked into Michael's.

He noted the startled stares of classmates passing by. "Looks like we're news all over again, now that the majority of the student body has returned from summer vacation."

"Ignore it. We're happy, and that's all that matters. I love you, Michael."

He stopped walking and tugged her closer to kiss her. "Love you, too."

"They're just jealous that they aren't as blissfully happy as we are."

"Well, at least we have a few classes together. We also have our projects; my crystals and your glyphs. And, of course, our soldier."

"Oh!" Her eyes lit up, and her features became animated as she tucked her hair behind her ear. "Speaking of the project, I think I've discovered what *Kotzuk Naka Xi* means."

"That's terrific."

"I'm not positive yet," her voice betrayed her excitement, "but I examined phonetic sounds from early Indio languages filtering into contemporary dialects."

"What did you learn?"

"Well, according to ancient translations, *Kotzuk* seems to be the Olmec word for mountain while *Xi*, can be interpreted to mean either 'us' or 'we'. That being the case, it stands to reason that *Kotzuk Naka Xi* means 'this is our mountain'."

"Then, those people in your dreams are Olmec?"

"Possibly. They could also be the ones known to the Cherokee as the Others, an older race. Whoever they are, they're claiming the mountain as their sole possession."

The two followed the walkway past the Library and University Center, and as they strolled, Alesandra spoke of her dream fantasy as a real life experience. "Michael, they were trying to tell me something. I'm sure of it. It may not be scientific but I know they were attempting to convey a message through the medium of time."

"You're right," he said. "It isn't very scientific."

"I know I'm going on intuition rather than the defined trial and error methods of a scientist. But I think that sometimes as an anthropologist, it's fruitful to surrender to a personal feeling, and I have a hunch about this."

Late that night, she poured over the cave glyphs. Analyses aided by computer research further convinced her of the relief characters being partial Olmec scripts blended with another obscure language. She deciphered several independent words and phrases, sending icy tremors throughout the fibers of her entire nervous system.

The implications thrilled her. Jared would understand her emotion even if he disbelieved the logic of her conviction. She sent him an email before shutting down her computer for the night, inviting him to meet with her.

The next afternoon she found him reclining on the grass outside the library, his head tipped back soaking up the warm rays of the sun. She dropped her canvas tote on the ground and sat next to him. "Hey, how's it going?"

Jared's head tipped in her direction, but with his eyes shielded by sunglasses, she could only assume he was looking at her. "Always good. This semester is gonna be a breeze."

"Must be nice. Why is it always the classes you see in the syllabus, and say, now that one should be a walk through, always turns out to have the most homework?"

"I've noticed that. So, your note said you had something new. Find that book again?"

"No, I think I found something regarding the translations of what I already have. And I had this really neat dream I wanted to tell you about." She recounted her dream and waited for his impressions. To her dismay, he began to laugh.

"You don't actually take that nonsense seriously, do you?" he chuckled. "It's just wishful thinking on your part. You're reading way too much into these relief symbols, if that's what they really are. The dancing spirits in your dream is the giveaway. They're the result of a romantic and very feminine imagination."

She sat rigidly, her anger flaring. "I resent that, Jared Brooks. That is the most sexist statement I have ever heard. I thought you of all people would understand. I suppose you think I'm too 'feminine and imaginative' to reach an unbiased conclusion. Well let me tell you something, buddy. I am as much a scientist as you or any other man can be."

"Nothing scientific about a dream, Sandy. Come off it. Don't you think you're overreacting just a bit here?"

"No, I don't think so. And I suppose the next words to come out of your mouth are that my anger can be attributed to my being a redhead."

He snickered, "Well, now that you mention it, the thought did occur."

"Well, if we're going to start drawing such 'scientific' conclusions, I can only conclude that the reason you're a jackass is because you have too much testosterone." She got to her feet indignantly. "And if you were any good in your area of specialty, you would have known that the drawings I brought you are related to the Olmecs, not the Mayans." She turned on her heel and started to stalk away.

"Now wait a minute, Sandy. Don't leave when you've finally said something intelligent. You're right, I think they are Olmec."

She stopped in her tracks and turned to look back over her shoulder. "Then why didn't you say so in the first place? Why did we go through all that song and dance in the library?"

He tried to disengage himself from her fury, not wanting to make an enemy of her. They had to work together in the Blaney Bunch, and although it was amusing to get such a rise out of her, he wanted to stay friends.

"Because at that time, I believed they were Mayan. I've done a lot of studying on them since then. I didn't want to offer you any preconceived ideas before I had a chance to study them further."

Her temper began to cool.

"And I do apologize about the dancing spirits comment," he added, almost as an afterthought.

With the argument apparently over, she returned to sit beside him. They agreed that the specimen glyphs possibly originated in east Africa prior to the Olmec civilization. She pulled the prints from her purse and spread them out on the grass to refer to.

Jared pointed out the Olmec system of bars and dots was a unique system of mathematics. "Each long bar equals the number five and each dot represents number one. Bars and dots appear on the relief drawings you gave me and might be some sort of calendar."

"I read something about that."

"Also, the Olmec people were believed to speak and write in the Manding language. The curved characters shown on your drawings, although not clearly defined, closely resemble Manding words for 'man' and 'death.' It could be interpreted as a danger sign of some kind."

"Maybe the spirit dancers were trying to warn me and..." she saw the mirth in his eyes and refused to finish her comment. Even if no one else took her seriously, she was haunted by the message communicated from beyond the ages.

Walking back to her dormitory for dinner, she decided Jared was too rigid in his follow-the-book approach to matters of science. He lacked imagination whereas she possessed an excessive amount. Michael, too, suspected she permitted emotion a bit more latitude in deductive reasoning than she should, but he maintained an open mind. She needed to consult with someone more knowledgeable of Indio culture; someone who might understand the meaning behind her dream.

Only one name came to mind. Mr. Bubba Grubbs!

Changing course, she headed to McCord Hall instead. She felt certain Michael would agree to accompany her to meet with the older man.

When she was seated cross-legged on his bed, she proposed her idea. "I like Mr. Grubbs, and he's always been really nice to us. He sure seems to know a lot about Cherokee tradition."

"Well, he's full of tales and legends, but I think he's a pretty busy man. He might be difficult to get hold of."

"For a busy guy, he sure seems to turn up on that mountain whenever we're there," she pointed out.

"True. Still, we should probably ask Blaney to help us get in touch with him. We don't want to waste time wandering around that mountain on the off chance that we might run into him."

"Okay, makes sense to me. Good idea. Let's go."

Carl Blaney leaned back in his chair looking at the books, papers, and rocks stacked haphazardly on his desktop, his shelves, the floor and other chairs. He kept the office decorated in a Midwest Tornado theme. With the phone cradled between his ear and shoulder, he spoke in low tones.

"You coming to spend the night with me? I really want you, baby. We haven't had the chance to see too much of each other all week." He smiled as Susan laid out plans for a late dinner and a night in his bed. "Great. I'll be there by 8 o'clock. See you then. Love you, too, Susan."

A rap sounded at his door as he dropped the receiver back in place. "Come in."

The door opened and Michael and Alesandra entered. "Hey, Professor. How's it going?"

"Fine. Busy as always at the beginning of a semester. Glad homecoming week is finally over." He glanced around the room, and seeing no surface uncluttered, decided he couldn't ask them to sit down.

"So, what can I do for you two?"

Alesandra spoke up. "Well, I was hoping you could tell us how we can get in touch with Mr. Grubbs. I've been doing some research for one of my classes, and I need to learn more about the history and legends of the local Cherokee tribes. He seems like the perfect one to talk to. He's always telling us stories whenever we meet him."

"I'm sure Mr. Grubbs would be happy to talk to you about Native Americans. However, I'd feel better if you consulted with Professor McBride-Hart. She's an expert on the cultures of Tennessee Indian tribes."

"I suppose I could talk to her, but I'd really like to speak with Mr. Grubbs as well, Professor. After all, he actually lived with the Indians. He knows first hand about their ceremonies and rituals, precisely what I'm concerned with at the moment."

Admiring the young woman's tenacity, Blaney raised his hands in surrender. "Okay, I'll give you directions and tell him to expect you."

The watcher looked out the window from where he sat at his computer and saw Gant place a cooler in the back seat of his Jeep. Alesandra came running across the parking lot and joined him. It was obvious they were planning another trip, probably to the mountain.

Grabbing his keys, he hurried to his own car and tailed them for two hours until they abruptly turned off the highway onto an old gravel road. Disgruntled when he realized the mountain was not their destination, he turned around and headed for home.

The long and winding gravel road managed to infiltrate the Jeep with dust and grit.

"Sandy, can you grab me a bottle of water out of the cooler? It's hotter than blazes today."

She turned in her seat and retrieved a bottle out of the ice filled chest, unscrewed the lid, and handed it to him.

"I'm so excited," she bubbled. "I'm sure Mr. Grubbs will know the significance of my dreams."

"Don't set your hopes too high," Michael warned. "He's an entertaining person with his tall tales and good ole boy manners, but he may not know as much as you think he does."

She smiled. "I know, and if we're wasting our time, then we can go talk to Professor McBride-Hart like the prof suggested."

"What time is it?"

"Just about one. We should be almost there."

"That must be the house down on the left. If the dust hadn't started to settle a mile back we would have passed it without even seeing it."

"Wow, what a run down place. I thought Mr. Grubbs had a job. This place sure doesn't reflect it."

"Look at those two brand-new black pick-up trucks parked in the driveway. I guess that's where he spends his money."

"There's Mr. Grubbs up on the porch."

Michael parked the Jeep, and they climbed out, smiling at their host.

"Welcome, welcome. Come on up here on the porch and set a spell." He rose from his unpainted rocker to greet them, at the same time shooing away two spotted hound dogs that sniffed their own peculiar welcome.

The screen door opened at the urging of a shapely young lady bearing a pitcher of sweet tea and three glasses. "Hi y'all," she said. "I'm Patty Ann. Set yourselves down. I'm sure you can both use a nice cool drink after that long trip."

Bubba introduced her as his housekeeper and winked at Michael.

"The professor called and said you two were a-comin' on out to the house. I told him, 'You just send my little mountain friends along.' So, you're interested in the Cherokee, are ya?"

Michael let Alesandra do the talking and sat back sipping his tea, glad to be on the shaded portion of the porch.

"Yes, sir. I'm doing a thesis on native dances, one dance in particular. I can't find the name of it, only a description. I'd really like to know the meaning behind its movements."

"Can you describe it for me?"

Trying not to divulge that it was a dream, she outlined the ceremony for him. "The dancers perform naked to the heavy rhythm of a drum in a circle around a young woman," she blushed. "They raise their arms high in a single motion and then reach down to pick up a handful of soil, then invite the woman to join them."

Bubba leaned back in his rocker. "That's not much to go on."

"I don't know much more than that."

"Did they sing or chant?"

"Yes, but I didn't really understand what they said."

Michael closed his eyes in anguish, and she realized her mistake.

"So, you've seen these dancers, haven't ya?" Bubba grinned.

"Uh, it was only in a dream, but it left a strong, lasting impression." She felt dismayed at how easily the older man tricked her. How could she have fallen into the trap?

"It's all right, little darlin'." He thought her a child in a woman's body, very impressionable, and he sought to learn more about her through friendly reassurance. Her male companion would be another matter.

"First, ya gotta understand the Indian. All tribes stem from the Old Ones, the Others. No one remembers their real name, but a branch descended from them are called 'Nicotani' or the Little People by the Cherokee. They're spiritual beings, not supernatural you understand, but very much a part of everyday life."

Michael interrupted. "You mean like the little people of Ireland? Leprechauns?"

"Yes, similar. They're invisible unless they wanna be seen, and the Indian fears 'em. To see one means a sure death within seven years. The Little People live in rock shelters, mountain caves, river thickets. They look like reg'lar folk, 'ceptin' they're much smaller with long hair that sometimes reaches the ground. They enjoy dancin' in a circle around a huge fire while the sound of a water drum keeps a steady rhythmic beat."

Alesandra's eyes widened as he described the dancing exactly as her dream unfolded.

Bubba continued, "A singer begins a chant which echoes among the dancers enticin' the younger tribal women to take off their clothes and join 'em."

"Why do the women have to remove their clothes?" she asked.

"Sandy," Michael groaned, exasperated.

Bubba took no notice. "It's a ceremony to carry on the tribe. The hot passion of the dance transfers itself to the women and makes 'em more, shall we say, 'receptive' to sexual desires. The Cherokee still observe that ritual in their pow wows."

She silently digested the story. "Mister Grubbs, why would I be having this dream?"

"I don't know the answer to that 'ceptin' to say that Little People are often mischievous and don't like bein' messed with. They're known to bother folks who interfere with 'em."

"But I, we haven't interfered with them. Why would they think something like that?"

"Sandy, you're taking this too seriously," Michael said.

"There's another way of lookin' at it, Missy," Bubba quickly interjected. "Could be they know about your visits inside their mountain. Could be you discovered somethin' sacred in there."

Sitting back, he watched the young couple exchange glances. He raised an eyebrow and continued. "Caves are dangerous, as you know, and maybe they don't want ya gettin' hurt. Little People like takin' care of their own kind."

"But I'm not their own kind."

"Think about it," he mused. "Here ya are in college spendin' a lot of time tryin' to learn about the Old Ones, and they, perhaps the Old Ones themselves, found out and adopted ya. Now they want ya to join 'em in body as well as in spirit."

He painted an eerie picture.

She shivered in spite of herself, and Michael became more impatient as the visit extended beyond his anticipated time limit. "Sandy, we've bothered Mister Grubbs long enough."

But Bubba was reluctant to see his guests leave. "Not at all, young fella. I'm happy as a speckled pup to have you folks drop in. I don't get many visitors out this way, and I haven't even told you about the prophecy yet."

Michael rolled his eyes, but Alesandra ignored him.

"I want to hear about the prophecy."

"Well, I don't hold much to it, mind ya," Bubba said in a somber, confidential tone. "Still, the Cherokee believe if a person takes somethin' from a cave where Little People gather, they're doomed to spend eternity locked up tight in the spirit world, unless–"

"Unless what, Mister Grubbs?" Alesandra's eyes grew large with wonder and anticipation.

"The red man swears the only way to get around that prophecy is to give what was taken to a tribal medicine man. He'll recite a special prayer and return the stolen object to where it rightfully belongs."

"I don't think we need to worry about the prophecy," said Michael.

"That's good. That's very good." Bubba stood up indicating the visit was at an end. "I just want the both of ya to know that I am a bona fide, genuine Cherokee medicine man, just in case. Ya never know when ya might need one."

The couple remained silent on the way back until they left the dusty gravel road and turned onto a paved highway. Looking at each other, they simultaneously burst out laughing.

Michael was relieved. “I thought you were falling for that hokum stuff he was feeding us.”

“No, of course not. But he does tell such delightful stories. I think he’s a very lonesome old man.”

“How can you say that? Didn’t you see that beautiful young woman he called his housekeeper?”

She giggled. “Anyway, I enjoyed our visit, although I am still a little puzzled about the circle dance.”

“I’m not at all puzzled. What he described was probably a typical rite in which the men selected sexual partners, not for marriage but for keeping the tribe supplied with babies. And he said the Cherokee perform that same dance in these modern times, so you better keep away from Cherokee men.”

“Are you afraid I might join in their dancing?” she teased.

“I was debating whether I should learn that dance myself.”

Revelations

She frowned, and Michael ran a thumb across her brow in an attempt to smooth it. They sat parked outside of McCord Hall, their journey drawn to a close. "I've dreamed about them twice now, Michael. I'm not normally carried away by the meaning of dreams, but I feel a strong bond with the dancers."

"I know you do, sweety. We'll find your answers. It may not happen today, or tomorrow, but we'll find them." He kissed her reassuringly.

As they strolled to the courtyard enclosed by Cooper Hall, she mulled over the information collected thus far. "Did I tell you Jared dropped some more information by the dorm for me yesterday? I thought that was rather nice of him, considering the fight we had."

"I thought you resolved that at the time."

"We did, but you know sometimes resentment can linger. Anyway, he went out of his way to keep searching for me, and I appreciate it. I just don't know where to turn next."

"What's your next step?"

"I need to delve deeper into the 'linguistic frontier' of pre-Olmec writings. Go where no man has gone before," she joked.

"Why don't you try Professor Blaney? I know it's not his specialty, but remember, he did extensive work in Central America before coming to UTM. He might be able to shed some light on things for you."

"Good idea. I'll call his office in the morning and make an appointment. Thanks for thinking of it, Pooh."

"Just trying to help, Piglet. He might not have the answers you need, but I think you should at least ask. Can't hurt. Just be careful how much you reveal. You're going to have to be more alert than you were with Mr. Grubbs."

"Gotcha."

Professor Blaney searched through the stacks of books lining the wall and finally pulled out two old, somewhat warped volumes. "In answer to your question there was a culture called the Jaredites that compares with the Olmecs."

"I'll bet Jared loves that. If he doesn't already know about them, please don't tell him. He's arrogant enough without claiming ownership to an entire society of people," she laughed.

He chuckled along with her at the jibe and continued in a more serious tone. "Without sounding too scholarly, the Jaredites left Babylonia at the time of the Tower of Babel when the languages were confounded. They arrived in Central America from the old world and were the first western civilization to develop a written language. The Jaredite nation, or Olmec, whether they were the same or separate, existed from 2200 to 600 BC. Their descendants were eventually destroyed in a great war and their people scattered northward into North America. Evidences of their civilization have been found as far north as Upstate New York."

"What about the term, 'The Others' used by the Cherokee today. Are the Jaredites who they're referring to?"

"I've heard that expression repeated by several different modern cultures," he replied. "It's pretty much a general definition for any people who preceded a current group, such as the Olmec or Jaredites."

"Did you find a connection between their symbols and an alphabetic language?"

He sat back and smiled. "Not personally," he said, "but one of the members of my team determined their symbols to be a link to specific words in a spoken language. One of our prize discoveries was a small cylinder seal with images inscribed in bas-relief on its surface."

She sat forward, captivated. "Really! I'd love to hear more about that."

"We found the seal, when inked, could be used to transfer images to other surfaces, much in the manner of a printing press."

Excitement rippled through her as she thought of the raised relief characters in the Chamber of Gods. "Professor, you mentioned a spoken language."

"Certain words and phrases carried over from Mayan and Aztec are still prevalent today in both Mexican and American Indian dialects."

"Would you say that a liberal translation is possible from Olmec to our language?" This was her primary question, and one for which she was eager to find an answer.

"Of course." He waited for her next question, but when she fell silent, he volunteered. "If you're seeking a translator, you could find none better, or nearer I might add, than Professor Delia McBride-Hart. I believe I mentioned her name before."

He sat back and studied the young woman. "Sandy, are you going to tell me what sparked all this interest? This is a little outside your normal realm of studies."

"Oh, well, I found a book in an antique store that had some intriguing markings in it. For some reason they seemed to really catch my attention. It's been sort of fun trying to translate them. I know it's not my major, but I'm considering taking a minor in it."

Blaney could tell by the way she looked everywhere but at him, that she was evading the truth, and he wondered why. What secrets could she possibly have regarding ancient writings that she couldn't tell him about?

"Well then, good luck to you, Miss Davis." He stood and opened the door to indicate the meeting had concluded.

"Okay," she grinned in surrender. "I'll go and see Miss Delia."

"I think you'll enjoy her. She's a southern lady through and through. UTM is fortunate to have her."

"Thanks, Professor. I'll call her office this afternoon."

Professor Hart, or Miss Delia, as she herself preferred, welcomed the attention of this young student, and arranged to see her early the next morning.

Sitting in her sunny, well organized office, Miss Delia greeted Alesandra and invited her to sit in a comfortable tapestry covered wing chair.

"I was just about to have some tea. Can I pour you a cup?" She lifted the dainty white tea pot with blue roses painted on it, and poured steaming liquid into a matching cup and saucer. Alesandra saw a second cup and saucer set on the tray and knew they were intended for her.

"That would be lovely, Miss Delia. Thank you. Cream, one sugar, please."

Miss Delia prepared it accordingly and passed it to the young woman. When they were settled comfortably with their cups in hand, the teacher asked, "Now, how may I help you?"

Alesandra explained with alacrity the details of her dream.

Delia noted the way the girl's eyes sparkled when she spoke of the dancing spirits, and nodded knowingly.

"Ceremonial circle dances are a familiar symbol. They are performed in a counter-clockwise direction accompanied by a steady drum beat. You may not know this, but dancing in clockwise circles is associated with witchcraft. Indians always go counter-clockwise. Nothing frightening about them, but it is strange you should have two such dreams."

"The dancers wanted me to do something, but I'm not certain exactly what it was."

Miss Delia was quiet for a moment. "You're the young woman from Professor Blaney's group who was trapped in the cave last spring, aren't you?"

"Yes, ma'am."

"I think you and your friend either found or experienced something unusual in that cave, something other than the cave-in, and it's troubling you."

"You're right. Of course you're right." Alesandra decided to trust the woman. "We discovered what appears to be inscribed glyphs on several stone pillars in one of the chambers. I believe they are Olmec in origin."

Miss Delia's eyes lit with excitement at the prospect. "Hmm, if that is true, it would be very exciting. Olmec monoliths have never been found in this area. I would be very interested in seeing them."

Alesandra opened her purse and removed the drawings, handing them over for inspection. "I traced these as best I could," she apologized. "I took actual charcoal rubbings of them. No one else knows they came from inside the cave." She felt a sense of eagerness as she watched Miss Delia study the drawings, intently comparing them, one against the other. At one point, she rose and walked to a glass-enclosed bookcase, retrieving a clothbound volume of loose pages.

"Come and take a look at this, Miss Davis."

"Oh, please, you can call me Sandy."

Miss Delia opened the book and explained. "This is one of my personal workbooks of literal translations from the Epi-Olmec or Mixe-Zaoquean language. Some common words are still spoken by their Gulf Coast descendants."

Side by side they sat, pouring over the word columns and examining the corresponding definitions.

Alesandra was amazed at the ease in which the translation charts were employed to decipher a portion of the symbols she traced in the cave. "I want to learn how to do this," she said. "Do you suppose it's too late to get into one of your classes?"

"My classes are all at maximum enrollment already, but if you can fit it into your schedule, I'd be glad to stretch the limit. I myself would love to see more of what you have. Possibly you would consider taking me to see them first hand someday?"

Alesandra smiled, feeling that she found more than a mentor in Miss Delia. She discovered a kindred spirit.

The professor was anxious to help. "Make copies of the basic translations," she suggested. "Study them thoroughly, and you should be able to know a few simple phrases."

"Miss Delia, do you use these charts in your classes?"

"Oh, yes. My students are quite familiar with them."

Alesandra gratefully tucked the folded charts in her purse.

"Thank you, Miss Delia. This has been a very informative visit, on many levels."

Alesandra handed Michael a dripping, cold can of Mountain Dew from the cooler in the back seat. He took a long drink before setting it in the cup holder. He felt her hand settle back on his knee and smiled. He liked the way she often set it there while they drove places together, and the mountain was still a few hours distant.

Alesandra relaxed, content Michael was keeping his word by returning for the soldier.

"Tell me more about your meeting with Miss Delia," he said. "We didn't get much chance to talk about it yesterday."

She eagerly shared the details of the interview. "With these translation charts and Miss Delia's assistance, I can work without Jared's help," she told Michael. "And when I stopped by the registrar's office yesterday at lunch, I was able to get into one of her classes. I'm glad the professor suggested her."

"Did you two figure anything out yet?"

"I stayed up half the night studying some of the more dominant features of the rubbings. One of the stone tablets appears to be of little historical interest from what I can tell. Another, however, contains references to *jama*, or spirit companions. I wonder if any other monoliths can be found in the cave."

He loved seeing her excited like this. She glowed with the prospect of a new discovery. "Well, we should have some time to look around. I don't think taking care of the soldier will take all weekend."

She sat back and fixed her eyes on the road ahead. "Lucky for us the football game was last night instead of today. You know, I can remember not long ago when I believed there was nothing in the world more important than making the cheerleading squad. But lately, I just seem to feel annoyed that games and practice take away from my time with the glyphs, and with you of course. I don't know what it is about that mountain, but I swear I feel it calling me."

When they left the paved highway and turned into the parking area a misty haze lay over the landscape sheltering the trails in a colorless camouflage.

"It's a good thing we know the way," she remarked.

Michael nodded as he shrugged his shoulders into the canvas harness of his knapsack before assisting her. "Yep, looks like the clouds are a little low today."

With the sun barely visible, he led the way around the mountainside. The mist dissipated swiftly and normal sounds of the woodland returned. It was a friendly trail now, and old familiar landmarks were recognized on either side. The two chattered happily until the disguised cave entrance loomed before them.

With practiced agility, they squeezed through the opening to find the knotted rope waiting to assist their descent. When they were both safely at the bottom, Alesandra reached out and clasped his hand.

"It's like a homecoming," she said.

"I know. I feel it too." Cool air brushed his face, and he reached up to turn on his helmet light.

They walked with a surety, familiar with the tunnels now, and quickly entered the chamber they sought. Their lamps focused on the seven stone pillars from which the glyphs had been copied. Alesandra allowed her light to stray elsewhere searching for something, anything possibly overlooked previously.

"I just can't believe these people left only the seven columns behind," she said. "There must be other signs of their existence here."

"Maybe they did leave something, and someone else found it." He tried to be realistic and at the same time, supportive. Curving an arm around her shoulders, he told her, "Don't be disappointed if we can't find what you're looking for."

"I don't know what I'm looking for, Michael. But those monoliths were placed here for a reason, and I want to know why."

She turned her attention to the individual columns. "They are so evenly spaced from each other they must have been positioned this way on purpose. Remember the first time we ever saw them? We were both struck with the impression that it was an altar of some sort. I think maybe our first instincts were right." As she peered through the darkness, disappointment was evident in her voice. "I'm sure they've left more. Why can't I find it?"

"Sandy, this chamber is just one room. Why don't we methodically investigate all the rooms and tunnels adjacent to the large cavern."

She smiled in appreciation of his support, although he failed to see it in the dark. "Thank you, Michael. You check along this wall, and I'll take the other one."

The Chamber of Gods revealed nothing further, so the couple headed into the larger chamber where they slept on past visits, and began their search. Minutes turned into hours, as more than once she loudly claimed a discovery only to rescind it after learning its true nature. Low murmuring moans and eerie banshee wails entertained as if ghosts cavorted around the limestone formations.

"Sandy?"

"I'm here." She stepped out from a small antechamber.

"I think you'd better see this," he called through the opening at the end of the soldier's tunnel, unable to hide the excitement in his voice. As she crawled under the barrier, she saw him standing at the fissure, the glow from within illuminating his face. He pulled her closer and aimed his light through the widened crevice.

She sidled in next to him. "Isn't this the chamber with your glowing rocks?"

"Yes, look above them." He pointed to the side wall.

Craning her neck, she perused the smooth wall where his light shone. Immediately above the glowing rocks, she saw it and caught her breath sharply in exhilaration.

"Time may have diminished the full scope, but I'd say we're clearly looking at paintings made by human artists."

Alesandra turned and threw her arms around his neck for a brief moment before turning back to scrutinize the artwork. "I knew it. This art has survived for nearly two thousand years! See the reptilian fish with large fangs or teeth? Just look at the green and red colors."

"These drawings would never have survived if they hadn't been in an area of the dry cave system." He cocked his head as he puzzled, "The thing I can't figure out, is how did anyone get into the chamber to draw them? There is no entryway."

Scripted symbols below the painting motif caught her attention. She stared for several moments, studying them. "I think I can read these. From what Miss Delia taught me, these symbols represent a warning message."

"What kind of warning? What does it say?"

"Death is a prominent sign. It reads something to the effect of 'Death to he who disturbs the eternal stones.'"

Michael was deep in thought. "Are you sure about the stones part?"

"Well, no. I'm not absolutely certain, but that's what I make it out to be."

Alesandra busied herself in photographing the wall painting. "I'll show these to Miss Delia when we get back. She might be able to tell us something about the message too. I don't see how we missed this the last time we looked at this chamber."

"Probably because it's not on the wall directly across from us. You have to turn your head at a funny angle to get a good look. It's easier because I've widened the opening. Besides, those rocks are a little beyond distracting in their own right."

Satisfied they had not overlooked anything else, they crossed the cavern and crawled back beneath the barrier, happily turning their attention to the Confederate soldier in the passageway. They found him just as they left him, a seemingly insignificant lump of discarded rags.

"I feel so sad," she sighed, "knowing he has been here all this time, alone and forgotten by friends and family." She knelt beside him while a lone tear trickled down her cheek.

Michael put his arm around her. "You know, Sandy, we can do something about that if we can just identify him. Let's get the body bag out."

"Sure," she rose to her feet. "I'll go get it."

She hurried to the main chamber where their equipment lay piled at the end of the room and quickly returned with the bag and Michael's backpack.

"Okay, I'm going to move his arms and hands onto the top of the uniform, so they don't fall off when we try to lift him." He carefully lifted the decaying sleeves trying to keep the appendages intact. As the bones shifted inside the tunic, they heard an odd rustling sound.

"I've never heard bones sound like that," she commented. "Is there something inside?"

Michael carefully unbuttoned the soldier's gray uniform tunic. Reaching inside, he retrieved a black, age-wrinkled notebook with penciled entries. Folded neatly within was a letter with faded but legible handwriting.

“I don’t know why we didn’t find these earlier.”

“Because we didn’t look close enough, that’s why,” she replied.

He shook his head in disbelief. “Some investigators we turned out to be.”

“Well, at least we were smart enough to come back looking for more. Let me have the letter, and you can read the diary, if that’s what it is.”

He handed her the letter but before they could open either item, the sound of approaching voices echoed across the adjoining cavern and carried through the passage as they grew louder.

“Douse your light, Sandy, and be very quiet,” he whispered as he grabbed hold of the body bag, dragging it with him into the shadows.

She needed no further urging. They tried to wedge themselves beneath the small outcropping, hoping it would provide them with adequate camouflage. Holding their breath, they awaited whoever else was in the cave with them.

A Soldier's Letter

Jack, as usual, assumed the lead position as he and Red maneuvered through the low-ceilinged tunnels and narrowed passageways. His massive torso literally filled the tunnel space providing little opportunity for his partner to see past him. Afraid of being left behind, Red followed closely, keeping his eyes focused on the cave's uneven flooring.

They worked well together. Former cellmates at Brushy Creek and now Bubba's right hand men, they took their duties seriously although their jobs were relatively simple.

"Keep the mountain free from trespassers," they were told, "and keep your mouths shut while doin' it."

Bubba provided room and board at the farmhouse in addition to a paycheck, but they preferred the freedom of the woodlands. The main cave offered suitable accommodations for overnight stays. It was dry, out of the weather, and except for occasional Indian acquaintances, away from prying neighbors.

Their primary responsibility, as they understood it, was to run the still while ensuring the seclusion of the boss' private vault deep within the mountain. Its contents remained a mystery to them, even though they had constructed a retaining wall around it.

The natural sounds emanating from inside the caves unnerved Red at times even though he was accustomed to hearing them. Reaching out, he clutched at Jack's arm, halting him.

"What was that," he asked.

"What was what? Are you hearing things again?" Jack pulled his arm away, frowning.

A distant sound echoed throughout the tunnels, and Red felt grateful the dark hid his jitters. "I keep thinking somebody is sneaking around in here," he complained.

"How many times do I gotta tell you, Red. It's only the wind or a fallin' rock. That's what you hear. How can anybody get in here without us knowin' about it?"

"Don't forget those two college boys. They found their way in somehow."

"But we took care of 'em, didn't we?"

"Yeah, we did, and if they ever show up again, I'll toss 'em down in that old Devil's Chasm."

Conversation ebbed as they turned a corner and entered a small chamber. "It ain't much farther now," Jack said over his shoulder.

"I think we're wasting our time coming down here so much."

His partner grunted. "Hummph, that's what we're paid to do, so stop grumbling."

Michael tucked himself as tightly around Alesandra as he could, pressing her out of sight under the outcropping. Footsteps resounded through the adjoining chamber, and tension made the young couple hold their breath, afraid the slightest sound might give them away. He squeezed her hand, and they both mentally crawled further into the protective darkness to wait until the danger passed.

Michael kept watch through the low hole at the end of the tunnel. He saw the light from their flashlights growing stronger as they drew closer. To his relief they passed without hesitation by the entrance to the tunnel he and Alesandra lay.

Voices echoed through the spacious cavern, loud enough to be heard.

"I told you, Red. Ain't nobody here."

"Well, might as well check things out while we're here. Save us from comin' back later."

Alesandra felt herself crushed against the rock from head to toe as the men passed by their tunnel. When the footsteps receded, they relaxed ever so slightly but remained hidden. Michael waited until he felt certain the men were gone before he rolled out from their hiding niche, pulling her with him.

"Aren't those the same men who were with Mr. Grubbs when we met him at the waterfall?" she asked.

"Yes, and I'm pretty sure one was the guy who attacked me outside the lab."

Her eyes grew larger, and her whispering became more audible. "And your stolen knapsack was recovered by Brandon and Lewis from these caves. I wonder what it all means."

His fingertips searched for her lips in the darkness, and he gently pressed against them to silence her. "Ssh. It means, my dear, that Mr. Bubba Grubbs is not the simple kind-hearted hillbilly he pretends to be."

She digested that for a moment. "Uh huh. Not only that," she added, "but I don't think he's a genuine, bonafide Cherokee medicine man either."

"No kidding." He rolled his eyes in exasperation, grateful she couldn't see him in the dark.

"What do you suppose they're doing in here?"

"Nothing good, I'm sure." He wanted to follow them, to learn more about their hijinx. Feeling Alesandra's hand grasp his arm reminded him that doing so would endanger her. He knew first hand the hired thugs did not tread lightly.

Keeping a wary eye on the direction taken by the two men, Michael unzipped his jacket and slipped the soldier's journal and letter inside his shirt for safekeeping.

"Those two men showing up in here means there's another way, maybe a better one, out of these caves, which we are going to need to get the soldier out. None of the aragonite crystals were disturbed the first time we came in here, so they must use a different route."

"Sure, they probably come and go in here all the time. But how do we know where to look?"

He hastily debated the options again and decided in consideration of the task ahead, the chance of exposure was necessary. "Well, it's kinda risky but we follow them and see where they lead us."

"We can't track them while carrying the soldier."

"No, we don't have time to take him right now. We've got to get on their tail before we lose them. I'll mark the trail like I did the day of the cave-in. That way we'll easily find our way back here to get him."

She bristled at the idea but was unable to offer an alternative plan. "What if they spot us?"

"Let's not think about that. We'll stay close enough to see their light without letting them see us."

"I'm scared, Pooh," her voice trembled, barely above a whisper.

Michael wrapped her in his arms and offered her what little security he could. "I know, Piglet. But I'd feel better with us on their tail than them on ours."

Michael tucked the soldier's sidearm in his backpack for safekeeping, then deftly unfastened the belt with scabbard and sword and secured it around his own waist. Taking a small bungey cord from the side pocket on his backpack, he secured the lower section of the scabbard just above his knee.

"What are you doing?"

"Protection. Just in case."

"Why are you strapping it to your leg like that?"

"So it doesn't bang against the rocks and tunnels and give us away. Come on, Sandy," he tugged her to her feet.

"He thinks he's Captain Jack Sparrow from *Pirates*," she muttered. "Lead on my swashbuckling hero."

He put a finger to her lips to shush her as he noticed the play of light returning in the chamber beyond. Waiting until the men were safely past them on their way back out, the students quickly slid under the rock barrier in pursuit. They scooted across the large chamber and detected the reflection of Jack's lamp in the depths of a tunnel extending from the north end of the room.

Michael gripped her fingers and whispered, "We're only going to use one light. Move as quietly as you can."

With her heart pounding in her ears and dread clutching at her throat, she held Michael's hand as they trailed behind Bubba's men. He paused to quickly arrange his trail signs using stones at each juncture.

Catching occasional sight of Jack's flickering lamp ahead, they emerged into a spacious cavern. They quietly scampered across the room and followed the light into another passageway which took them on an upward slope. When the ground leveled out again, they wove through a number of quick twists and turns. Alesandra was glad Michael was marking the way, certain she'd never find her way back otherwise.

Suddenly, a beam turned back in their direction. They ducked into a small crevice, barely large enough for both to squeeze into. As the men neared, the glow from their lamp became brighter and their words more easily distinguishable.

"Jack, I swear I heard somethin' back here."

"All right, but I'm tellin' you it was only the mountain makin' its peculiar sounds. You prob'ly heard one of these overhead rocks fallin'. Happens all the time, and you should be used to it by now."

"I ain't never gonna get used to all the noises in these caves. They sound worse than in prison."

"Yeah, well you don't wanna go back, do you? Now quit with the nonsense. We're late, and we gotta meet the boss in town."

Michael and Alesandra slipped from their hiding place and resumed their quest as the men retreated again, their lanterns bobbing up and down.

The journey ended at a large room illuminated from the outside. They observed a pile of bones in the center of the room with sleeping bags and a large, homemade, white lightening still.

"Looks like they live in here," she noted.

"Yeah, that's not all they do." Michael hurried to the open entrance. "They're gone. I think we can easily bring our soldier out here."

"Let's hurry before those men come back."

"I don't think we need to worry about that. They said they're going to town. Let's just do it, and get out of here."

No need for caution now, they swiftly headed back into the depths of the cave system to gather their equipment and the soldier. Carefully, they lifted the uniform and remains into the body bag and zipped it closed. Michael donned his backpack, and they lifted the body bag by the handles and retraced their steps.

He led the way, watching for his trail markers until they emerged from the mountain into daylight through the newly found opening. He pulled his compass from the side pouch on his backpack and quickly checked their direction.

"I think we need to go this way, Sandy," he pointed toward a small copse of trees. "Hopefully we'll find some familiar landmarks soon."

"Between our usual entrance and the waterfall, we passed several false cave openings. We can leave the soldier in one of those."

"That's the plan. Problem is, we don't know how far we are from the old opening."

"He isn't really heavy, Michael. Just a bit awkward."

"Okay. We'll manage all right."

The trail they followed was unfamiliar but a sense of urgency compelled them onward. They needed to find a suitable location for the soldier's body and be long gone before Bubba's men discovered their presence.

While on their way to the cave earlier, they observed several likely places to leave the soldier. There did not seem to be any false caves now that they had him in tow. Several times they needed to stop and rest with their cumbersome bundle. They almost passed their usual entrance without noticing it.

"It really is well concealed," she remarked.

Once again on familiar ground, their spirits lifted, and they trudged ahead, hopeful of finding a resting place for their soldier. They investigated several possibilities before selecting an appropriate one.

"This one looks good." He had gone alone to inspect the small indentation above an outcropping ledge in the rock face. Relief was evident in her eyes, and they hurried to hoist the body bag into place.

"I think we should put him as far back into the cave as we can. That's where he would have crawled if he had actually died here, and would justify no one ever finding him before us."

"Okay, Sandy. That sounds reasonable."

With a little effort and a copy of *Gray's Anatomy* in hand, the soldier was lying in approximately the same position they found him in the cave. "Even if we don't have him laid out perfectly, animals would have disturbed the bones in this location anyway." Michael moved some rocks to offer a natural looking barricade, helping to conceal the remains.

When finished, Alesandra knelt beside him. "Soldier, I'm sorry, but this is the best we can do for you at the moment. We're going to try and find your family, so you can get a decent burial."

"Sandy, after all these years–"

"I don't care. It's what he deserves. We can at least try."

Silence between them became prolonged, and he recognized the determination in her voice. "Yes, honey. We can try."

They turned to head out of the cave when she stopped him. "Wait a minute. The sword. And the gun."

"What about them?"

"You forgot to leave them with him."

"I'm not leaving the sword behind."

She quirked her mouth and gave him a puzzled expression. "Well, what are you going to do with it?"

"I'm gonna keep it."

"Whatever for?"

"Never mind, Sandy. It's a guy thing."

"What about the gun?"

"Geez, it's not a gun. It's a Colt .44 revolver."

She rolled her eyes and tugged him along. "Come on. It's getting late."

After a quick journey back inside to the Chamber of Gods to retrieve the remainder of their gear, they resurfaced to find the sky overhead transformed into a panorama of colors, and shadows from the mountain advanced across the landscape. The sun prepared to drop below the horizon, and they had yet to descend the mountain.

Darkness overtook them as they reached the Jeep. "It's too late to start back now," Michael said. "Why don't we spend the night at that motel we stayed at when we came with Blaney?"

"That's fine with me. I'm tired anyway."

After a light supper, they retired to their room exhausted. She lay on the bed and closed her eyes only to bound up quickly as she remembered the soldier's journal and letter.

"Do you want to look at them now? Can't it wait until morning when we're not so beat?"

"I'm not too tired to read his letter."

He retrieved it from the pocket of his backpack where he put it upon checking in at the motel. She lay it flat on the bed, gingerly touching it so as not to damage the aged paper.

"It's a letter to his wife," she said. "Listen to what he says." She looked to make sure he was paying attention.

"My Dear Emmaline. It has been a long time since I've had an opportunity to write you, and this may be my last letter until I can once again hold you in my arms. We just returned from a raid into Missouri. I will tell you all about it after I look into your eyes and show you how much I have missed you."

She paused and dabbed at her eye with a tissue.

"Sandy, if you're going to get all teary-eyed over this letter, you better let me read it."

She shook her head and continued.

"I never wanted to see you as bad as I do right now. The war isn't going well for us, and we are holed up waiting for new orders. We lost some of the boys I enlisted with at Lenoir City. John Barstow and Rufus Goode fell at Elizabethtown. I saw James Owens take a minnie ball in his shoulder and bleed to death before he could reach the hospital tent. You remember him from the dance just before he and I transferred into the 7th Kentucky."

Again she hesitated. "It's so sad knowing he never made it home to see his wife."

Michael reached out and took her hand in his. "A lot of soldiers never made it home."

"I know, but I feel as if we know this one personally."

Turning her attention back to the letter, she went on.

"Only a few of us Tennessee boys are left. These Kentuckians are a lot like us, and the Colonel is a damn fine fellow. He rides a mean horse and is always out in front of the fight."

She stopped and gently refolded the unfinished letter along the crease lines. "That's all he wrote, and his name doesn't appear anywhere. How will we ever find out who he was?"

Clearing his throat, Michael announced. "He was 2nd Lieutenant Peter Crumpleton, born in Sweetwater, Tennessee, on June 22, 1843 and participated in the battle of Fort Donelson, among others."

She stared at him, stunned. "How do you know all that?"

He grinned. "I peeked at his journal."

Family Reunion

It was a typical small notebook issued to officers in the field. Once covered in black leather but now cracked and flaking, it showed the ravages of more than a hundred and forty years of neglect. A small oval with the initials "CSA" in light gray was prominently displayed. Inside appeared the handwritten signature of 2nd Lieutenant Peter Crumpleton. The journal contained only a few pages, none of them dated, but it related the tale of the Lieutenant's brief service with Morgan's Raiders.

Michael, in a soft voice showing reverence for the moment, read while Alesandra listened intently.

"We returned from the Missouri raid in good fettle and high spirits. It was my first taste of battle with Morgan's Raiders, and the smell of gunpowder was strong enough to choke a mule. We took the Yankees by surprise and kilt the entire column, taking their field rations along with bullion. Major Beauregard had assumed temporary command and praised our action because the Confederacy dearly needs every bit of it.

"We hid it all in a mountain cave until such time as we can transport it south. My troops are charged with protecting it until our campaign is over here in Tennessee. We will remain in this vicinity for some time to recruit additional horses and men."

Michael thumbed through the journal. "The rest is filled with other military excursions but I don't see anything else about the gold."

"Read the final entry, Michael. What does he write there?"

"Okay, let's see. 'The regiment is breaking up because of the amnesty offer. Many of the men are taking their mounts and heading out to sign the papers because they want to go home. My unit has been relieved from the mountain, but I have been personally ordered to dynamite the cave.'" He leafed through the remainder of the journal but found only blank pages. "That's the last entry he made."

"If he did blow up the cave, maybe he got caught in it and died from the explosion."

He pondered the idea before answering. "I don't believe he ever got to fulfill that order. We never saw any evidence of an explosion. Something like that would reverberate through those tunnels and cause a whole lot of damage. I think there's a good chance the gold is still in there somewhere."

"If that's true, it must be well hidden because it doesn't look like a lot of people have been searching for it."

"That's something else I'll have to tell the government," he said, then added, "but only if they ask." He noticed Sandy's eyes had closed and leaned to kiss her. "Come on, baby. Let's go to bed."

At breakfast the next morning, Alesandra let her eyes stray across the restaurant. "I wonder if there are any Crumpletons in this area."

Michael sipped his coffee. "It's possible, but our Lieutenant was from Sweetwater. That's almost a hundred miles east of here."

The waitress appeared laden with two platters filled with bacon, eggs, home fries and toast. Her gray hair hung in a tidy braid down her back.

Michael smiled and had his fork ready before the plate was even set down before him. "Thanks."

"You're welcome. Enjoy."

"Can I ask you something?" Sandy queried.

"Sure."

"Have you ever heard of anyone with the name Crumpleton in this area?"

"Can't say as I have, and I've lived here all my life."

Alesandra looked disappointed. "Okay, thanks."

The waitress stood appraising them, her eyes narrowing slightly. "Aren't you the two kids that got caught in that cave-in last spring?"

"Yup, that's us," Michael agreed between bites.

"Thought I recognized you. I was up the mountain cooking for the rescue workers. A young gal by the name of Susan helped. Friend of yours, I presume."

"Yes, she's my best friend," Alesandra smiled. "Thanks for helping.

We both appreciate it more than you can ever know."

"Just glad you both got out without serious injury." She stuck her hand out. "My name's Martha Sue. Breakfast is on the house. Remember me to Susan. She was a great gal."

The young couple smiled. "Wow, thanks, Martha Sue. That's so nice of you. And, yes, we'll be happy to remember you to Susan."

Smiling, the waitress left their table to hand menus to a table of customers being seated.

Michael happily ate while Alesandra fretted over her soldier. "You know we have to go to Sweetwater now."

"I was afraid you were going to say that."

"It's only a few hours away, and we can make it back to campus before dark. Neither of us have classes today. Please?"

He smiled. "Well, do I at least get to finish my coffee?"

"Of course. But hustle. Time's a-wastin'."

Following road signs, they drove through several small towns, across creeks with odd names and lakes on which early-rising fishermen were trying their luck. It took longer than Michael thought before they crossed over the Tennessee River and entered Monroe County. The little town of Sweetwater lay directly ahead.

"Let's ask at the post office first." Her excitement began to effervesce at the prospect of finding their soldier's family.

A customer standing at a nearby counter placing stamps to a stack of envelopes overheard their conversation and remarked, "You might be referring to the Whitten place off the Niota Road. I think Mrs. Whitten is a Crumpleton."

"That's right," the clerk agreed. "Her place has a long driveway flanked by a white cross rail fence and a row of Juniper's lining the laneway leading to the house. She calls it Rolling Hills Farm. Ya cain't miss it."

Taking note of the directions, Michael drove across the Interstate and followed the Niota Road until Alesandra recognized the long unpaved driveway, just as it was described.

"There it is," she pointed.

The fence on either side managed to keep the few heads of cattle from straying onto the roadway, but its paint flaked badly and obviously needed some repair. A mailbox bearing the name "Whitten" stood at the edge of the lane, about a hundred yards from the house. Michael turned in, and the Jeep was accompanied the full distance by a large barking dog. Alesandra leaned closer to Michael as they pulled into the front yard to be greeted by a young man in a straw hat and bib overalls with grease streaks where he apparently kept wiping his hands.

"Howdy, folks," he waved as he appeared from the other side of a tractor with a monkey wrench in his hand. "Can I he'p y'all?"

Michael stepped out of the Jeep, and they shook hands. "We're looking for members of the Crumpleton family," he said. "We may have some information about a long lost relative from the Civil War."

"Ya don't say! The Civil War, huh? That was a purty long time ago, wasn't it?"

"Yes," Michael chuckled.

"Well, come on up to the house and you can talk to Me Maw about it. Tell your lady friend she's welcome too."

Alesandra opened the passenger door and stepped out to be met and sniffed by the scruffy-looking dog.

"Pay him no mind, Missy. Bo is a good dawg, and is just sayin' 'how'ja do'. He ain't hardly ever bit nobody." To Michael he added, "His name's really Bosephus, but he answers to Bo."

He clapped his hands together, and the dog obediently dropped to the ground.

As they approached the house, the screen door swung open and out stepped a spry little lady in her sixties, wiping her hands on an apron. "Sakes alive, I thought I heard a car door out here," she said.

"This is Me Maw," said the young man. "By the way, I'm Jesse."

"Thank you, Jesse." Michael faced the woman. "It's nice to meet you, Mrs. Whitten."

He introduced himself and Alesandra, and they were invited into the house. They found the living room tastefully furnished, with a stone fireplace and a black piano displaying an array of photographs.

"We're always happy to have folks stop by," she said as they made themselves comfortable. "I don't believe we've met before."

"No, ma'am. The truth is, we've come to locate relatives of a Confederate soldier who never made it home after the war. His name was Peter Crumpleton. Someone at the post office said they thought that was your maiden name."

"No, actually it was my mother's maiden name. My own husband, bless his soul, passed away two years ago. Paw Paw left me and our grandson Jesse, but we have a good many close family members around to keep us company. Some, but only a few, still carry the Crumpleton name."

Alesandra explained how they found the soldier's body still in his army uniform and identified him from papers in his possession. "He apparently enlisted here in Sweetwater and served in the 7th Kentucky Cavalry. We're hoping to find his descendants so we can tell them where to find the body."

Me Maw's eyes lit with surprise at the news, but she curbed her enthusiasm. "I think Tildy is the one you need to tell about this. She takes care of the family tree. Hold on a minute, and we'll get her." She yelled for Jessie.

"Ma'am!"

"Call your Aunt Tildy, and tell her we have us some folks here who want to talk about the Crumpleton family history."

"Yes, ma'am."

"If I know my sister, she'll be here in two shakes. She's always lookin' up stuff about the old days."

As predicted, Aunt Tildy, a bustling woman with white hair and busy hands, soon arrived with a car loaded down with assorted kinfolk, fried chicken, potato salad, black eyed peas, a sweet tater pie, and a strong desire to talk to the two young visitors about the older Crumpletons.

Michael and Alesandra were amused to note a continuous stream of new faces trickling into view as though a general call had gone out to converge at the Whitten place. They arrived in several cars and pickup trucks, and the front yard quickly converted into a parking lot.

Everyone moved outside where four picnic tables were soon laden with food and goodies. Jugs of lemonade and sweet tea were continually replenished. People scattered across the yard with tablecloths spread out on the grass. The grape arbor provided a pleasantly shaded area where anyone could simply reach overhead for a handful of juicy grapes from large, full clusters.

Me Maw directed the assemblage, and it was readily apparent she was in her proper element. This was obviously not the first dinner on the ground manufactured at a moment's notice.

Aunt Tildy was the unofficial historian for the family. She came equipped with charts, lineages, anecdotes and scrapbooks, and presided over the occasion. Waving for Michael and Alesandra to join her on a large blue gingham tablecloth, she spread out her accumulated materials.

Once the children stopped running and screaming across the yard, and the food and dishes miraculously disappeared, the grownups gathered around to hear about Peter Crumpleton.

"Mind you," Aunt Tildy said, "we're not at all unfamiliar with him. I have an old photograph of the two of them on their weddin' day."

She presented a small oval photograph of a man and woman standing side by side. The woman in the picture wore a lace fischu with a small cameo suspended from a white ribbon tied at her throat. Her hair was pulled back and tucked into a snood with a ringlet hanging in front of each ear. The young gentleman sported a large moustache drooping at each end. His high cut vest topped by a frock coat looked dapper. He held a top hat in the curve of his right arm, while the woman's hand was daintily tucked into his left.

Alesandra felt tears brim in her eyes as she beheld the face of the young soldier who had come to mean so much to her. Eagerly, she told the gathered clan what little they knew of the life of Peter Crumpleton. A hush fell upon the congregated family when she extracted the yellowed pages from her purse.

"My dear Emmaline," she read aloud. The opening words shot like electricity through the coterie.

"Well, I swan!" cried Tildy. "It's true. This is Granny Em's soldier she waited for, and he never came home."

A buzz went around as Tildy explained. "They were married for only a month when his unit was activated, and he left for the war. She kept watch for him the rest of her life."

"That's right," someone else joined in. "She used to set in her front porch rocker ever night, a-lookin' and a-prayin' for him, and a-tellin' her little baby about the daddy he would never know."

"What does his letter say," someone asked.

Alesandra read from it. "I saw James Owens take a minnie ball in his shoulder and bleed to death before he could reach the hospital tent. You remember him from the dance just before he and I transferred into the 7th Kentucky."

"Wasn't James Owens the one who wanted to dance with Granny Em and Grampa Peter hit him with his fist? Knocked him clean over the horse trough."

Alesandra smiled, enjoying the tales of their soldier. "And Granny Em really spent the rest of her life waiting for him to come home? That's so sweet, and so sad. She must have loved him very deeply to never give up hope."

Michael told them, "He belonged to one of the fiercest Confederate Cavalry regiments of the war. Morgan's Raiders attacked Northern forces behind the lines and were often chosen to escort President Davis on his inspection rounds."

Aunt Tildy added how strange it was that no one was able to learn what happened to him. "A lot of the soldiers drifted home one by one, but old Grampa Peter warn't one of 'em. We're grateful to the both of you for a-tellin' us what became of him. I wonder how we go about bringin' him home for burial?"

Michael suggested, "There's a local chapter in Knoxville of the Sons of Confederate Veterans. Why don't you contact them? I'm sure they would help recover the body."

"I'll do it," said Aunt Tildy. "If you'll write out directions where his body can be found, I'll get in touch with them. They might even want to hold a ceremony in his honor."

"That's a possibility." Michael wrote the directions and handed them to her. "It may be difficult to find, even with these instructions. I've written my name and number down here at the bottom," he pointed. "That mountain is littered with caves. If they want my help, I'll be happy to meet them and take them to the one Peter's resting in." It was with great reluctance that Michael finally looked at his watch. "I'm afraid we have to start for home. We have a long drive ahead of us."

The couple said their goodbyes, shaking hands and being hugged by all in attendance. Even Bo came to the Jeep to lay his head against her before they drove away.

"I wish we didn't have to leave so soon," she told Michael. "They seem like nice people."

"I think so. Well, girl, you accomplished what you wanted. And they were happy to see us, I think."

They turned from the long laneway onto the Niota road. Alesandra closed her eyes, thinking of the many faces they just met. "There must have been thirty people or more gathered around, and all of them, or nearly all of them, descended from our Johnny Reb soldier and his Emmaline."

The miles sped by, and the hours confided the distance they traveled. Headlights from passing cars became hypnotic, and the two fell silent with only the radio keeping them company. The soft music lulled her into a warm and fuzzy feeling, and she reached her hand across to lie on his thigh. He, in turn, was satisfied with the day's events, but even more so with having her next to him.

Night had long since fallen when they arrived at the university. Michael parked the Jeep, and they walked hand-in-hand toward their dorms. Reaching Alesandra's building, they pressed their bodies close together in an embrace, their lips finding each other as they caressed and whispered words that lovers share. Finally they parted, each going their own way.

The moonless night cast lengthening shadows across the campus, producing bizarre and unrecognizable shapes shifting from one moment to the next. From the protective seclusion of the darkness, a man emerged lighting a cigarette in his cupped hands.

Max Dugan slowly exhaled a long thin stream of smoke as he observed the tender scene.

A Confidence Betrayed

The two-story brick house with tudor-styling on Mockingbird Lane resembled others in the neighborhood with respect to size and elegance. Comfortable, richly upholstered couches befitted the bachelor who owned them.

Although a professor's salary was not astronomical, Carl Blaney accrued more than a modest nest egg giving him financial security. Still a young man, he joined the University of Tennessee with the intent of retaining his tenure until retirement.

Blaney's post graduate studies were reflected in the Aztec and Mayan replicas on the walls and mantles of his home. Not a rah-rah type of individual, he exhibited his school ties by displaying a small banner in his den showing the UTM colors: royal blue, orange and white.

The Blaney Bunch originated from his habit of conducting frequent excursions to field sites. While his intent was for them to uncover additional artifacts, he occasionally salted the digging areas to whet lagging appetites. Various sciences were represented by the members, and several went on to establish successful careers.

Along with the home, he inherited a housekeeper. Mrs. Watanabe, a woman of Oriental descent, instinctively knew his needs without specific request or demand. She maintained an immaculate household and supervised the cooking and catering for his occasional guests with maximum efficiency and minimum effort.

Being a private person, Blaney naturally avoided the social party atmosphere of university life. However, he frequently hosted a Friday poker game for his most intimate friends such as Jacob Turner, John Winthrop, of the Mathematics Department, geology professor, Colin

Curtis, and Chancellor Galen Jeffreys.

The Blaney Bunch gathered at his home for a burger bash and pool party on Saturday afternoon. Scrambling out of their vehicles like school children wildly galloping to recess, they rushed through the front door without bothering to knock, towels across their shoulders and boom boxes under their arms, heading noisily straight to the pool.

"Hey! Mrs. Watanabe," the professor asked, "did you open the gate and let these uncivilized hellions in?"

She threw her hands into the air as if to disavow any blame for the intrusion. "No, sir, professor-san. They alla samo samo take over house. I no have nothing to say."

The girls shed the clothes worn over top of their swimsuits and kicked off their sandals. Valerie jumped off the diving board, and rose to the surface behind Brandon. Lewis filled the pool with various toys: a ball, an inner tube, and a few styrofoam noodles. Susan chose the slower method of entry, down the steps in the shallow end.

Alesandra came to stand next to Michael at the side. "You don't have your suit on."

"No, I don't think I'll go in yet. But don't let that stop you. Go ahead. Have a good time. I think I'll just sit over there and get some sun."

"You sure that's what you want to do, Michael Stanley Gant?"

"Yup."

Before he could stop her, she tucked her fingers into the back pocket of his jeans, flicked his wallet out onto a nearby chair, and jumped into the deep end, pulling him along with her.

When he thrashed his way to the top, he found her grinning unabashedly at him.

"Geez, Sandy, what is it with you and water? You're not a safe combination."

She giggled and looped her arms around his neck while he reached for the wall. "I just didn't want you to miss out." Her legs wrapped securely around his waist. "You look so sexy when you're wet," she whispered in his ear.

He gave her a lopsided grin, and tightened an arm behind her back. "Then I suppose I'll have to forgive you, won't I?"

Smiling, she nodded and kissed him.

The sound of squealing alerted Blaney to look just in time to see Lewis running headlong toward the pool. He shouted at him, "Lewis! Don't do a ..."

Splassssh!

"... cannonball."

The resultant wave drenched everyone in the vicinity of the pool. Miss Delia, accompanied by Jim Dougherty, Associate Professor of Mathematics, chose that moment to come through the back gate and was greeted by the spray of water dousing her. Delia laughed melodically as she looked down and saw her white lacy bra showing through her now wet blouse.

Leading the way around the deck chairs, she turned to talk over her shoulder. "Come on this way, Jim. Looks like we're just in time for dinner."

Blaney tried to include at least one faculty member in his gatherings. Miss Delia was known by many of the group, while Jim Dougherty, on the other hand, was a first year faculty member at UTM and remained in the background, safe from the wisecracking and joking that prevailed. He considered Blaney's Bunch to be immature and unamusing, but he was there as a favor.

Mrs. Watanabe bustled about bringing out the hamburgers already nestled in their poppy-seed buns, along with a variety of salads, baked beans, deviled eggs and cola drinks. Ringing a bell, she called out, "Come get it, or I feed to hungry children in Mongolia."

First to reach the table, Brandon flipped open the lid of the ice-filled cooler. "Prof," he complained, "I don't see any beer to go with these eggs."

It brought a quick retort. "That's cause you're a delinquent, and I don't serve juveniles."

Jared and Max played a game of eight ball rather than swim. Trailing water in his wake, Lewis left the pool for the first round of food.

Max towered over the diminutive housekeeper, his empty plate in hand as he looked over the feast. "As always, Mrs. W., you've put together a great spread."

She frowned in jest. "No make smooth talk," she said. "Best to eat before other hoodlums steal table." She nodded her head at Lewis, piling his plate until it spilled over the edges.

"Great grub, dudette," Lewis smiled at her as he added one more burger to the top of the edible tower on his plate.

The others continued to swim and cavort in the water. The sun shone brightly, keeping the temperature in the high 80's throughout the afternoon. The professor enjoyed their exuberance and energy.

Michael and Alesandra emerged from the pool long enough to eat but quickly returned to the water afterward, while Susan slid into a lounge chair next to the professor and Miss Delia to listen to them converse.

Jim Dougherty wandered through the house looking at the collected relics. His eyes fell on a framed photograph on the fireplace, and he stepped closer for a better look. Picking up the silver frame, he studied the picture of Blaney and Delia with their arms around each other atop one of the many pyramids in Oaxaca. They both looked deliriously happy.

He returned the photo to its spot on the polished maple mantle and stopped to read a wooden plaque on the wall.

Go my sons, burn your books,
Buy yourselves stout shoes,
Get away to the mountains, the deserts
And the deepest recesses of the Earth.
In this way and no other
You will gain true knowledge of things
And their properties.
Peter Severinus

With a disbelieving snort, Dougherty walked to the back door. Looking through the screen, he watched Blaney and Delia talk together, wondering if there was more to their relationship than met the eye.

As the day wore on, the noise around the pool began to subside. Alesandra changed into her cheerleader garb, while Michael gathered together their belongings.

"Sorry, Professor," she apologized, "but I have to get to Graham Stadium for tonight's football game."

"Thanks for having us over, Prof." Michael said. "We had a great time."

Soon after, the rest of the young people slipped away until only the faculty remained. Mrs. Watanabe dutifully waited until then to bring out the brandy. The three gathered in chairs around the canopied table. She poured each of them a glass and discreetly retired.

"They're a good bunch of kids, Carl," Delia said. "I'm sure they enjoyed themselves, and so did I. Especially Sandy. I like her. She is a real go-getter, copying those glyphs while in the cave, and all. That demonstrates ingenuity. She has a sensitive soul. I can tell because her dreams were obviously brought on by her sympathy for the spirits of the Others."

Blaney listened quietly before commenting. "Lots of kids copy those glyphs, Dee. Every time I take a new group in. It's always been the exciting part of the caving experience for them."

"I don't mean those few in that cave up near the dig site. I'm talking about the other ones. The ones she copied from the cylinders."

"Oh, those." Carl had no idea what Delia referred to, but he knew if he let on she would clam up, and he would never find out. So, he played along. "Yes, they're quite interesting, aren't they?"

"I should say they are. What I don't understand is why you didn't tell me about them. It's been months since that cave-in, and you haven't said a word. It isn't like you to keep something this spectacular a secret. Not from me. You have to know what a discovery like this can mean. Evidence of the Jaredites has never been found in this area before."

He felt shock course through him at her words but struggled to maintain a calm disposition. Jaredite discoveries in Tennessee? If indeed it were true, Delia was right. The impact of such a find would be monumental.

"I wasn't keeping you in the dark. Remember, I'm the one who sent Sandy to show you her copies of the glyphs. Who else would I send her to? You're the best in the field, Dee."

"I guess. I'm just surprised you didn't tell me yourself."

"So, you agree that they are Jaredite in origin then?" he prodded.

"Oh, certainly. Not a doubt in my mind. They match up perfectly with the things we collected in Central America. Not even the slightest variation to them. It's been fascinating. Something puzzles me though."

"What's that?"

"Well, on one of the cylinders there were references to something they called eternal rocks. I'm not certain what they're alluding to. It's very curious."

"Indeed it is," he murmured. "Very curious." He stared at the glint of the setting sun on the water in the pool, watching as it danced and sparkled. He wondered why Alesandra and Michael kept this information from him. After all, he was their mentor, their group leader. Why didn't they confide in him? How many times had they returned to the mountain, and was there more to their visits than he thought? Memories of a conversation with Michael around the campfire late one night surfaced in his mind.

Michael had asked him, "If you saw rocks that seemed to glow on their own, what could cause that? What if the rock didn't need another light source to instigate the glow? What if it glowed independently of its environment?"

He thought they were purely hypothetical questions at the time. Now, he wasn't so sure. Maybe they discovered something akin to glowing rocks in that cave. If that was the case, it could represent a possible danger to them.

Jim Dougherty was not the least bit interested in the discussion. He swigged down the remainder of his brandy and checked his watch. "I'm sorry to put an end to this, but I have things I have to do before it gets too much later. Delia, would you mind terribly if we go now?"

The professor saw his guests to the door, bidding them a safe journey home, then dropped some Jim Brickman piano music in the stereo and returned to sit by the pool.

On her fifth time cruising by the professor's house, the front door opened to expel the last of the lingering guests. Turning her head quickly, she sped past hoping she had not been noticed.

Carl sat by the pool mulling over the situation. The more he thought about it, the more rankled he became. Coupled with the anger was concern. He felt certain his prize students were way over their heads in something. He finished his brandy and lifted the decanter to replenish his snifter.

As he debated the information learned this night, he turned to see Susan closing the back gate behind her and got to his feet to greet her appropriately.

"Gee, Carl. I thought those two would never leave."

"I know, honey. I was hoping you'd come back tonight. Would you like some brandy?" He took his glass and the bottle into the house and got another glass for her. Filling it, he handed it to her, then slipped an arm around her waist and led her to the bedroom.

An hour later when they lay sated together, Susan sprinkled kisses across Carl's chest as he waited for his pulse to slow. He settled a hand on her breast while she snuggled against his neck.

"I love you, Susan."

"Mmm. I love you too, baby."

"How would you feel about moving in here and living with me next term?"

She lifted her head in amazement. "Are you serious? Is it safe? I don't want to do anything that will cause you trouble, Carl."

"You don't have any more classes with me, so there won't be a conflict of interest. And I think if you have a wedding ring on that hand, there's nothing the university can say about it."

Tears sprang to her eyes, and she smiled tremulously. "You want to get married?"

"Yeah. Interested?"

"Yeah."

He reached out, opened the drawer of his night table and removed a small velvet box. "I hoped you'd say that. I bought this for you."

She took the proffered box and lifted the lid. An emerald cut diamond twinkled in the evening light. "Oh, Carl."

"Susan, I love you. Will you marry me?"

"Yes, Carl, yes. I love you."

He slid the ring on her finger and captured her lips with his own. After allowing her time to show her gratitude, he laid back against his pillow with an arm behind his head.

"Susan. There's something I need you to do for me."

"Of course, darling. Anything you want."

"This has to stay secret for now. It has to be just between the two of us. You've proven that you're capable of keeping a confidence, so I hope you won't have a problem with this."

She couldn't see his face clearly in the darkening shadows. "I'll do whatever you ask."

"Good. I need you to search Alesandra's room for me without her knowing about it."

The Skyhawks were not exactly a power team in the Ohio Valley Football Conference this year, and their record reflected it. However, this game with the Golden Eagles of Tennessee Tech was a thriller with a tied score at the end of the third quarter. The stadium rocked when the Skyhawks scored the winning touchdown. Weary but happy, Alesandra left the stadium with Michael in the midst of an ecstatic throng.

"This has been an exciting week," she told him.

He chuckled. "It was a busy one, all right. We finally got your soldier squared away."

"Now I feel free to devote my time to translating those writings."

They settled on a bench in Centennial Court in the quad where they could talk. “I have to go to Nashville next week,” Michael said. “Want to come along?”

“What's in Nashville?” “The Treasury Department. Don't forget, that gold bar needs to be turned over to them. The sooner the better as far as I'm concerned. I'm getting nervous about keeping it. I really think it's time, Sandy. We got your soldier out of the cave, so it's not a threat any more.”

“Yes, that was my only reservation.” She watched a robin hop across the lawn and considered his proposal before answering him. “Oh, Michael. Government people make me nervous. I'd rather not, if you don't mind. I think you'll do better without me. I'd really rather spend my free time concentrating on learning more about the Others.”

“Okay, not a problem, hon. By the way,” he slid his arm around her waist. “Did I tell you how cute you looked today in your short skirt and pom-poms?”

“No, you didn't, but thank you for saying so now.” She rewarded him with a long kiss.

“I especially like your pom-poms,” he grinned.

The Hot Seat

The problem with a conscience is that it frequently changes direction more than once before deciding on a course of action. It happened to Michael as he waited to be ushered into the private sanctum of Supervisory Special Agent R. D. Fraser.

Fearful of spending the entire day there, he studied the framed pictures on the wall and pondered what the initials "R. D." possibly stood for. *Robert David*? *Raymond Daniel? Really Dumb?* Various alternatives occurred, while he contemplated whether to simply leave before it was too late.

But no, the gold bar rightfully belonged to the United States Treasury. He wrapped his hands around the lump in his backpack to assure himself it was still there.

No one else entered the waiting room and nobody left, making him question if Agent R. D. Fraser himself was present. He didn't blame Alesandra for not wanting to come along. What was it about government offices anyway that made visitors squirm in discomfort? He attributed it to the waiting time and the hard seats. He stretched to keep from falling asleep, and as he did so the door to the inner office opened. A tall, well-dressed man of about forty motioned for him to enter.

"Sorry to delay you, Mr. Gant. Come in, please." He displayed a firm handshake and a professional smile. "I understand you have some information for me. Why don't you sit down, and tell me about it?"

Michael glanced around the room observing the obligatory American flag behind the Agent's desk next to a large plaque on the wall in the outline of a badge. He cleared his throat to relieve his nervousness.

Fraser patiently waited.

Michael began. "I recently became lost inside a cave not far from here and found an object stolen from the U.S. Army." He removed a plain wrapped parcel from his backpack and set it on the agent's desk.

"Is that the stolen object?"

"Yes, I want to turn it in."

"Mr. Gant," the Agent leaned forward, "if it was stolen from the Army, why don't you surrender it to them?"

"Uh...because General Grant's not around any more?"

The agent looked at him quizzically. "I beg your pardon?"

"Inside that package you'll find a bar of gold that was destined for the U.S. Treasury during the Civil War. The army was transporting it as part of a shipment when Confederate forces seized it. I just want to see that the Treasury Department gets it back."

Fraser stared intently at the package on his desk before activating his desk intercom.

"Ask Jennings to step in here." Silence stretched until they were joined by a younger man. Fraser pointed at the package. "I want you to witness what I am about to do," he said.

"It's not a bomb or anything," Michael assured him.

Fraser explained, "Don't be alarmed, Mr. Gant. When evidence of any sort is delivered into our custody, it's normal procedure for another Agent to act as witness."

He carefully unwrapped it to reveal the aged army dispatch case bearing the initials *U.S.*. Inside he found the single gold bar. The two Agents examined it closely.

"Mr. Gant, I can tell you from the engraved marking that this is indeed part of a shipment of gold bullion hijacked from the Army in 1864."

"That's what I said."

"Yes, you did. May I ask exactly where you found it?"

"Well, I already explained. I was caught in a cave landslide and after finding my way out, I noticed something unusual in a small mountain recess. When I got closer it turned out to be the skeleton of a soldier in a Confederate uniform. He was lying on top of the dispatch case with the gold bar in it."

The two Agents eyed one another with skepticism. "Can you describe the uniform he was wearing?" Jennings asked.

"Sure. A short gray jacket with fancy embroidery on each sleeve and ten brass buttons on the front in two rows. He wore a yellow epaulet on each shoulder around a single bar of rank and another bar on his collar. His cavalry hat had a single gold braid around it. His pants, however, were blue."

"A good description, Mr. Gant. You're very observant. Your man was obviously a Confederate Lieutenant. Tell us again where you found his body."

Michael repeated his earlier description.

"What was the area like around the body? Were there any marks of any kind on the ground, such as would be made if he had been crawling?"

Michael looked at the man like he was an imbecile. "You expect there to be marks like that sitting around in the dirt after a hundred and forty years? Come off it. I am a geology student you know. We found him lying against the rear wall of the small recess."

"Who was with you, Mr. Gant?"

"With me?" Michael tried to appear as though he misunderstood the question. He did not want to bring Alesandra into the story.

"You said, 'we found him.'"

"I did?"

"Yes, you did."

"Huh, wonder why I said that?"

"Mr. Gant, was someone else with you when you found the gold bar?"

"Er," he fidgeted uncomfortably before finally admitting, "yes, there was another student with me."

"I see. Did you find anything else on or near the body, such as a sabre? Cavalry officers carried sabres as well as a sidearm."

"He had a Colt .44. I gave that to his family when we located them. No sign of a sabre though," he lied. Shrugging his shoulders, Michael was silently grateful Alesandra had not accompanied him. She would have blabbed about the sword, and he didn't want to give it up.

"Okay, we'll let that pass." Fraser pressed him further. "Military dispatch cases usually carry messages or other documents. Did you find anything like that?"

He had momentarily forgotten about the journal. Rooting in the bottom of his backpack, he dug it out and handed it to the agent. "I intended to give this to you also. It's a record he kept of his brief service with the 7th Kentucky Cavalry."

The agents poured over the pages, impressed with the handwritten notations Lt. Crumpleton made. "Listen to this," Fraser read aloud to Agent Jennings. "We hid it in a cave until we can move it south. My troops are charged with protecting it until our campaign is over here in Tennessee." He turned the page and read the final entry. "My unit has been mustered out, but I have been ordered to dynamite the cave personally."

Jennings broke in with a question. "You said you found his remains in a rather shallow cave. Did you see any evidence of an explosion? Maybe it was once a larger cave, and the detonation closed off adjoining tunnels?"

"No, sir."

"Any loose rock or rubble lying around?"

"No, sir. Well, except for the landslide in which we were trapped ourselves. But that was in a different cave altogether."

SSA Fraser again: "Mr. Gant, I assume you understand that all of the stolen gold is still U.S. property."

"Yes, sir."

"The government wants to recover the rest of it, so if you have any idea where it might be located within that mountain, I'm asking that you tell us."

"I don't know where it might be." Michael felt intimidated as questions seemed to fire at him from both of the federal agents. Tired and ready to walk out of the interview, he started to stand.

"We aren't finished yet, Mr. Gant." Fraser gave him a look invoking prompt compliance. Michael resettled on his chair. "What's the name of the mountain where the cave is located?"

"I don't know its official name. We all call it Blaney's Mountain after our geology professor. He takes us there on digs."

"I suppose we can always find out from him," Fraser said. "What school do you attend?"

"UT at Martin."

"We'll need to talk to the other person that was with you in the cave."

"I'd rather not divulge the name." He wanted to protect her from being subjected to this type of intense interrogation.

Jennings raised an eyebrow, wondering if the young man was trying to conceal something of import. "I understand, Michael, but it's a matter of moiety. You see, the government pays a reward for information such as this, and you are both equally eligible to receive it. However, we need both of your names before it can be paid out."

Michael acknowledged the sudden use of his first name. Up until now he was addressed as mister, so they must have an ulterior motive for becoming more friendly with him. He realized they could easily find out her name by visiting the university and asking questions, or by looking at back issues of The Tennessean newspaper. It had run a number of articles last spring about the cave-in. He decided it was pointless not to cooperate.

"Her name is Alesandra Davis."

"Thank you, Michael." Fraser scribbled the name on a notepad on his desk. "Now, I would like a stenographer to take a signed statement from you, and we'll begin to process the moiety application. It could amount to as much as twenty-five percent of the recovery value, tax free, with a limit of $250,000 for each of you. A sizeable amount, to be sure."

"Really? But I want you to know, I didn't surrender this gold bar because of any reward."

"I know, Michael, and we appreciate what you're doing. We will speak to you about this again at a later date."

"Sure, I guess so. What happens now?"

"We need you to confirm which mountain is involved."

"I don't know if I can identify it on a map, but it's part of the State Forestry Reserve."

Jennings left the room for a moment, returning with a map of the state which he spread across the desk. "Show us where the mountain is. Do your best."

Michael leaned over the map looking for a familiar landmark. Finally, he pointed to a town. "There's a motel here we stay at when we go to the dig site." He knew from the moment he pointed it out that it would be a race against time. The agents would be all over that mountain, and he may never get another chance to recover his glowing rocks.

The Agents exchanged glances and shook hands with him indicating the interview was concluded. "Thank you. We'll be in touch."

His statement was taken, and he quickly read it through and signed it.

"That's it, Mr. Gant. You're free to leave," the secretary smiled.

He needed no further urging. A heavy weight lifted from his shoulders as he left the building. Climbing behind the wheel of his Jeep, he sensed he had not seen the last of the U.S. Treasury Department.

Fraser wasted no time either. He issued orders to notify the field agent of the latest developments in the case, then hastily arranged a conference with representatives of the Tennessee Bureau of Investigation. Since the mountain was apparently under state control, it would be advantageous to have the cooperation of the TBI in a concerted search for the gold, negating the need to obtain a federal search warrant.

He next placed a call to banker Allan Cornelius in Knoxville. Cornelius was their informant through which payments had been made to recover individual gold bars in this case. "We're about to wrap up the gold investigation. You're not to accept any more bars from our suspect. Stall if he shows up, and we'll send someone right over to arrest him."

Finally, he set in motion an affidavit for the issuance of an arrest warrant for Wilbur Grubbs on the charge of unlawful possession and conversion of federal property.

Michael ate his breakfast the next morning, thanking his lucky stars Alesandra had not accompanied him to Nashville. To call it stressful was an understatement, and she would certainly have lost her temper at the insinuations of the Federal Agents. He understood it was their job to glean as much information as possible to determine where the gold was stashed, as well as discerning any culpability involved.

When he left the University Center, he found her waiting outside on a bench.

"Hey, hon."

Her face lit when she saw him. "Good morning." She kissed him. "I missed you yesterday. I'm glad you're back."

"Believe me, so am I. It was no picnic." He ran his fingers through her auburn strands, glistening in the morning light, as he told her the details of his experience.

"Michael, do you mean they're going to search the caves?"

He watched as a myriad of emotions flickered across her face, wavering between anger, fear and frustration.

"I'm afraid so." He ran his hand up and down her arm in consolation.

"They're going to go bumbling around like crazed bulls in there, destroying those Olmec artifacts, and who knows what else? Stuff we haven't even found yet."

"I've been thinking about that, too" he said.

"You have?"

"Yep. With the government involved now, they'll move in rather quickly. We might have time for one last visit before they get there."

"You think so?" she asked eagerly. "I would really like one more look around. Once they've been there, it will never be the same again."

"I keep thinking about those glowing rocks. I want to retrieve at least one to see what they're made of, and how old they are. I'll have to bring some better tools to widen that crevice so we get one."

They looked at each other with sly grins.

"We'll have to move fast. I can already hear those government wheels turning, just waiting to dive inside our mountain. Our only advantage is that we know where the entrance is, and they don't. Let's skip classes for the day. Go pack what you need, and I'll meet you in half an hour. There's one more thing I have to do before I'm ready."

He swiftly crossed the campus to the EPS building, taking the staircase three steps at a time. It was early in the morning, and many of the classrooms were still dark. The door to the chemistry lab sat open.

Thinking his glowing rocks might be too hot to handle, he went to the cupboard where the Geiger counters were stored and signed out a small palm unit. He knew chances were good the stones were radioactive, and if so, he wouldn't bother with them. However, it was worth a chance to see if they possessed some internal properties causing them to radiate as they did.

Dr. Turner saw him leaving the lab. "Mr. Gant. Just the man I was hoping to see. Can I speak to you for a minute?"

Rolling his eyes in frustration, Michael hesitated.

"Morning, Dr. Turner. I'm in a bit of a hurry this morning."

"Those latest crystal samples you brought me are very interesting, my boy." He took off his spectacles and settled back in his chair.

"Hey, that's great, sir. I'd love to talk with you about them, but right now I'm kinda rushed."

"Hah, you young people. Always in a rush to go somewhere. Is that a Geiger counter you have there?"

"Uh, yes." He quickly stuffed the tool into his backpack.

"Doing a little testing of your own, huh?" He walked over to one of the examination tables. "Did you get one that detects Alpha, Beta and Gamma rays? I should warn you, I already ran the crystals through the spectrum without any noticeable results. Speaking of which, I'm pleased to tell you..."

"Thank you, sir. I've really got to go. I'll talk to you later." He left the lab at a run, bursting through the doors at the end of the hall.

"But, Mr. Gant..." Turner shook his head in disappointment. He spent the past twenty-four hours trying to reach the young man to impart some mind boggling news. It would obviously have to wait a little longer.

Sudden movement from the corner of his eye caught his attention. He turned to see one of his students quickly jamming his belongings into a backpack. As he did so, something spilled out onto the lab counter. It was quickly snatched up and hidden again, but too late. Jacob Turner saw it, and panic gripped him.

Professor Blaney's first class started in half an hour, and he liked to get there early. Students often wanted those extra minutes to talk with him, and he resented when it cut into his lecture time. As he approached the geology lab, Jacob Turner jumped into the hallway, his hair in its usual frenzied state.

"Carl. Thank God you're here! I've been beside myself with worry."

Confused, Blaney laid a hand on the older man's arm. He frowned as he saw the alarm exhibited in his colleague's eyes. "Take it easy, Jake. What is it?"

"Young Gant. He's in trouble."

"What kind of trouble?"

"He was here about twenty minutes ago. Checked a Geiger counter out of the lab." He grabbed the younger man by the sleeves. "You've got to save him, Carl."

"I don't understand the problem."

"He was in a hurry. Going back to that mountain, I think. Back into those caves again."

"We're not allowed back in the caves. Michael knows that."

"Don't be naive, man! He's been back there plenty of times."

Carl replayed the conversation in his mind in which Michael mentioned glowing rocks. Now he was taking a Geiger counter? He was probably getting himself into trouble, but Carl still couldn't comprehend Turner's anxiety.

"He's not going alone this time. Someone else was here. One of your Bunch. He overheard our conversation and ran out of here. I saw it, Carl. The feral gleam in his eye. He's going to kill that boy."

"Jacob. You're not making sense. Why would someone kill Michael? Who is it? Which one of my kids?"

"He had a gun. It fell from his backpack. He snatched it up quickly enough, but I saw it. He's on his way to kill Gant so he can claim the prize for himself."

"A name, man, give me a name."

Jacob blurted out the name, and Carl's eyes closed in dismay for a brief moment before he took off at a run.

"Cancel my classes for the day," he shouted back over his shoulder as he dashed for the stairwell, hoping to avert a tragedy.

Justice Served

Susan came out of her bedroom in time to see Alesandra lugging a duffle bag and backpack through their living room at the end of the hall. Perhaps she and Michael were taking a few days off again to go away. They seemed to do it often, although not normally in the middle of the week.

The door to Alesandra's room opened and Valerie came out, juggling an armload of books trying to get her key from her purse.

"Hey, Val, hang on a second."

Valerie turned to find Susan standing behind her shoulder. "Hi, Sue."

"Glad I caught you. Sandy said I could borrow her blue sweater. Mind if I go in and get it?"

"No, go ahead. I'm late for class though, so I have to go. Here's my key. Lock it when you leave, okay? You can return it this afternoon in Lit. class."

"Of course. Thanks, Val." Susan wiggled her fingers and slipped through the doorway, closing it firmly behind her. She waited until she heard the door to the suite slamming shut before clicking the lock in place.

She surveyed the room, trying to decide where to start her search. Carl said to look for anything that might have been brought from the cave. She had been uncomfortable with his request until he explained Sandy was in trouble, and he needed the information to help her.

As she opened the top drawer of the dresser, she caught sight of the diamond glittering on her finger and smiled.

Careful not to disturb the neatly folded clothes in dresser drawers and in the closet, her hands deftly slid between dainty undergarments searching for things of a suspicious nature.

Opening the deep drawer of the computer desk, she quickly perused the contents of the files hanging inside. One caught her immediate attention. She found a large number of photographs of glyphs, both painted and carved relief. Maybe this was the kind of thing Carl wanted.

She smuggled a handful into her purse and closed the drawer. Glancing once more around the room to ensure there was no trace of her covert act, she slipped back into the hall, locking the door behind her. If Alesandra was in some sort of trouble, she needed to get these to Carl as quickly as possible.

The receptionist knocked before entering Agent Fraser's office. "Sir, there's a call for you on your private line. It's the case agent at Martin."

He waited until she closed the door behind her before addressing the agent. "Did you receive the information on the Gant interview?"

The caller acknowledged the update, and Fraser continued. "Are you sure they're headed back to the mountain at this moment?...Uh huh...Okay, I agree. We'll have to move fast. I'll have the team assembled and on their way. See if you can pinpoint Grubbs' location so we know where to pick him up."

Carl Blaney jogged across the campus toward the parking lot. He felt a tug on his arm and stumbled to a stop.

"Susan," he panted, "I don't have time now, honey."

"I did what you asked. I think I've found what you need." She drew the photographs from her purse and handed them to him. He paused long enough to give them a cursory glance, then stuffed them in his shirt pocket.

"These are great. Exactly what I was looking for. I'm sorry, but I'm in a real hurry. I'll get back with you soon. Thanks, babe."

Bewildered, she watched him climb behind the wheel of his van and race out of the parking lot. She felt strangely abandoned and disappointed by his abrupt departure.

He watched Michael and Alesandra loading gear into the back of Gant's Jeep. Pulling out his cell phone, he dialed Bubba's number.

"Hey, Bubba. It's Max. I just wanted to let you know those crazy college kids are on their way back...That's right. They're heading to the mountain right now...I couldn't stop them. You might want to take care of them personally this time...Okay, I'll try, but no telling what they might be looking for in there. I overheard them talking about some kind of treasure...Sure, I'm sure. That's why I'm calling you."

He saw Gant's Jeep at the foot of the mountain and parked beside it. Knowing they couldn't be too far ahead, he began the trek upward. He was familiar with the first part of the trail, having traversed it many times before with Blaney and the Bunch.

Not expecting anyone to be trailing them, Michael and Alesandra settled into a comfortable pace and soon arrived at their disguised cave opening.

After shimmying through the rocky orifice, they shrugged their gear back on and followed the tunnel until they came to the aragonite slope. Lowering themselves down the knotted rope, they followed the passageway through the mousehole leading to the Chamber of Gods. They felt instantly at home in the familiar environment.

"Hang on a minute, Michael."

He turned and noticed her light was extinguished. "What's up?"

"My batteries are puckeroo. I meant to change them after our last trip and forgot. I need your light so I can put in new ones." She flipped open the casing on her flashlight and took out the dead batteries while he hunted through the side pocket of her backpack for replacements.

She cocked her head and listened. "Did you hear that?" Her eyes grew large with fright. "Do you suppose it's those men of Mr. Grubbs again?"

"No. It's just the same old sounds we always hear in here. Not like you to be nervous." He watched her facial features relax. "Ready to get to work?"

"You bet."

He watched as Michael and Alesandra suddenly left the trail and headed toward the rock facing where they seemingly disappeared. Moving closer to investigate, he discovered the optical illusion that shielded the cave opening from casual view.

Deciding the entry was too narrow, he left the backpack behind. He listened for the sound of their retreat as he took the pistol and tucked it into the waist of his jeans before squirming his own body through the portal. Once inside the black hole, he sat huddled in silence, hearing only his heart pounding in his chest. Taking a moment to relax and calm his breathing, he detected sounds to his right. The problem was, he had not anticipated just how dark it would be inside the cave. He did not remember it being so fully vacant of light when he went in the other cave with the Bunch. This was a spur of the moment trip, catching him unprepared. An idea sparked, and he reached into his jeans pocket for his car keys. The key chain had a small penlight on it. With the tiny beacon in hand, he listened for the tell-tale evidence of movements ahead, and set out in pursuit of the young couple who trekked onward oblivious of possible peril.

Arriving at the edge of a slope, he saw no other route and determined they must have descended. Placing his feet carefully on the slanted floor, he managed three steps before tripping over a jutting rock and sliding precariously headfirst the remainder of the way down. His hands flew wildly, grasping for anything that might give him anchor. The razor-edged Aragonite crystals randomly cut deep slices through his hands, arms and face as he skidded along, finally landing in a haphazard heap at the bottom. As he lay in the damp darkness trying to catch his breath, the gun digging into his belly, he heard the keys skitter to a stop across the floor.

Blaney tailed his students up the mountain. Leaving the camouflage of the forest behind, he stepped into the clearing, startled to feel a hand clutch his arm. Panting from the exertion of the climb and worried about his students, he let out a yelp.

"Ssh. It's just me, Professor."

Blaney stared at him in astonishment. "Geez, Max! What are you doing here? And how the hell do you manage to sneak up on anyone wearing those damned Hawaiian shirts?"

Max snorted. "Well, Prof, you didn't think you had a monopoly on all this fun, did you?"

"It's not fun, Max. This is serious business. Michael and Alesandra are in trouble."

"What sort of trouble? I hate to tell you this Prof, but those two come up here all the time. They know their way around."

"This time is different, Max. This time it's dangerous. I want you to get out of here. Go back to town and call the police." Expecting his orders to be immediately obeyed, he headed to the opening.

Wondering about Blaney's involvement, Max grabbed his arm again pulling him up short. "Wait a minute. The police? Just what sort of trouble do you think those two have gotten themselves into?"

"Jared just entered the cave behind them, and he's got a gun." Carl tried to shake off Max's grip, but the younger man held on.

"How do you know that?"

"Dr. Turner saw it in his knapsack back at the lab. I really can't stop and talk about this, Max. I've got to stop him. Just go back to town."

"All right. Listen, I'm going in after them, but I want you to stay right here. Don't follow me because I don't want anyone behind me."

"No. I'm going in. Those are my kids. It's my responsibility to see that nothing happens to them. I have to stop him."

"Professor, you have to trust me on this. I'm on their side, believe me. Let me take care of Jared."

Blaney stared into his eyes and saw something there that convinced him to agree. "All right. I don't like it, but you can come along. I hope you know what you're doing."

"So do I, Prof. So do I." Max scrambled up to the mountain facing and stood alongside the opening. Trying to wedge his well built muscular frame through the crevice provided a serious challenge. "Geez, how the heck does Gant get through here?"

"He's not exactly a football player, Max."

"Right. Well, let's just hope the passage doesn't get any tighter than this."

Michael worked at chipping away the ledges of the small window to the chamber housing the glowing rocks. With chisel and hammer in hand, he continued to enlarge its accessibility.

Alesandra clutched his arm. "Look at this," she said excitedly, shining her light at the wall painting they discovered during their last visit.

He stopped working long enough to give her his attention.

"What is it?"

"Look at the painting. There's something there I didn't notice before. It's quite small, but it looks like an eye. Yes, just like someone's eye." Her voice took on a mystical quality he was becoming familiar with. "It's their way of saying they're watching us."

"Well, they're pretty good if they can see us after all these years, them being dead and all."

She slapped at his shoulder and frowned. "Don't be facetious. You know what I mean. It must be another warning of some sort."

"Hon, right now I just want to get hold of those glowing rocks."

"You know, maybe it's not such a good idea. Standing here looking at it, I can't help but be uncomfortable with that warning sitting smack there in front of our eyes. '*Death to he who disturbs the eternal stones.*'"

Agent Jennings led the excursion to the old farmhouse in search of Wilbur Grubbs. His team consisted of several additional Treasury Agents plus TBI Investigator Ralph Hooker and an investigator from the State Bureau of Mines and Land Management.

The men spilled out of two dark sedans onto the front yard and stood waiting, their expensive, tailored suits a stark contrast to the dilapidated surroundings. Jennings climbed the steps of the ramshackled front porch and rapped on the screen door, while Hooker was subjected to a sniffing hound dog.

An attractive young woman appeared from the shadows of the darkened interior.

"May I he'p you?"

"Mrs. Grubbs?"

"Lawdy, no. I'm the housekeeper. Bubba ain't here just now," she drawled. "He got a phone call and high-tailed it out of here like a scalded dawg."

Jennings asked, "Can you tell us where he went?"

The woman pursed her lips as she thought about it. "I do believe he muttered somethin' about a mountain. Cain't tell ya anythin' more than that."

"Any idea exactly where on the mountain he might be? It is very important that we find him."

"No, but ya might ask old Injun Joe. He's out back there somewhere."

The men walked around the house to the barn. It took a moment for their eyes to adjust to the dark interior after being in the bright sunshine, but when it did, they spotted Injun Joe.

His face was wrinkled with the deep ruts of indeterminate age and he wore a long-sleeve checkered shirt, broad suspenders, and a dirty Stetson with a single eagle feather protruding from the rawhide hat band.

The agents hid grins as they watched him busily engaged in filling gallon jugs with whiskey from a homemade still. It provided all the leverage they needed.

So involved was Joe that he failed to notice the newcomers until a host of badges flashed in front of his nose.

Investigator Hooker addressed him. “Now, I suppose you’re gonna tell us you don’t know that what you’re doing is against the law.”

Injun Joe looked at them uncertainly. “Bubba said it was all right. I just work for him.”

Hooker shook his head. “I’m afraid Mr. Grubbs is dead wrong, Joe. It is Joe, isn’t it? You don’t mind if I call you Joe, do you…Joe?”

The Indian shook his head and pulled a rag from his pocket to mop the back of his neck, his eyes reflecting his discomfort.

Hooker continued. “It ain’t all right, and I guess we’re gonna have to arrest you.” He started to pull his handcuffs out to make his point. “That is, unless you decide to help us.”

“Help ya? How?”

“Maybe Mr. Grubbs has a good explanation for what you’re doing, and if he does, we might not have to arrest you. Problem is, the housekeeper says he ain’t home. Gone up to the mountain, I hear.”

Joe nodded slowly.

“You know where the mountain is, Joe? We’d surely like to get this cleared up with Mr. Grubbs right away. Don’t want to arrest you if we don’t have to.”

“I can take ya to him. I know where he goes up there.”

“Why don’t you do that? We’d be mighty obliged. You can ride up front in the first car and show us the way.”

Jack and Red huddled inside around a small open fire although the amount of heat it produced was negligible in the damp lair. Red tipped back the bottle of moonshine, swigging down a large gulp to warm his innards before passing it to his friend.

“Look alive, you two,” Bubba barked. “We got visitors somewhere in the caves. Those damned college kids again. I don’t know why they have to keep comin’ back. They’re gettin’ to be a real pain in my–”

“Watcha want us to do with ‘em, boss?” Jack asked.

“Just scare the hell out of ‘em, so they don’t come back. Red, you stay here and guard the entrance in case they show up.” Turning to Jack, he nodded his head in the direction of the tunnel. "You and I'll go lookin' for 'em."

Michael's stomach churned with a sinking feeling. He saw the determination in her eyes. He didn't often argue with Alesandra, but he felt an altercation brewing on his horizon and wondered how long it would be before she forgave him for not letting her win.

She took hold of his arm as he once again started chipping at the opening. "Michael, I don't want you to think I'm crazy or anything, but I can hear the voices of the Others. Honestly, I'm not making this up. They're talking to me."

"Sandy, we're so close. Please, don't freak out on me now."

"They're all around us. They're telling us to stay away from the stones. 'Nupin nas, nupin nas.' It means blood will spill."

He felt a distinct chilling of the air as he looked through the enlarged crevice at the glowing rocks. The hole was almost wide enough to slip through.

She refused to relinquish her grip on his arm, preventing him from working. "They're doing that dance, but now they're between us and their eternal stones. I don't think we should get any closer."

He refused to be swayed by her flights of fancy. Firmly disengaging her hand, he raised his arms and began hammering at the rock. "Sandy, it's what we came here for. We can't quit now. I'm going to find out what makes them glow."

Jared squirmed through the darkness of the mousehole, following the sound of their voices. Their words were indistinct, yet he could discern from their tone they were arguing. He knew he was getting closer when he saw the chamber ahead brightly illuminated.

As he came to the end of the tunnel, he sought their location before entering the cavern. When he saw them standing with their backs to him, he crept up to them, their bickering covering the fall of his footsteps. He tried to remain in the shadows, not wanting to reveal himself until he was ready.

Drawing closer, he saw an ethereal brightness emanating from a crevice in front of them. It had to be the glowing rocks he heard Gant speak of; the ones he himself dreamed of for months.

He took a chance and moved closer to get a better look. In his eagerness, he dislodged several pebbles underfoot.

They turned in alarm and saw him. She lifted her flashlight and shined it in the intruder's blood-covered face.

"You followed us?"

"You two have been coming back here for months. I want to know what you found so intriguing about this cave. Is that it over there? Is that your discovery, Gant? The one that you're going to cash in on for mega bucks and fame?" He stepped closer, mesmerized by the sight. Shoving Michael aside, he edged his foot into the crevice, wanting to examine the rocks himself.

"Don't go there, Jared. I think they're radioactive."

"Right, and that's why you've been knocking a bigger opening in the wall. That's crap, Gant. You've found something valuable, and you don't want to share it. Well, my friends, I want in on it. If there is any glory to be had in whatever those things are, it's going to be mine. All mine." He started toward the rocks, and Michael grabbed his arm, yanking him back from the opening.

"Let go of me, you moron." He wrenched free and struck Michael with his fist. The punch offered little more than a glancing blow. Michael landed a retaliatory fist in Jared's stomach, doubling him over, followed by a clubbed fist on the back of his head. Jared went down. As he scrambled to regain his footing, he pulled out the revolver.

Alesandra saw the gun and screamed, running to Michael's side and clutching him in fear.

"Are you a lunatic? You can't shoot that in here," Michael warned. "Don't you know the vibrations could bring this whole mountain down on us?"

Jared's face twisted as though in agony. "It's over, Gant. I'm tired of losing out all the time. Always second best. Well no more. This is my time, my prize. The winner takes it all. And you, my friend, lose."

His finger hovered over the trigger as he pointed the weapon at Michael. "Sorry it had to come to this, Sandy. I always liked you, even though you got a bit flaky at times with all your visions and nonsense. It's a shame I have to kill you both, but it's the only way. You see that, don't you?"

The pistol fired. Alesandra screamed again as a force knocked both she and Michael to the ground. The professor lay on top of them as bits of rock crumbled and fell from the ceiling.

"Drop it, Jared." Max stepped from the shadows, a gun of his own pointed at his classmate. "It's over."

"No. It's not over. It's never over." He stepped into the cavity and picked up one of the glowing rocks, clutching it to his chest. "They're mine. You'll never take them from me." His gun fired again, the explosive reverberation bringing Michael's prophecy to pass.

The ceiling buckled and fell, obliterating the chamber of eternal stones, followed immediately by the collapse of the wall at the far end, revealing the gaping jaws of the Devil's Chasm behind it. Completing the sequence of destruction, the floor beneath the stones dropped into the chasm as though someone tipped it over with the flick of a finger, putting the dispute of ownership forever to rest.

Injun Joe led the stream of Law Enforcement officers, to the cave entrance and was allowed to unobtrusively slip away.

Red leaned over the fire, seeking what little warmth it offered and did not observe their presence until too late. Seeing his rifle across the chamber propped against the wall, he knew he couldn't reach it in time, so he barreled at them in a foolhardy attempt to stop them from entering the cave. They easily dodged the rush, overpowering and placing him under arrest. As they snapped on the cuffs, they heard a distinct underground rumbling, and the mountain shook violently beneath their feet.

The staggering force of the quake knocked Bubba and Jack to the ground. Their hands flew to cover their faces as the dust and grit gusted through the tunnel to wash over them. Struggling to their feet, they heard voices echoing in the aftermath from the direction of the main entrance.

"Sounds like somebody's comin', boss. Red don't make that much noise."

"Damn that Red. Cain't he do nothin' right?"

Common sense told Bubba to retrace his steps and get out of the quaking caves as quickly as possible. However, he deduced the commotion at the entrance was far greater than two college kids could stir up. Going back could be more trouble than going deeper and taking another route. Besides, he needed to be sure his gold was safe.

The colors faded into darkness as the group lay scattered on the floor, praying it didn't give out beneath them, taking them to an eternal resting place at the bottom of the chasm. Too shocked to speak, they remained transfixed as though in a state of suspended animation.

When the quaking earth finally ceased, the professor got to his feet and switched on his light. Seeing Alesandra and Michael close by, he helped them up. "Max, you okay?" he called.

Max shook off the debris that blanketed him and slowly rose, rubbing his shoulder. "I'm fine, Prof. How about you?"

Blaney shone his light over the other two and replied. "I think we're all okay. Battered and bruised, but still alive to talk about it."

Max looked to where Jared stood when the ceiling came down. Shining his light at the empty space that used to be a chamber of glowing rocks, he groaned in despair.

Alesandra stared, refusing to accept the reality that faced her. "What about Jared? We can't just leave him here."

"He's gone, Sandy. There's no way we can even retrieve his body now." As much as it was true, Max hated being the one to have to state it, knowing it would cause her pain. He watched as she turned and folded herself into Michael's embrace and sighed. It hurt, but he accepted that she would never be his.

Slowly regaining his own equilibrium, Michael turned to the others. "Why did you follow us here, Max? And professor, you too? Thank God you did. If you hadn't knocked us out of the way, one of us would probably be dead right now. But, I don't understand what brought you here?"

"It's a long story." Max tipped his head and warned, "Ssh." With a shooing motion he looked at the professor. "Get them out of here. I have some unfinished business. Go. Now!" He clutched his pistol, ready and waiting as he watched light bounce off the walls of the adjacent tunnel.

Bubba lurched down the passageway and emerged into the cavern with Jack at his heels. He stopped suddenly when he became aware of the others. "What are y'all doin' in my cave?" he demanded.

"Hello, Bubba."

"Hey, Max, I'm surprised to see you here."

"I came along just in case you needed my help. Hello, Jack. Where's Red?"

Cutting the chit chat, Bubba bellowed, "Never mind about him." He flashed his light at the fallen rock and inhaled sharply. "Look here. That damn cave-in knocked part of my wall down. Good thing you're here, Max. You can help us fix it."

In the beam of light, Max noticed a recess previously concealed. "What have you got in there, Bubba?"

"Now, don't ask foolish questions, Max. You still work for me, ya know, and I need your help here."

"I don't think I can do that, Bubba." He strolled across the chamber and peered inside. A smile played at the corners of his mouth as his suspicions were confirmed. "Looks to me like you got some kind of treasure hidden in there. It wouldn't be gold bars now, would it?"

Bubba squinted at Max, his lips curling as he asked, "What do you know about my gold?"

"Well, if it *is* gold, I know it isn't yours. It belongs to the United States Government."

"Bull. That's my gold, and ain't nobody touchin' it."

Max pulled his badge and held it up to show the mountain man. "Wrong on both counts. I'm a federal agent. Wilbur Grubbs, you *are* under arrest for possession and conversion of U.S. property."

Bubba threw back his head and laughed. "Ain't nobody gonna take my gold or me. Sorry it had to turn this way, Max. I kinda liked ya." Without taking his eyes from the younger man, he lowered the rifle he was carrying. No need for him to get his hands dirty; that's what he hired muscle for. "Jack, finish him."

The man hedged nervously. "I don't know, Bubba. Shootin' cops ain't no part of the deal."

"Do as I tell ya, or I'll shoot ya myself," Bubba barked. "This is my mountain. Ain't nobody gonna come between me and my mountain."

Jack had no reservation that Bubba would do just that, but he also had no intention of going back to Brushy Creek. Turning tail, he headed back into the tunnel, hoping to escape before Bubba could exact his justice.

"Jack!" Bubba turned to see his right-hand man fleeing down the tunnel, abandoning him. Raising his rifle under his arm, he had no compunction in pulling the trigger and shooting Jack in the back. The echoing blast in the narrow confines caused the already-weakened ceiling to rain down upon their heads.

Prophecies Fulfilled

The doorbell rang, and Carl excused himself to answer it. Finding Susan on the doorstep, he drew her into his arms.

"I'm so glad you're here, honey. I really need you."

She held him tightly, feeling his tension. "What is it, Carl? What's wrong?"

"Come on inside, babe. I'd rather go through it just once." She entered the living room, finding the rest of the Bunch and Dr. Turner already gathered. She sat in the only available chair, and Carl planted himself on the arm of it, his hand resting comfortably on her shoulder. Eyebrows raised as the gesture was noted by the others present.

"Well, it looks like we're all here," he declared.

Lewis interrupted. "No, Jared's not here yet. We should probably wait."

"Jared's not coming, Lewis," Max informed him. "That's one of the reasons we've called this meeting."

"You mean he got the boot? How come?" Lewis looked from the professor to Max and back to the professor again.

"It's a long story," the professor began, and Susan felt him squeeze her shoulder. She placed her hand reassuringly over his.

"Susan, what is that you're wearing?" Valerie bounded out of her seat and across the room, grabbing hold of Susan's hand. "It's a diamond. It's a whopping big diamond. You're engaged?"

Susan raised her eyes to Carl's for his consent, and he nodded. "Yes, I've asked Susan to marry me."

A moment of silence hung in the room, followed by a spontaneous burst of exclamation.

"Aren't you a bit old for her?" Brandon asked.

"Shut up, Brandon," Alesandra reached over and swatted him.

Valerie turned and frowned at him. "Yes, Brandon. Do be quiet until you can think of something intelligent to say." She turned back to Susan. "That ought to keep him quiet the remainder of the day."

"You old dog, Professor." Lewis clapped him heartily on the back and shook his hand. "Stealing our Susan right out from under our noses. Congratulations, dude."

The group clamored to their feet to hug and shake hands with the happy couple.

"So, when did all this happen? I didn't even know you two were dating."

"Oh, they've been seeing each other since the cave-in expedition," Dr. Turner said.

Carl's face reflected surprise as he looked at his friend. "How do you know that?"

"Not much goes on at this university that I don't know about. People think me a doddering old fool, but I keep my eyes and ears open."

"Okay, okay, everybody. Susan truly deserves this to be a happy occasion, but this isn't the reason we've called you all here." The professor waited for the group to reclaim their seats before continuing. "We have a story to share with you, and it can't be told by just one person because so many things factor into it. It seems that day of the cave-in set a whole big ball of wax in motion. Michael, I think you and Sandy should tell the story, and Max, you cut in when you need to."

The group sat enthralled as they listened to the account of what had transpired within their midst but without their knowledge over the past six months. Their gazes shifted in amazement back and forth between Alesandra and Max as the adventure unfolded. They heard tales of an ancient civilization, a Confederate soldier, and of gold and skullduggery. When the story finally concluded, the group remained speechless.

Lewis finally found his voice, though trembling, and asked, "So Jared's gone? That's what you're telling us? The dude died?"

"The painting on the wall said, 'Death to he who disturbs the eternal stones.' I knew it. They told me so. Michael thought I was crazy." Under the circumstances, she felt no satisfaction in being right.

"Prophecy fulfilled, I guess." Michael lowered his eyes feeling guilty for not believing her. "You know what else? Jared's last words were, 'They're mine. You'll never take them from me.' I guess he was right about that."

Valerie let out a whimper of grief, and Susan's eyes closed as tears streamed down her cheeks. She leaned into Carl for support as he answered, "Yes, Lewis, I'm sorry to say, Jared didn't survive. We felt it was important that this group hear the news first, just the way it happened before the rumor mill hacks it to pieces. If any of you have questions, we'll try to answer them as honestly as we can."

"So they'll never get him out of there?"

"I'm afraid there's no way. He's several hundred feet down that chasm. As for Bubba and Jack, they're buried under some pretty large boulders. I imagine the state will eventually excavate and find them," Max surmised.

Brandon sat staring at Max. "So, you're not really a student at all. You're a fed?"

"That's right, Brandon. I'm an agent with the Treasury Department. I've been here undercover since January."

"Whoa, you sure had us fooled. How did you manage to pull it off? I mean, I have a struggle keeping up sometimes, and I'm supposed to be a student." Lewis gave Max a half-hearted grin.

"Yes, that rather amazes me too, now that you mention it," Professor Blaney added. "I sure wasn't notified about it in order to make it easier for you."

"No, sir. The Department got me enrolled, but I've had to make it through on my own merits."

"The man has a Ph.D from Georgia Tech, Carl," Turner interjected as though it was common knowledge.

"You knew about this, Jacob?"

"How did you know, Dr. Turner?" Max, too, looked surprised by that revelation.

"It was obvious that the work you submitted was not the work of an undergrad student. So I did a little checking. Summa cum laude in engineering. Nothing to sneeze at, young man." Turner gave him a nod of admiration.

"I simply enrolled in a number of classes I've already taken, so it wasn't too demanding. Although, if I needed it, Bubba could have gotten me registered with no problem."

"Grubbs? How do you figure that?" Blaney sat forward with interest.

"One of the Trustees, a fellow by the name of Walker, was on Bubba's payroll. Kept the old coot informed on things happening with the Bunch and was paid a tidy sum to enforce the ban against the group from returning to the mountain. That's why it took so long to get permission reinstated."

"Walker! Well, that explains a lot." Carl scratched his head. "Remember when you all planned that secret trip back to the mountain, and I got there just in time to stop you? Walker was the one who snitched on you. I always wondered how he knew about it before I did."

"He knew because I told Bubba we were going, and Bubba obviously passed that information on.

"Will he be arrested too?" Brandon wanted to know.

"No. While his actions were unethical, they weren't illegal. That doesn't mean the university won't take action against him, though. I really can't speak for them." Max turned his attention back to Blaney. "As for my being here, you're absolutely right, Professor. The department didn't fill you in on it, because you're the one I was sent here to investigate."

"What?" Carl thought all the secrets had already been revealed. "Why me?"

"We knew of covert operations somewhere in the region of the mountain. We considered you might be using the digs to mask criminal activity."

Carl sat stunned by the implications, amazed that he had been under suspicion by the federal government. "Well, you pulled it off beautifully, Max. But, I can't help wondering, if the government knew all along that Bubba was marketing those gold bars, why wasn't he arrested a long time ago?"

"It's true we could have picked him up at any time, but our main objective was to locate the hidden gold. We didn't know where he had it stashed. It could have been anywhere."

He took two more sandwiches from the tray offered by Mrs. Watanabe. "When Alesandra and Michael started making regular trips back to the cave, we hoped they might locate it. We wanted to recover the entire stash, not just the one bar. Anyway, under federal law we had insufficient probable cause to obtain a search warrant until the bullion cache was uncovered behind that false rock wall."

Alesandra's mouth dropped open. "You mean you knew we were making all those trips back to the mountain?"

Max smiled, and Dr. Turner commented, "My dear girl. Of course he knew. Didn't everyone?"

Michael and Alesandra looked at each other in surprise. All their attempts at nonchalance had been for naught. They weren't the sneaky pair they thought after all.

Max explained, "If we obtained a warrant for Bubba's house and farm property, we wouldn't have found the gold because it wasn't there. The search would have tipped him off that we knew about it."

"You know, he told us he was a genuine, bonafide Cherokee medicine man. He really should have known better."

Michael rolled his eyes.

She continued, "Miss Delia told me that according to Indian beliefs, anyone using the Native legends for their own gain will suffer a punishment equivalent to seven times the consequences threatened in the tale told."

"Well, then the prophecy is fulfilled on that score also," Max said. "Bubba used legends of the mountain for his own gain, and in the end, the mountain exacted its price from him. Come to think of it, he got what he wanted, too. His last words were, 'This is my mountain. Ain't nobody gonna come between me and my mountain.' He's right. Ain't nobody gonna come between them now."

Michael asked, "How much gold did he actually convert to cash? You sure wouldn't know he had any money looking at his house. Maybe he was keeping it in a Swiss bank account."

"As a matter of fact, we uncovered several foreign accounts and placed holds on them through international agreements. He hasn't had access to them for some time, so the only funds he really had were in local banks. We now have them confiscated."

Blaney was curious. "Any idea how much bullion is actually involved, or its value?"

"It originally consisted of three wagon loads. Let's just say that according to current market standards, it's worth millions. Bubba decided it was 'finders keepers' and considered it his own private hoard, drawing from it as his need arose."

"What will you be doing now, Max? I assume your duties will take you elsewhere."

"Yes, I'll stick around long enough to take signed statements from everybody, conduct a few other interviews, but then I'll be gone. The Department will have another assignment waiting for me."

Max turned his attention to Michael as he stirred sugar into his coffee. "By the way, why did you lie about finding the soldier in some false cave?"

Michael flushed with embarrassment, and Alesandra quickly jumped in. "What makes you think it was a lie?"

"It was obvious. There's not much chance he would have been where you claimed to find him with the gold bar still in his possession, so to speak. He would have been subjected to too many wild animals and hikers over the past hundred and forty years. It's not even a logical assumption."

She bridled. "Well, we were afraid a bunch of thoughtless policemen would destroy the artifacts inside the mountain if we told you where we really found him."

"My dear, Alesandra, that's why we took a state land management specialist along to be certain our thoughtless agents preserved the integrity of the cave system."

She quirked a smile and blushed at his teasing. "Professor, I don't understand something."

"What's that, Sandy?"

"It's Jared. I mean, he was one of us. Why did he go crazy like that?"

"I admit, I'm as perplexed as you on that score. We may never know what finally made him desperate enough to bring a gun into the cave."

"Then allow me to shed some light, if you will," Dr. Turner interrupted. "Jared Brooks was the type of person who didn't want to be just one of the guys. Excessively competitive, he needed to be successful and make a name for himself. He was an extremely bright student, but I saw a change in him after Michael's discovery of the crystals." The old chemist set his cup and saucer on the end table beside him and continued. "He envied the attention it created, and in my opinion, he became obsessed with obtaining the glory for himself. Even his grades began to suffer because of his jealousy toward you, Michael."

"Jealousy?" Michael listened in disbelief. "Surely my finding the crystals didn't affect him all that much."

"Ah, but it did, my boy. I warned you."

Michael looked at him puzzled. "You did? I don't remember any warning."

"I emailed you on more than one occasion. I felt certain it was Jared behind the break-in's but couldn't prove it at that point in time."

A light of dawning appeared in Michael's eyes. "You're Jacatom?"

"Yes, indeed, my boy. I thought you were clever enough to decipher that. Jac, short for Jacob. Atom, the basis of chemistry. Who else could it possibly be?" He watched the transformation on Michael's face as the young man suddenly comprehended. "Now, as I was saying, Jared saw how Alesandra became enamored with you following the cave-in incident, and how the two of you obviously shared some intimate secrets. That bothered him very much. When he saw you take the Geiger counter, he surmised you were returning to the cave for an even bigger discovery."

"I still find it hard to believe he pulled a gun on us, even though I was there to witness it with my own eyes."

"He wasn't thinking straight," Max said. "We're just lucky Professor Blaney and I got there in time, or things would have turned out very differently." His words returned the group to a somber mood as they considered the ramifications.

Lewis could only take so much melancholy and decided it was up to him to change the course of the conversation. He turned his attention to Alesandra. "I want to hear more about these artifacts."

The doorbell rang. "Hold that thought until I get back," the professor told them as he left the room. At his front door, he welcomed his poker playing friend, Chancellor Jeffreys, with a handshake. "Galen, come join us. The group is all here."

"Sorry I'm late. Have I missed much?"

"No, we haven't gotten to the exciting stuff yet." He led his friend into the living room and quickly retrieved an additional chair from the den for his guest.

"Everybody, you all know Chancellor Jeffreys." The room grew a little more formal in atmosphere.

"Relax, kids. Nobody's in trouble," Blaney teased. "Now, Lewis was asking about the artifacts Alesandra found. I think this is a very good time to tell you, Sandy, the extent of your extraordinary scientific discovery. The evidence in the caves indicating the presence of Jaredite people in this part of the country, is something never before suspected."

He waited for the murmurs of excitement to die down before continuing. "Writings and glyphs left in your cave by these early tribes have been partially translated by Miss Delia."

Chancellor Jeffreys concluded, "What you don't know, Sandy, is that Professor McBride-Hart has been in touch with the National Geographic Society. They are sending a team to verify the authenticity of your discovery."

"Going back into the mountain? Is that safe?"

Blaney answered. "Not really. You won't be permitted to accompany us, I'm afraid. Miss Delia and I will lead a small team of their specialists into the mountain. Your Chamber of Gods suffered little damage in the cave-in. We won't be able to get in beyond that chamber. It is permanently inaccessible. Once they're satisfied that the glyphs are real, they plan to interview you and do a pictorial spread. This may be the most important archaeological find of the decade."

A squeal of delight betrayed her pleasure, resulting in congratulatory hugs from everyone in the room, including the chancellor. They milled around her, happy that one of their group was about to become famous.

"Hey!" said Brandon. "The National Geographic! That's the magazine with all those pictures of naked ladies in Africa and the South Pacific."

"You would think of that, dude. But you're right," Lewis agreed. "How 'bout it, Sandy?"

"You're both idiots. I'm not posing for nude photos." She swung at them playfully.

"Well, since good news seems to be on the agenda, maybe I can offer more," the chancellor said. He waved a hand, motioning them to their seats. "I know you've been through a lot, and this has been quite an afternoon for revelations. I'm going to further add to that. I've been invited here this afternoon in regards to Mr. Gant."

That quieted the group immediately.

"Me, sir? What about me?" Michael was instantly alert. "What have I done?" he asked, fearful of expulsion from school for returning to the cave in violation of the administrators' ban.

Dr. Turner spoke up. "I tried to tell you at the lab, but you were in such a rush I didn't get a chance."

Jeffreys cleared his throat and addressed all present. "As you know, Dr. Turner and Michael Gant conducted extensive tests on some crystal specimens discovered at Blaney's Mountain. The results have been duly prepared in a paper by Dr. Turner, and are scheduled to be presented to both the American Physical Society and the International Association of Science and Technology. Mr. Gant, we expect you to present the paper," he paused for emphasis, "to the Royal Society of Chemistry in London, England."

"I'm going to England?" Michael's eyes grew large with excitement. "Cool."

Galen Jeffreys surrendered the floor to Turner who expounded further.

"The laboratory tests determined the crystals possess an innate composition which changes when bombarded with electrons to produce an enlarged magnetic flux. In short, a new element is being added to the Periodic Table. This element has officially been given the name *Gantium* in honor of its discoverer, Michael Stanley Gant."

A round of applause followed, and Michael and Alesandra embraced while tears ran down their cheeks. Embarrassed, Michael swiped at them quickly with the back of his hand.

When the first wave of spontaneous exclamations died down, Dr. Turner continued. "We further learned that increasing the flow of electrons altered the field of magnetism so that either the positive or negative poles could be strengthened by deliberate design. The possibilities are endless with respect to transportation, military usage, and the space program."

"You should be able to adapt the new Gantium element with no problems, Michael," Jeffreys said. "Even more so because the university has been awarded a government grant to develop specific applications for the crystals. The school is offering you a full scholarship to complete your doctorate. Let me be the first to congratulate you."

"Wow, dude, I always knew you'd amount to something."

It seemed a fitting expression as the Blaney Bunch reflected upon the past year and the year to come. They each grew a little taller, somewhat wiser, and considerably closer together as a group.

Blaney's mountain stands ready to welcome another avid edition of the Blaney Bunch, perhaps somewhat tattered in places but still offering its venue to artifact seekers and to story tellers.

The panther and the bear remain within its sacred interior as venerable dancing spirits celebrate ancient rituals. The mysterious rocks continue to glow buried deep within its heart, ensuring they remain forever free from human interference.